PRAISE FOR (

THE SECRET WAYS OF PERFUME

"Sensuous, evocative, intriguing and emotional—and like all good perfumes it lingered long after. An absolute treat."

—Veronica Henry, author of *How to Find Love in a Bookshop*

"Evocative, atmospheric and engaging."

—*Daily Mail*

"An intoxicating quest . . . A feast for the senses."

—*Daily Express*

"A beautiful and well-constructed tale."

—*Elle*

"A stunning story. An astonishing storyteller."

—*Vanity Fair*

"*The Secret Ways of Perfume* is a lovely, elegant story that will allow readers to transport themselves into a heady adventure. Elena's journey is intriguing, beautiful and inspiring."

—The Reading Nook Reviews

The
BINDER
of
LOST
STORIES

ALSO BY CRISTINA CABONI

The Secret Ways of Perfume

The BINDER *of* LOST STORIES

CRISTINA CABONI

TRANSLATED BY PATRICIA HAMPTON

AMAZON **CROSSING**

Text copyright © 2017 by Cristina Caboni
Translation copyright © 2020 by Cristina Caboni
All rights reserved.

Previously published as *La rilegatrice di storie perdute* by Garzanti in Italy in 2017. Translated from Italian by Patricia Hampton. First published in English by Amazon Crossing in 2020.

Published by Amazon Crossing, Seattle

www.apub.com

Amazon, the Amazon logo, and Amazon Crossing are trademarks of Amazon.com, Inc., or its affiliates.

ISBN-13: 9781542000147
ISBN-10: 1542000149

Cover design by Faceout Studio, Spencer Fuller

Printed in the United States of America

The

BINDER

of

LOST

STORIES

PROLOGUE

The gold charm sparkles in the girl's hands. It's her family crest—a circle containing a pair of wings.

Clarice knows it's precious; she keeps it next to her heart. It was her mother who gave it to her, along with her violin and the stories she holds and cherishes deep inside, the things that make her who she truly is—a von Harmel.

"As long as you remember me, I shall live on," her mother had said to her one evening, many years ago.

That was the last time Clarice saw her.

Now the memory feels distant, faded with time. It shouldn't hurt her like this. And yet, thinking of the mother she loved so much still cuts her to the quick.

The candle flame lights up the smooth table where she places the sheets of paper. At the bottom, in slight relief, is the same shape as the gold charm. She embossed it herself.

Quickly, she folds them to make sections and, after lining them up on the frame, binds them together with a thread. The book is almost ready. Now, all that's missing is the cover. Fans, little fruits, and graceful garlands bloom on the leather amid the gold powder and the bitter smoke of the red-hot stamp, telling their own secret story.

"Have you finished, my little sparrow?"

She nods, her eyes on the book. "Yes, master."

She can feel the man's gaze on her. "You are my pride and joy."

A sweet feeling fills her. "Am I a bookbinder now?"

"The best."

They stay like that for a moment, and then the silence is broken, as if magic has just left the room. Noises filter down from upstairs. Their time together is over.

"You must go now. Hurry. I don't want them to find you out."

She obeys because she has no other choice. This is a world that's forbidden to her. Because she's only a woman. But one day everything will change, she's certain. She climbs the stairs in silence, her bare feet on the stone, a slight smile on her lips. She looks at her hands and at the scratches she'll be obliged to explain tomorrow morning.

One day she'll fly away on the wings of freedom.

CHAPTER ONE

Indeed, the searching heart feels that something is missing; but the heart that has lost it, feels something has been taken away.

—Johann Wolfgang von Goethe, *Elective Affinities*

The book was magnificently bound in red morocco leather with decorations in gold leaf. It was one of the first editions of Goethe's *Elective Affinities*, including his dedication and autograph. Despite being under a glass cover, it exuded a mysterious power that captivated the guests.

The attendees at the Galileo Society's gala dinner pressed close to stare at the main attraction. Some knew the work's literary merits, while others were merely amazed that some pages written by a dead man could draw so many visitors.

Sofia Bauer had waited patiently for her turn, and now that she found herself in front of the glass case, she felt her heart beat faster. A host of questions rose in her mind, one after the other, as she noted a detail on the frontispiece.

This particular copy of the book had led an adventurous life. Apparently, it'd been given by the author to a mysterious lady, as indicated by the dedication, and had then been taken from her. After remaining in the shadows for over a century, it had only recently come to light in a small used bookshop in Bucharest.

When Sofia learned it would be presented in Rome, her hometown, she managed to get herself an invitation. It wasn't difficult, since she'd worked at the Bibliotheca Hertziana for a few years.

"It's beautiful," said a voice next to her.

Yes, it was. Sofia smiled at the girl. The book was truly magnificent and well preserved. She would have liked to touch it, browse through the pages, smell them. This desire was so strong, she felt her palms getting damp.

People bustled around her, all looking forward to the lecture that would begin shortly. She greeted a few of them, but briefly. Since her marriage, she was no longer part of that scene, and being around it again made her uneasy. She chose a seat at the back of the room and stayed just long enough to hear the secretary of the Galileo Society give an account of the unusual circumstances that had led to the Goethe volume's rediscovery. As the secretary handed things over to the speaker who was to describe the work in detail, Sofia discreetly slipped out.

She waited a few minutes on the terrace, allowing the breeze to fan her long hair and the hem of her dress. Then she walked slowly down the steps that led from the villa to the road, taking everything in. This wasn't the first such event she'd been to, but it'd been quite a while. In fact, it was one of the first evenings she had decided to go out on her own since she'd been married. She felt uncertain, as though her decisions were made of cut glass, unable to withstand the slightest tremor.

While she wandered through the garden of the villa, Goethe's *Elective Affinities* returned to her mind. Love engulfed everything. Judgment and reason were minor impediments in its path. With a touch of bitterness, she wondered if there had ever been a love capable of feeding on itself alone.

The night air was warm, and the flowers went on blooming undisturbed, as though autumn hadn't yet decided to show its face. It was like time had paused, a sort of parenthesis between a before and an after.

The villa where the Galileo Society was holding the event was one of the oldest and most beautiful in Rome. The darkness did not prevent Sofia from recognizing, in the near distance, the ruins of what had once been a tower. The garden was surrounded by a magnificently preserved columned portico. Behind a low wall, the orderly lawns revealed the predilections of their designer. Here, time was suspended. Here, it was possible to rest a moment without having to do anything you didn't want to, without having to be someone you were not.

She came across one of the guards by the main entrance. "Would you call me a taxi?"

"Of course, signora."

Sofia waited in silence, her gaze lost in the darkness.

"Twenty minutes. If you'd like to wait in the front garden, I'll call you as soon as it arrives."

"Thank you."

She walked in the direction he'd gestured. Beneath glowing lampposts was a series of benches. Some of the guests had stopped there, taking advantage of the fine evening. Sofia walked on. A wave of exhaustion came over her, making her steps heavy and her thoughts slow.

She chose a cast-iron bench. Laying her head back, she let out a long sigh and closed her eyes for a moment. When she opened them again, the night was velvet black above the trees and the stars were sparkling.

"There's nothing that makes you feel smaller and more alone than the immensity of the sky."

She jumped, scanning the trees.

"Over here, to your right."

Sofia saw a tall, elegant man leaning against a column. He didn't move, just went on looking at her with a kind expression. She turned her attention back to the sky. "That depends."

He approached her, stepping out of the shadows. "On what?"

"On who's looking."

"Interesting." The man paused. "May I ask you what you see?"

She was surprised by the ease with which her answer came. "Peace." Was that what she was lacking? "I apologize for my intrusion. I didn't see you standing there."

He looked surprised. "You mustn't apologize. If I had kept quiet, we would both have found what we were looking for here—isolation for me and peace for you. But in that case, we also wouldn't be having this pleasant conversation." He paused. "And that'd be a true shame."

Sofia was speechless for a moment. "You're a very kind person."

Silence, then a deep breath. "Really? I'd like to know how you managed to come to that conclusion. How many remarks have we exchanged? Five or six? I don't really think that's enough to know."

It certainly was. Sofia stood up. From this spot, she could see the villa's stunning flight of steps, lit up as though in full daylight and dotted with guests. The water in the pool mirrored the flickering lights. She looked at the stranger. Some moments were special simply because they were so fleeting.

She observed him. High cheekbones, full lips. A hint of a beard softened the hard, angular face, which was interesting rather than handsome—like his voice, she thought. Perhaps what intrigued her was his reaction. He didn't like being called kind, probably didn't like being judged at all. Yet the man had made her smile—a rarity of late. She decided that he deserved an answer.

"It isn't just what's said that's important. How it's said often tells you a lot more. Thank you again. Good evening."

She didn't wait for his reply, but made her exit. Her taxi should have arrived by now.

"Evening," she said to the driver as she got in. "Piazza di Spagna, please." It wasn't far from her apartment, and Rome at this hour held a particular charm; she would take a little walk.

As the vehicle set off, she thought back to the book and the excitement she had felt while looking at it. Staring into the darkness, she asked herself once again what had ever persuaded her to leave the life she loved and the work she had trained for at the library.

Books had always fascinated her. They were possibilities, new opportunities. They were answers. Looking after them, offering them to people, was far more than a job. It was a vocation. She never should have given it up.

When she got back, the house was silent. There wasn't a trace of Alberto, her husband. She took a shower and then went out onto the patio. The night air made her shiver, but she decided to stay out a bit longer. Her knees pulled up to her chest, she allowed her thoughts to roam. It couldn't go on like this. She had to make a decision. Possibilities whirled around in her head. After a while, the light went on behind her, but she didn't turn around.

"Did you have a good evening?"

What trite, empty words. She had spent hours, days, months, years with her husband, sharing thoughts and laughter, and now they were little more than strangers.

"Not bad. Marcello and the others say hello."

"Nice of them."

It seemed to her that he wanted to add something. She shut her eyes.

"I'm going to bed."

Sofia didn't answer. She went on looking out at the night.

The next day, when she returned from her morning run, she found her husband's carry-on bag in the hallway.

"Are you going somewhere?"

She hoped her voice didn't betray her relief and hope. She wanted to be alone, needed space to think. Living together had become a challenge. It was as if they were always at odds, sizing each other up, trying to find new ways to inflict pain. She had to tell him it was over. But whenever she tried to say the words, courage abandoned her. And so she turned away, hating herself for her cowardice. Then she looked at the suitcase again. This trip was a sort of break, a time that she would use to make the decision she'd been putting off for far too long now.

"I told you about it last week, regarding the Posillipo acquisition in Naples. There might be some issues with the contract, and I have to make sure everything is still on track."

No, he'd made no mention of a trip. "Perhaps you forgot to tell me."

She saw him stiffen. "You're the one who has to take pills for everything, not me."

She didn't reply, just put her keys on the table. She asked herself what had happened to the man who used to wake up singing and managed to find the good in everything. He had been replaced by this stranger who blamed her for everything, criticized her constantly, and was never content. The stranger chose his words carefully to hurt her as deeply as possible. The real question was: How long would she let him go on doing it?

"I'm going to take a shower." She didn't stay to hear her husband's reply. She pulled her clothes off and threw them angrily into the laundry basket. When she came out of the bathroom, there was no trace of him.

I'll call you from the airport.

The note was lying on the table. She crumpled it up and threw it into the wastepaper basket. She ate breakfast lethargically. It was such a familiar sensation lately that she wondered if she would ever really get rid of it. Her thoughts felt heavy, somehow preventing her from looking beyond the coffee she was holding in her hand. She put down the cup and stepped out onto the patio.

This was the part of the house she liked best. The sun, the sky, the air. Whenever it seemed as though she could no longer breathe, she would take shelter among the plants and wait for the knot in her throat to loosen, the tears to retreat. She started watering the large pots, then moved on to the smaller ones.

"Hello, Sofia. Good morning."

She raised her head. "Joice, I'm sorry, I didn't see you."

Her neighbor waved. She was a few years older than Sofia and had a kind expression and an endless passion for cakes and pastries. From her Japanese father, she had inherited her dignity and pride. From her mother, a passion for cooking and a strong Roman accent. Their patios were separated by a simple wooden fence.

"Would you like a slice of cake?"

For a moment Sofia was tempted to refuse, but she couldn't resist the woman's plaintive expression. "It's your fault if my clothes don't fit me anymore!" She turned off the tap and dried her hands.

Joice snorted. "I'd kill for a figure like yours."

Alberto didn't see it that way. He'd look at her and say, "You should make up your mind to lose some weight." Sofia wasn't overweight, and she knew it, but that did little to mitigate her sorrow. It was always painful to feel she was being judged.

Still, there was one thing that pained her more than anything: her instinctive need to please him. She had tried for a long time, she really had! She'd only stopped recently when she'd realized that nothing would ever be enough, that nothing she could do or say would make any difference. She'd started to confront her dependence on him, but the habit felt too deeply ingrained to break.

And yet, while she knew that this was not love, there were still other demons to face.

She climbed over the piece of wooden fence that hadn't yet been overtaken by Joice's giant wisteria.

"Coffee? It looks like you need some."

She shook her head. "Actually, what I need is courage. Got any of that?"

Joice took her time answering. "Your problem, Sofia, is that you think too much. If something isn't working, there's no use persisting."

She ran her hand through her hair to smooth it. "It's hard to accept you've made a mistake. I'm thirty-two, Joice. I should have learned by now, don't you think?"

"Why? Perfection doesn't exist, you know. Everyone makes mistakes at different times. They fall, and then they get up again." She handed Sofia a slice of cake. "Things happen because it would be impossible for them not to. And out of those, others arise. You don't put the roof on a house without building the walls first. There are sequences."

It was a curious way of looking at life. Accepting everything that happened and trying to move forward anyway. Was it really possible to live like that? "I'm tired."

Joice touched her hand. "You must fill your time with beautiful things that make you happy. What do you want from life, Sofia? That's the question you have to find an answer to."

Sofia stayed out on the patio a little longer, then accepted a hug from her friend and went back inside.

While she was changing, she heard the phone ring. "Hello?"

"Ciao, *Liebling*, how are you?"

"Grandpa? It's so good to hear from you! What would you say if I came to get you and Grandma, and we all went out to lunch?"

"We're in Munich. Can you make it by midday?"

Her eyes widened. Her grandparents were over eighty. Even though Munich was Max's hometown, he hadn't been back for years.

"Munich? Does Mom know?"

Sofia had a difficult relationship with her parents, who had traveled often when she was young, leaving her on her own. Years ago now, they had moved to France, where her mother had been born. Fortunately, she'd always had her grandparents close by.

"Adèle doesn't know. And don't tell her, please—she'd tell Peter, and you know what your father's like. I've got things to do. God willing, I'll be back before they realize I'm gone."

She doubted strongly they would be able to trick her parents. But in the case of Maxim and Therese Bauer, anything was possible. "You should just tell them to mind their own business."

"It isn't that easy. One day you'll have children, Liebling. Then you'll realize what a nuisance they can be. On the other hand, you'll know that your life would be practically useless without them. Anyway, don't you say anything. Your grandmother and I may just extend our trip. Perhaps we'll pay them a surprise visit. We haven't been to France for some time."

Sofia imagined the expression on her parents' faces if Max and Therese appeared on their doorstep. She almost burst out laughing. "I won't say a word, I promise. When do you think you'll be back?"

A sigh and a cough. "That depends. Do you think you could go and look after my babies? You've got the keys, don't you?"

Yes, she did. It wasn't the first time she'd looked after Max's orchids, though it had been a while. "Of course."

"Ah . . . your grandmother wants to know if you need anything, if you've eaten, if you're well . . ."

She smiled; it was typical of Therese to ask all those questions at once. "Tell her everything's fine."

"Thank you, darling. Say hello to Alberto."

"Er, yes. Of course I will, Grandpa." A charged silence descended on them.

"Everything's all right between you two, yes?"

"Yes, of course, of course," she said quickly, hoping Max wouldn't notice she was upset.

Another sigh. "Liebling, you've never been any good at lying."

Sofia felt the tears welling up. It had been so long since she'd seen her grandparents! A wave of love and shame rose inside her. "Don't worry, I'll work things out."

"Do you remember what I told you the morning you got married?"

"That I still had time to change my mind, and you would personally put me on a plane to Bali?" Max had been the only one to see the fear hiding behind her smiles and flowing words.

He laughed softly. "No, the other thing. The thing about love. Remember?"

The words rose from the depths of her memory and started to take shape in her mind. She didn't reply; she couldn't. She put her hand over her mouth.

He cleared his throat. "What are we born from?"

It was one of the first poems Sofia had learned. Max was the one who'd taught it to her. Goethe had written it two centuries ago, and since then, things hadn't changed a bit.

Max paused for a moment. "From love, Liebling. And how would we be lost? Without love. What helps us to hope? Love. Can we find love too? With love. What stops us from weeping for long? Love. What must join us forever? Love." He paused again. "Without love, we are nothing. Remember that, and everything will turn out for the best."

She made an effort to recover her voice. "Grandpa, I love you so much."

"Me too, Liebling. Me too."

CHAPTER TWO

> Love, she was convinced, would arrive all of a sudden, with thunder and lightning—a heavenly storm descending on life, turning it upside down, wrenching at willpower as though it were dead leaves, dragging the whole heart down into the depths.

—Gustave Flaubert, *Madame Bovary*

The lions stared at her menacingly, their teeth bared. Sofia lingered to gaze at them as memories of childhood filled her mind. She'd always loved the gargoyles that Gino Coppedè had placed on the buildings of the neighborhood bearing his name.

With her hands deep inside her pockets, Sofia thought about how exciting it must have been when the architect imagined those disconcertingly beautiful, asymmetrical shapes. Pure magic. Seeing the statue in the stone, discovering the melody in the notes, feeling the emotions in the words yet to be written.

She looked up at the darkening sky and decided to hurry. As she was crossing the road to her grandparents' building, a shadow fell over her face. Earlier that day, she'd had a brief chat with Alberto and, before hanging up, he told her to pick a place where they could go once he was back. A few days alone—just the two of them.

She gripped the phone tighter. "We don't need a vacation. We need to talk."

"Come now, there's nothing that can't be worked out."

But there certainly was. "Alberto, it's obvious we're not happy anymore."

"Then we'll have to try harder."

Try? Of course you had to work at it, but that wasn't the only thing that held a marriage together. All that remained of what should be a union was routine—a series of automatic responses. She and Alberto were running on parallel tracks, and they were both alone. "Stop it," she'd said before hanging up. "I'm fed up with your solutions."

She entered the downstairs hall and said hello to the doorman who came over to greet her.

"Signorina! It's been too long."

"How are you, Felipe?"

"Well, thank you, signorina. And you are always becoming more and more beautiful. You remind me so much of your grandmother."

Sofia smiled at him, surprised and embarrassed by the admiration in his eyes. As she climbed the marble staircase, she ran her hand along the bannister. How she had missed this place.

She knew every nook and cranny of the apartment, like how the morning sun lit up a precise spot on the living room floor, and that if you lay down there, you could admire all the constellations on the frescoed ceiling. She thought back to the games of chess she'd played with her grandmother; the times Max had cooked *Kürbissuppe*, the sweet smell of pumpkin filling the house. She remembered the long hours in front of the open fire in the library as they played their games, guessing the meanings of obscure words. A knot formed in her throat. Had she really been so busy chasing her new life that she hadn't found a little time to spend with Maxim and Therese?

Sofia paused at the door before gathering the courage to turn her key in the lock. She walked along the corridor, past the china vases that only

Therese was allowed to dust, the abstract paintings she still didn't understand, studying her own reflection in the big, metal-alloy mirrors—her grandmother's pride and joy.

Her favorite mirror stretched from the floor to the ceiling. The surface, framed by solid silver spirals and geraniums, had deteriorated so much that it hardly reflected her face. A pale oval with delicate features, eyes more green than blue, and long blond hair tied back in a ponytail. Felipe was right: she looked more like Therese than Adèle. And not just physically. Her mother would never have let anything stand in the way of her objectives. Her parents loved one another ardently and shared the same basic ideals, but all the rest was a matter of compromise. When Sofia had met Alberto, she'd thought they might have something similar.

She went out onto the large balcony, the part of the house she liked best after the library.

Evening had fallen abruptly, and golden light softened the buildings' edges and arches. Even the lion on the opposite cornice didn't seem so fierce now. She gazed at the olive trees and bougainvillea.

From the Fontana delle Rane at the center of the square, water rose high into the air and then fell again, producing a sort of hypnotic chant. Everything was different in the Coppedè neighborhood. Where symmetry dictated the rules of style and beauty elsewhere, here the exact opposite was true. A vision somewhere between madness and creativity. She loved this place, felt she belonged to it—to its light, its space, even its shadows. She allowed herself one last look, this time up at the dark sky that had clouded over like the depths of the Tiber River.

I should be getting home, she thought, but made no move to rush.

She entered the small greenhouse and relished the embrace of the damp warmth and the perfume of the flowers. She checked on the plants, exchanging a word or two with each as she stroked their leaves. It was like a tiny corner of jungle right in the city center. The colors of the petals were so bright, they took her breath away. She checked the thermostat and made sure there was enough water in the humidifier. Everything was in excellent shape. *Why did Grandpa want me to come?*

Inside the apartment, the library smelled like old paper and leather bindings—the smell that had helped her choose a life path so long ago. She opened an old edition of Flaubert's *Madame Bovary* and smiled at the frontispiece, printed with such loving care and restraint. Title, author, publisher. She ran her fingers over the old paper, yellow with time and use. The book's various owners had left their marks—little folds, notes on slips of paper, a few dried flowers between the pages. They were like messages.

Time seemed to expand as Sofia's finger traced the engravings, questions forming in her mind. The author's name was plain as day, but who had done the binding? Who decided what fabric, leather, and drawings would do the story justice? And why had these colors been chosen? The stamps, the decorations?

Suddenly, she shook herself. It was as though something inside had taken over in those moments, a sort of automatic machine, oiled to perfection during the years when her passion for books had been the subject of her studies and then her work. It'd been too long since she'd felt this interested in something, anything.

There hadn't been room in her new, modern house for antique books, so she'd had them sent to her parents'. Her marital obligations had distanced her from her passion. Not immediately, but over time. It had been the family dinners, birthdays, meetings she couldn't attend because there was always something more important to do, like spending time with people her husband liked. Gradually, he had become more demanding, complaining about her work, her hours. "We can live very well on my salary, you know."

For a while, she'd held out. But faced with Alberto's long silences, his snide comments, his judgments of the people who mattered to her, she'd decided that perhaps it was better to let it go. Books, art, music—all her own interests had been moved to the back burner until, finally, she'd abandoned everything, and he had become the center of her world. She'd married young and given up so much in their five years of marriage. But it hadn't been enough for him.

She put back the book and went into the kitchen. After cleaning off the wood-and-granite countertop, she made herself a cup of tea, then sat on one of the velvet divans, sipping it slowly.

She needed more time alone to think, like the stranger from the villa had said. Being alone meant having space, the opportunity to look around and see herself as Sofia Bauer and not Alberto De Santis's wife.

She finished her tea, then stood up, rinsed the cup, put on her coat, and left her grandparents' apartment.

The warm air bore the sweet perfume of the season's last flowers. She paused to take it in, to linger and meet people's eyes, exchanging smiles instead of walking straight past, as she normally would have.

She passed a group of tourists admiring the Palazzo del Ragno and crossed the road. Suddenly, she stopped, her eyes on a little pool of light up ahead on her right. It was a bookshop. Or, at least, it had been.

When had it reopened?

She moved toward it instinctively, urgently, guided by memories and the pleasure they brought her. It was what remained of those carefree afternoons of her childhood, a time when she'd been happy. She stopped in front of the doorway. She could still see the old sign, carved into the wood, reading "Books, Atlases, Maps, Antiques, Vinci & Son."

Beneath the sign were two shop windows, one on either side of the entrance. In front of the smaller one was a little table filled with vases of flowers and herbs. There used to be bookshelves along the outside wall, but they were no longer there. Neither were the wooden boxes in front of the doorway, which used to contain secondhand books. She'd always found treasures in them.

When she opened the door, Sofia was welcomed by the tinkling of a bell.

She looked around and noticed an elderly man sitting behind the counter. He hadn't moved. The man was formally dressed and bent over a book, his elbows resting on the counter, a hand propped under his chin. His fingers seemed to be stroking the pages as he turned them slowly, one after the other.

Sofia smiled and wondered what he was reading. She knew that sort of rapture, so she decided to wait for him to finish.

It took him a while to raise his eyes, peering at her from behind thick glasses. "Oh! You must excuse me, signorina, I didn't hear you come in."

Sofia looked into that face where time had traced deep furrows, as though the bookseller himself were a map—one of those the shop had been famous for at one time.

"Don't worry."

He closed the volume and placed his glasses on top of it. "Can I help you?"

"I'd like to take a look at the books."

"'I question them and they answer me, and for me they speak and sing . . . Some drive away my worries and bring back a smile . . . Others teach me to know myself.'" He smiled. "Sorry, every now and again I get carried away. Of course you can look at the books, and if you'd like to buy one, that'd be even better."

She smiled back. "I'd forgotten Petrarch's epistle on reading. Thank you for reminding me of it. It really is beautiful."

"Oh yes, I'd go so far as to say comforting. Don't you agree?"

"I like that—'comforting.' I used to come here when I was a little girl. I thought the shop shut down a long time ago."

"You're not wrong. It belonged to my father. His name was Andrea Vinci. Like mine. You're too young to have known him, though. My cousins kept it open for a while after he died. I've only just returned to Italy."

That explained his accent. "Spain?"

The bookseller smiled. "A bit farther than that. Chile." He stood up behind the polished wood counter. "I should do some renovating," he said sadly, taking a long look around.

Sofia followed his eyes.

"No, why? It's so beautiful here." She looked up at the vaulted ceiling with the old, wrought-iron lamps hanging from it. The walls were covered with books of different shapes and sizes, their spines in relief, the scrolls, the maps. On the opposite side were wooden shelves darkened with age, long tables and armchairs placed in front of a fireplace, and in one corner, a lectern. She ran her fingers over the keys of an old typewriter; beside it was a ream of paper and on the walls dozens of handwritten pages that someone had fixed to a panel, using colored pins.

"Don't you have a computer system?"

"What on earth would I do with it?"

"Then how do you know how many books you have and what they are?"

"The catalogs." He gestured toward a series of volumes. They all looked the same: dark spines, simple bindings. He took one and opened it. "You see? Here are the titles, the authors, the genres, and the locations. All handwritten. But what really counts"—he tapped his forehead—"is memory. It's all here inside. See up there?" He pointed to a shelf with glass casing. "Those are all first editions. The essays are on the right, the travel books and adventure stories are on the wall behind you. Then there are the cookbooks and fine arts. Novels are in back, though, because there's more room and some armchairs."

Sofia's surprise grew. "There are thousands of them. How can you possibly remember the location of each title?"

"You know, what comes next is not always progress," whispered the bookseller. "If Manzoni was already saying that in his own time, I wonder what he'd say now." He smiled sheepishly. "Please excuse my plunging back into the past. It's almost obligatory for us old people to take refuge in what we know best. Literature, for example, always provides good shelter. We feel the need to show off the knowledge we've gained and the time we devoted to acquiring it." He smiled again. "We need every advantage we can get to compete with you young people." He fingered the book he was holding in his hands, as though it were proof of what he was saying. It looked extremely old. She'd noticed the red cover immediately.

"I'd like to say I have a great memory," continued the bookseller, "but that's not the case. It's an old system. You divide the available space and fill it according to a specific order. Genre, for example, then author. My cousins used alphabetical order from left to right."

"Of course, that makes sense. I think there's more to it, though."

The man's smile grew, causing a new series of wrinkles to appear around his eyes. He looked down to clean his glasses, his eyes sparkling. "You know what's never lacking in a bookshop?"

Sofia raised an eyebrow.

"Time. And even if it were, a true bookseller would never allow his other commitments to keep him from reading. So, you see, signorina— what did you say your name was?"

She hadn't. "Sofia."

"A fine name indeed. So, as I was saying, it's a matter of constant application. Books have no secrets for someone who is always reading, and they certainly do not hide their position on the shelf."

Coming from him, she could believe it.

"Tell me, Sofia, are you looking for something in particular? A special book, perhaps?"

Why not? Although she doubted there would be a manual for cases like hers. "Got any books that teach people how to find themselves again?" Her tone was glib, and she immediately regretted it. What had gotten into her? She was just about to apologize when he pointed to a spot behind her.

"Of course. There's a book for every need—didn't you know that?"

She didn't answer, partly because she didn't know what to say and partly because she was ashamed.

He was squinting at the top shelf.

"No, *Beloved* isn't the book for you. Even though it's a revelation. You need something different. There. *Home* would be more suitable— also by Toni Morrison, of course. It's the story of a journey back. Retracing your own steps is often the only way of finding the courage to move forward." He fixed his eyes on hers. "Don't misunderstand me, though. You won't find the solution you're looking for in that book unless it already lives inside you. However formidable they are, books, my dear, are just sparks. The fire is only lit where there's wood to kindle, so to speak."

"You don't beat around the bush, do you?"

"I'm too old for that. But I wasn't always this way, you know."

Who knows what he'd been like when he was younger. Good-looking, thought Sofia, because he still was, and strong, like the expression in his eyes. "You remind me of someone."

"Someone good, I hope."

Sofia allowed herself a broad smile. "One of the best. Aren't all grandparents?"

The bookseller nodded, his eyes lighting up. "You said you used to come here when you were a child. Do you live in Coppedè?"

Sofia shook her head. "No, my grandparents do. Maxim and Therese Bauer. I've always lived in other parts of Rome, but this is where I have the best memories."

"Ah . . . You're very lucky."

Sofia found the remark curious, but decided to let it pass. "I'm sorry. I'm taking up so much of your time."

He looked at the book in his hands. "You said you were lost, but you know a lot about books and the power they have. How could such a sensitive, kind, educated girl have lost herself?"

A bitter smile came to Sofia's lips. "In the usual way, I suppose. Ignoring your own needs, making the wrong choices, putting things off . . ." She paused to think. "After I graduated, I worked in a library. It was what I'd specialized in. But then I got married." There wasn't much more to add. "That's an antique book you have there, isn't it?"

The bookseller raised his head. "Yes, early 1800s, but the binding has serious problems. I should get it restored before putting it up for sale."

Sofia stretched out a hand. "May I?"

"Of course." But he didn't pass it to her right away. "It's by Christian Philipp Fohr. The first volume in German of his only work: *In Praise of Perfection*, consisting of *Discourse on Nature*, *Discourse on Humankind*, and *Discourse on Thought*. It was the first edition from this printer." He handed her the volume.

Amazing, thought Sofia. She loved Christian Fohr. She'd come across him almost by chance while writing her thesis on the Romantics and had been enchanted. It was his heart—the essence of his soul—that Fohr had put into prose. As she'd read, she'd had the feeling he was there with her, smiling at her, guiding her through the reasoning that had led him to imagine an ideal world.

"You know him? You know German?" The surprise on the bookseller's face turned into delight.

"Yes, my grandfather is from Germany. He taught me the language when I was a child." She turned over the book, her eyes on the spine, her heart beating fast. "Not as popular as Goethe, but just as significant, don't you think? A realistic portrait of his times and the anguish over what they should have been. A utopia, the dream of a man who comes up against the contradictions of a rapidly changing society." Her voice was professional and detached, but she was trembling inside. Her attachment to Fohr was pure, unadulterated admiration. That man had been capable of offering himself completely to his reader and to the unforgiving society of the nineteenth century, laying bare his soul and risking condemnation and derision.

Silence fell between them for a long moment. Then Sofia took a deep breath.

"You said you need to have it restored before putting it up for sale . . . Tell me, what would it cost for me to take it as it is?"

"But it's in poor condition."

"Don't worry, I'll look after that." Now that she could see it better, she realized that the cover was a work of art. "How much?"

The bookseller hesitated.

"I imagine it's one of the most valuable books in your catalog. Name your price."

The man shrugged his shoulders. "But you can see how damaged it is."

Sofia took out her wallet. "I like it as it is, with all the traces of its past. And I know how to restore it." Of course, some years had gone by since she'd last repaired a volume, but she had the skills. Elaborate antique covers, leather, wood, and metal inserts had fascinated her since she was a child. And so, after a few clumsy attempts, she had spoken to her grandfather, and he enrolled her in the first of many specialized courses.

The thought of taking care of Fohr's book made her heart race. She couldn't wait to start.

"I can't let you pay for it," the man finally said. "Let's say it's a gift, with one condition."

"What's that?"

"Will you promise to come back and show me how you've restored it?"

On an impulse, she leaned toward the man and gave him a quick hug. "I'm sorry. It's just that—thank you."

"Signorina, in all my years, I don't think I've ever seen anyone moved almost to tears by receiving a book."

No, that wasn't why Sofia's eyes were prickling. Or rather, not just that. It was the feeling of taking the first step back toward herself. "I'll take Morrison's book, as well."

After paying for it, Sofia said goodbye to the bookseller.

"I'll take good care of the Fohr and bring it back restored."

He nodded. "I'll be expecting you."

CHAPTER THREE

We love only what we do not wholly possess.

—Marcel Proust, *The Captive*

There was something special about Villa Borghese. Not only because of its size, even though it was one of the largest parks in Rome. Sofia went for a run there every morning, venturing down a different path each time. She always found a distinct feeling of novelty there—the light falling on the lawns, the walls, the pillars, the statues, the stretches of water reflecting tall trees, the people she passed and with whom she exchanged a few words, a smile, a sensation.

But today she wasn't thinking about that. Sitting against a tree trunk, hugging her knees, she stared into the distance. Her mind was on Fohr's book and what she had discovered while browsing through it. On some pages there were notes written in German, in elaborate, old-fashioned handwriting. Mostly they were comments on the concepts of freedom and equality, which were at the heart of Fohr's project.

"Sofia? Is that really you?"

She raised her head, her eyes still hazy with thought. "Ilaria, what a surprise! How are you?" She stood up, incredulous, and fell into the arms of the girl who had been one of her dearest friends in college days.

"I'm well—and you? How long has it been since we saw one another? Four, five years? I'm so sorry I couldn't come to your wedding."

"They told me you were abroad. I tried to call."

"I know, but things were quite complicated for me at the time. I was pregnant." Ilaria smiled. "I have a son. His name's Alessandro. Look," she said, pulling out her cell phone. "Here he is."

A little blond boy with a mischievous smile, waving a hand.

"He's beautiful. I didn't know you were seeing someone then."

Ilaria shrugged. "There are experiences that bring you together and others that keep you apart. You were so wrapped up in Alberto that we lost track of one another."

Sofia scrutinized Ilaria's face—she looked like the same cheerful girl as ever, with her kind brown eyes, red hair, and the spray of freckles that used to make her despair. Yet Sofia heard a veil of reproof behind those words. "You're right, I was too wrapped up. But tell me about yourself. Do you live in Rome?"

"Just around the corner. I work as head of HR for an American multinational company. And you? Do you have children?"

Sofia shook her head. "Not yet." She'd wanted kids, initially, but Alberto kept postponing the idea. Later, she changed her mind.

Their steps led them to one of the park's little kiosks. Ilaria pointed to a table. "Let's sit down. Do you feel like a coffee?"

"Tea, please."

They ordered and then looked at one another for a moment without speaking. It used to be a game of theirs—tuning in to each other like that. Ilaria was the first to speak. "Is something wrong?"

Sofia reached out and grasped her friend's hand. "I've missed you so much."

She felt like an idiot for giving up on her youth so quickly. How lost she'd become; in the very years when she should have been experimenting with life, she'd thrown herself headfirst into something that existed only in her imagination. *It's the facts that count,* she thought, repeating one of her parents' life principles. And now that disappointment had swept away all the distractions, Sofia could see how things really were.

"Let's talk about more cheerful things. Tell me about the others: Davide, Luigi, Serena . . . Have you kept up with them?"

"Yes, of course." Ilaria told her about their friends and their ambitions. About Luigi, who'd written a book, and Serena, always chasing an absurd new project. Sofia found herself laughing more than she had in a long time. They talked for a little longer about all the dreams they'd had during college. When Sofia searched for a subject of conversation that wasn't linked to her marriage, she realized there was one thing that deserved some attention. "Yesterday, a bookseller gave me a first edition of Christian Fohr's *Discourse on Nature*."

"You've always been lucky like that."

"What?"

"Winning the admiration of others. It's as though you see details other people miss, as though you have the key to some sort of unattainable world. You have something in you that attracts people." Ilaria looked at her carefully. "It's still in there, all that magic, you know? You haven't changed."

Although Ilaria's words were kind, Sofia shifted uncomfortably. She shook her head and looked away. "You're exaggerating. And I didn't charm the bookseller—he's my grandfather's age, anyway. The book's in a very bad state. It's probably not even worth much. It's just . . ." She searched for the right words. "I felt like fixing it. Restoring it and perhaps finding out a bit more about that particular volume." She looked up at the sky and then back at Ilaria. "There are notes in the margins." Inside the cover, there was also a strange symbol, a circle containing two wings.

Ilaria's eyes flashed. "Fascinating. Who knows whom it belonged to, the story behind it, how it got to Italy . . ."

"Exactly."

"So you intend to restore it?"

"I'd really like to."

Ilaria nodded. "Books can conceal such surprises. I'm a little sorry I went into a different field." She looked at her watch. "I have to get back to work, but what do you say we have dinner together tomorrow? I could call the others too."

"That would be wonderful."

Sofia knew Alberto would be back by then and that he wouldn't approve, but she felt like spending an evening with old friends, and that's just what she would do. She said goodbye to Ilaria, and as she walked through the park, she thought about how special the relationships with school friends are. You spend so much time together, in the same places, sharing the same experiences. It doesn't take much to reconnect—you just have to want it.

But perhaps, willingness is what any relationship is based on, she thought as she left Villa Borghese to head toward the city center. She remembered an art supplies shop next to Piazza di Spagna. She would buy the materials she needed to restore Fohr's book—synthetic rabbit-skin glue, rice paper for the pages, creams and solvents for the cover, and all the tools, from spatulas to cutters. Fortunately, she still had her bookbinding frame somewhere; it was something she'd never give away. And thread, she needed needles and thread.

And there it was! The shop was right where she remembered.

The heat of the morning was still strong, flushing the faces of the passersby. Tourists were joined by office staff and workmen on their lunch breaks. Sofia let herself be carried by the flow of people, thinking how each of them was driven by an objective, including those standing speechless in front of the church facade, the obelisk, or the fountain. She smiled and stepped into the shop.

After making her purchases, she decided to stroll for a little longer, her mind on old friends. They were all so curious and energetic in those days; classes were never quite enough. They'd spent so many evenings talking about nothing, everything, politics, poetry, philosophy. The discussions meandered, ebbed, and flowed. They all had such a hunger for knowledge. Above all, there was the pleasure of discovering new things together.

On her way up to her apartment, Sofia ran into Joice.

Her neighbor smiled. "Did you buy out a whole store? Marvelous. Wait, I'll give you a hand." She took a bag. "What do you need all this for?" she asked, peering inside.

Sofia opened the door. "I'm taking your advice. I'm going to restore a book."

"Well done." Joice didn't ask for further explanations. "Where do you want me to put this?"

"There, on that table." Sofia pushed aside the armchairs in the study and arranged her bags. "The binding frame can go in the middle." She paused. "But I need something to protect the table."

Joice thought a moment, then raised a hand and made for her own apartment. She was back almost immediately with a sort of thick cloth. "This should work."

They spread it over the table together. As Sofia bustled around, arranging things, the study began to look like a real workshop. It became a luminous and welcoming place dominated by two wide tables full of tools, all framed by a few chairs and the sliding glass doors screened by curtains the colors of sand and sea. "It's perfect."

"Yes, it's lovely. What now?"

Sofia got out Fohr's book and placed it on the table. As she opened it gently, she saw the puzzled expression on her neighbor's face.

"Beautiful, isn't it?"

Joice tilted her head to one side. "Well, I wouldn't say beautiful. Interesting, maybe."

"You'll see when I'm finished."

"There's room for improvement in everything."

She smiled at Joice's optimism.

"I can see you're itching to get started. See you later."

After seeing Joice out, Sofia sat down in front of the book. Everything around her seemed to disappear. Questions rose up from the binding and the cracks in the thin pages, so transparent they seemed to reveal what lay behind. The headband was badly damaged in several places. As she gingerly opened the volume to test the paper, the spine fell apart. She pressed her lips together, grateful it had held on this long.

She sighed and examined the damage. The thread that had bound the volume had disintegrated. Using a pair of tweezers, she picked out pieces of thread and set them aside. Then, with a bone folder, she lifted the endpaper. There was something else stuck to the inside of the cover. She frowned.

For a moment she gazed, puzzled, at the inside of the board, beside the hinge. It was as if someone had crafted a secret pocket. She groped for the tweezers, fearing her discovery might disappear if she took her eyes off it. Slowly and with great care, she pried open the little pocket. When she finished, she stared at the folded sheet of paper tucked inside. She moistened her lips and pulled on her cotton gloves, her heart hammering in her chest.

Sofia slipped the antique paper out of its place. A sea of conjectures churned in her mind. She checked the paper, smelled it, looked at it against the light. It wasn't a fake. She was willing to bet the sheet had been hidden there by the person who had done the binding. But who? And why? She would have to look for an explanation in the contents of that page, written in German in elegant, spidery handwriting.

> *I have waited a long time for the house to become quiet. For darkness to fall.*
>
> *What I must do requires silence, time, and light. But not the clear light of day. The light of which I speak is slow, tremulous, and partly formed of shadows. It is the light of truth. Of what has been, of the tears and bloodshed. Of death. And of life.*

These memories are buried, hidden in a part of me I rarely visit. Candles burn on my desk, but darkness never leaves me. I have opened a window so that the warmth of this summer night may help me to remember what has been, what I must put down in writing. Yet, despite my strong desire to tell the story, there is something else in my soul that rebels, urging me to be prudent, to keep the secret that has been guarded for so long. My eyes wander along the tapestried walls, the paintings, the fabrics, and the furniture—the symbols of my prestige. I could lose everything. I could put my own children in danger.

Yet I can no longer stay silent. What I have been hiding belongs to everyone. It is his, his best work, his finest. And it is mine as well.

Words run away, darting like fish and slipping through my fingers. I must concentrate. I must begin my story.

The curtains shift, brushing against the wood. As my pen runs across the paper, the breeze brings a familiar perfume. It comes from the rose bed that a kind man planted for me many years ago beside the villa. But it is not him I wish to think of. I must force myself further back in time. To when I was a little girl and life was one long discovery. Munich was expanses of pure white snow, the affectionate embrace of a father and the love of a mother. Once, I had a brother. He held me in his arms. With him I discovered joy and laughter and the cold sweetness of snow dissolving in your mouth. This was before death transformed it all, and everything became outrage and fear.

I must stop and catch my breath. Emotions kept hidden for so long escape my control and overcome me. I must quiet my soul or I shall not get to the end, and then the truth would be lost. What he achieved would no longer be recovered. Our secret. I do not have much time left, and none of my riches can make any more for me. What is the sense of possessing the world when you cannot command the minutes, the days, and years that slip away?

What fools, those men who revere money above all things. Possession is not what makes us happy.

It is the ability to create.

My thoughts are like a river following the current of memory. As I write, I think of words, their immense power. They are threads that reach beyond time. Words have made us what we are. Progress has been entrusted to them.

The Fabriano paper feels thick beneath my fingers. Like the leather and silk I have been keeping ready for this moment. No one in my family ever saw them. No one knows their story. I've kept them for years behind a secret shelf. They are all that remains of a forgotten time when, hiding behind a wall in Frederik Schmidt's workshop in Vienna, I spied on the bookbinders hunched over their benches.

I still remember the bitter smell of the strips of alum-tawed skin, the ink leaving marks on paper and stains on hands. The sweet smell of the glue. The dim light catching on cracked skin, blood between the fingers, lips pressed together over teeth. The silence broken by the scalpel and the groaning of the mechanical devices. My heart drumming in my ears and in my throat.

One man keeps watch over everything. He has a long white beard, hands like vices, and little protruding eyes.

He has taught me to be in the world. But I'm a woman, and no one must know what I do.

My name is Clarice Marianne von Harmel, and to this book I entrust the truth.

What is Nature without humankind and thought?

CHAPTER FOUR

It was that way with everything: even sadness passed, even pain and despair, as well as the joys. Everything passed, faded, lost its depth, its value, and finally there came a time when one could no longer remember what had pained one so. Pains, too, wilted and faded.

—Hermann Hesse, *Narcissus and Goldmund*

Vienna, 1804

Clarice didn't know what to think about that patch of sky peeking out between roof tiles and attics. To her, a girl who'd grown up at the foot of blue mountains with snowcapped peaks, it seemed but a mere scrap. But since it was all she had now, she found a stool to climb on and placed her little fingers against the frozen, snow-covered glass.

Since she'd come to live with her aunt and uncle in Vienna, her life had changed drastically. Her *amme* was no longer there to look after her. Her uncle, Kurt Vogel, would not let the woman get into the carriage with them. "Clarice is nine years old. She doesn't need a nanny anymore." So her amme had been left at the castle, like the others. What remained in Clarice's heart was the last look her amme had given Clarice before hiding her face in her apron. Clarice had never before seen her nanny cry. But since her parents and brother had died of the fever, nothing had made much sense.

Her aunt Marta was kind, but even though she looked a lot like her mother, she wasn't at all. As for her uncle, Clarice didn't know what to make of him. He was hardly ever there in the tall, dark house where she'd gone to live. One thing she did know for sure: Vienna was tremendously cold, despite the big fires burning in the fireplaces and the braziers scattered around the house. The smell of burning wood was so strong, it made her eyes water. Now and again, when fear took her breath away, she clutched the charm her mother had fastened around her neck a few days before dying. It was a circle with two diamond wings inside, the family crest.

There were so many strange and puzzling things in that house. The hours spent praying, for example. Not that she disliked God, but she did wonder if he really listened to the invocations of Herr Krauser, the most terrifying man Clarice had ever set eyes on. She didn't even understand who he was. He wasn't a relation or a real priest. Herr Krauser came to visit her aunt once a week, always when her uncle was away, and frightened the servants with his continuous talk of redemption and modesty. And how the world was full of swindlers capable of robbing a decent woman.

Liliana, Clarice's mother, had taught her to look into people's hearts, and she managed to always find something good in each person she met. But not Herr Krauser. Perhaps it was because of his clothes, rigorously black with a high collar buttoned up to his chin, which made him look like a crow. Or perhaps it was the severe looks he gave her, reprimanding her for a dress that was too brightly colored or for not tying back her hair like the other girls did.

Of course, the man criticized everyone. According to him, the staff were careless and slow, and there was always something wrong with the food he was served. Her aunt endured the complaints in silence, her lips pressed together, her eyes on her plate. And so Clarice had started to copy her, thinking this was model behavior.

One day, Clarice was looking at a picture book her uncle had brought back from one of his journeys. Krauser came into the room and approached her on the carpet in front of the fire.

"Where is your aunt?"

Clarice shook her head. "She's not feeling well. She isn't receiving guests today."

He started walking to and fro. Then he turned back to her, his eyes flaming. "It's your fault. You said something to her about me, didn't you?"

"I don't think so," Clarice replied, bewildered.

The man raised a fist threateningly. "You're an ungrateful hussy. You should make yourself useful, earn your keep."

It wasn't the first time he'd said that, and Clarice wondered if perhaps she should explain. "If my aunt hadn't wanted me, she would have left me with my amme."

"You insolent child!"

From then on, Clarice ran off to hide every time he came to the house.

Fortunately, the inhabitants of the house were nothing like Krauser. Milly, the cook, for example. Even though she was taller and stouter than Uncle Kurt and shouted so loudly she made the windows shake, she made the most delicious chocolate cake. And Milly always gave Clarice the first slice.

"All children are a gift from heaven, but little girls are its magic," Milly told her one day after showing her a special door—the one the servants used. If Aunt Marta was the mistress of the house, Milly was the mistress of the kitchen. "Half an hour," she would say, pointing at the door, and Clarice would rush out after pulling on a cape she kept by the oven. Her aunt was a good person, but very apprehensive and never wanted Clarice to go outside, especially not on her own. In the time the cook allowed her, the little girl explored the streets near the house, made friends with children in the neighborhood, and discovered you could have fun without a pony or an ice-covered lake to skate on. Milly often gave her a coin or two, so Clarice could buy milk or a roll for her friends—a brother and sister, Lucas and Ruth—who stood near the church, asking for money. They didn't have parents either, just like her. Clarice could see in their eyes that they understood her, and this was why she liked them best.

One time, she had a very close call. Her uncle appeared on the street unexpectedly and started walking toward her. Clarice knew that if he found out she'd been leaving the house on her own, she'd be in trouble. But then, just before making eye contact, the man turned back. She couldn't tell if he had seen her or not. Since he didn't mention anything that evening, she didn't, either. Soon after, her uncle left on one of his journeys and wasn't due to return for a long time.

That morning, Clarice watched as the snow fell softly to the ground. Her desire to go out and play in it was so strong, it made her skip all around the room. She ran downstairs to say good morning to her aunt, who reciprocated with a brief smile. She was the least talkative person Clarice had ever met. How could she be so different from her sister? Then she rushed down to the kitchen to see Milly. But today, Milly didn't even glance in her direction.

Clarice noticed that the cook's eyes were red, and every time she bent over the cooking pot, her shoulders shook. Clarice went thoughtfully back upstairs. In the end, she decided that if she couldn't go outside, she could at least look out the window.

She loved snow. When it used to snow at the castle, her brother would hug her tightly to him as they'd plunge down the slopes together on the toboggan. If she closed her eyes, she could still smell Oscar and feel the happiness and warmth of being with him.

"Fräulein, get down from that stool immediately! What will people think?"

Clarice furrowed her brow. "That I want to look at the snow?"

"Not another word! As a punishment, you will stay in your room all day. You will only come down for prayers, and you will ask God to forgive you for your insolence."

Dava was a tall, thin woman with a scar on her pale face that seemed to divide it in two. She had appeared in the house a few weeks after Uncle Kurt's departure. Clarice was afraid of her, or rather, of her eyes, similar as they were to Herr Krauser's. He had been the one to recommend her as a housekeeper. It wasn't until later that Clarice realized the two were related.

Since the woman had begun working, Clarice noticed that all her own dearest possessions had disappeared. Her mother's mirror, the lace curtains, her paper and paints. The books, too, had been taken away. Her room had been reduced to a little bed against the wall, a table, and nothing else. Dava had even taken the washbasin and blue enamel jug. Clarice couldn't understand why beautiful objects would be considered immoral. Some of her clothes started to disappear too, and were replaced by mud-colored garments that made her skin red and itchy.

During this time Clarice grew used to being alone. She would think back to her life at the castle, her father in front of the fireplace reading stories of far-off lands. "It seems they have such long noses that they almost touch the ground when they walk," she could still hear him say. She would climb onto his lap to get a better look at the illustrations. "And look at these, Liebling, don't they look like horses whose necks have stretched up to the treetops?"

Their library was immense, with high walls completely covered with books, and a ladder that she was strictly prohibited from using. Sometimes her father would gather a few worn volumes and give them to an old monk, Father Loretto. The ancient man talked as though he were singing. He would let her stay by his side as he opened the books and redid the sewing with his needle and thread. Then he would cut out the leather or fabric, giving her the leftover bits and pieces to make necklaces for her dolls. When Father Loretto was finished, the books were as good as new. Her father would arrange them happily on the table. Then he would beckon to her. "Look, Clarice, books aren't just stories. Everything about them is art. Do you know what art is, my little princess?" She shook her head, her eyes on the books. "It's one of the highest expressions of human genius, my darling. Without it, we wouldn't be much at all." The memories of those happy days were often so clear, they brought a knot to her throat. Dava could take whatever she wanted from the room, but she couldn't steal what Clarice kept in her mind and heart.

That winter was a particularly hard one. There was no news from Uncle Kurt, and her aunt grew more and more silent. She often spent whole hours bending over her embroidery frame. Clarice would read to her and, when Dava wasn't there, she would sing the ballads her mother had taught her. Sometimes she danced, just as she used to at the bonfires the peasants would light in the fields during harvest festivals. Other times, she would play the violin, the notes high and heartrending. In those moments, Aunt Marta seemed to light up and become as beautiful as her sister, Liliana. Herr Krauser turned up on one of those afternoons and complained bitterly at Clarice introducing such deplorable behavior into a respectable house like the Vogels'.

As Aunt Marta's health deteriorated, Dava, supported by Herr Krauser, took over running the house, firing much of the staff—Milly included. More than once, Clarice tried to go to Aunt Marta's room to see her, but Dava was too quick. "Go away, your aunt doesn't wish to see you."

Clarice didn't believe it. Her aunt was a very good person, but she was deeply sad. If her husband returned, Aunt Marta was bound to get better. Melancholy was an illness as bad as any other. Her amme always said so.

The morning they caught Clarice slipping out of the house with the intention of seeking news of her uncle, she was locked in the cellar.

"When you've learned the value of obedience, you can come out; until then, you'll stay in there."

Despite the chilly treatment from Dava and Herr Krauser, Clarice had never really felt in danger before. Her aunt and uncle had always stood between her and the Krausers. But as Herr Krauser pushed her backward until she fell onto the sacks of potatoes, she felt a spasm of terror. Was she no longer safe? Had her aunt died, just like her own parents?

Darkness and confusion descended on her like a hood, forcing her to curl up in a corner, sobbing. The floor was freezing cold and, without her cape, she began to tremble. She got up and wiped her face with her sleeve. Around her was the smell of salted fish and sweet wine.

Clarice set about looking for a way out of her prison, searching the cellar from top to bottom. Then, all of a sudden, she saw a shaft of light filtering from behind the wine barrels. She slipped between them and the stone wall. In the corner, there was a sort of niche opening. That was where the light was coming from. She crept closer and her hand found a wooden panel, closed like a little door. "I'm here," she whispered softly. Then she shouted, "Help me. I'm here!"

With what seemed like great effort, the panel was forced back, and the biggest man Clarice had ever seen stuck his enormous head through the opening.

"And who are you?"

"Clarice Marianne von Harmel, sir. Can you help me, please?"

Crossing the threshold, Clarice found herself in a place just like her uncle's cellar but lit by dozens of candles.

"This is the book workshop, isn't it?"

Lucas and Ruth, her friends from the street, had shown it to her through the window. On occasion, if he was lucky, Lucas would run an errand or two for the workmen, so he knew their names and had been inside the workshop long enough to witness incredible things.

"The gold dust settles like a shower of light on the covers." Both she and Ruth would hang on his every word. "Stags and eagles come out of the red-hot iron."

Clarice remembered Father Loretto and how he, too, seemed to make the books come alive. But Lucas's stories were even more fantastic. The images took shape in her mind like paintings. And they made her think of her father.

She looked around her, her heart racing. There was light everywhere and a comforting warmth that reminded her of the kitchens at the castle. Even the bellows for the fire were similar. "I've never seen a more beautiful place than this."

The man, Frederik Schmidt, stepped back, dumbfounded by this little girl who had emerged from the wall. She was small, with bright eyes full of wonder and something else he couldn't quite define. "Why were you shut in there? Tell me the truth, or I'll put you back. And if you're lying, I'll know!" He wasn't usually so gruff, but surprise had gotten the better of his manners.

"How will you do that?"

"What?"

The child waved a hand. "How will you know if I'm telling the truth?"

Frederik found it hard not to burst out laughing. He stepped closer. The girl hardly came up to his belt, but there was no fear in her eyes, just curiosity.

He was about to answer when she slipped around him and went up to the table with the binding frame. Binding was one of the humblest jobs in the profession, and Frederik usually had it done as piecework. But the particular book he was working on was too precious—a single copy that could not be reproduced—so he had decided to do it himself. The child pointed to the frame and looked at him. "Teach me."

The order took him by surprise. He'd been on earth long enough to recognize the manner of someone wellborn, and he could tell from this

41

little girl's attitude that she was, no doubt, an aristocrat. The rags she was wearing could not disguise her delicate bones, the finely chiseled features, the hair sleek as burnished gold.

"Why should I do that?"

She paused a moment in thought. "Father Loretto didn't want to. Are you also afraid God would punish you because I'm a girl?"

What rubbish was this? And then he understood. "Fear of God has nothing to do with the noble art of bookbinding. But young ladies have delicate fingers. They might hurt themselves."

"I prick myself when I'm embroidering"—she held out a hand—"and I hardly ever cry."

This time Frederik laughed out loud, and when Clarice frowned, he shook his head. He went up some steps, disappearing behind the door leading to the upper floor, and came back carrying a small basket. "How long is it since you ate, little princess?"

She stared at the bread and honey, her eyes wide. "I'm not a princess, but I did live in a castle once."

"If you're not a princess, what should I call you?"

She thought about it for a moment without taking her eyes off the basket. "I think Clarice will do. You're the bookbinder, aren't you? Thank you for your kindness, but I can't pay for your food. I only have my lucky charm, and I must keep that with me always. I promised my mother." In truth, fearing that Dava would take it from her, Clarice had slipped the necklace with the charm between the floorboards in her room.

"This food is not for sale. And so, Fräulein Clarice, there is no chance that you might pay for it. Why not be my guest instead? In exchange, you could tell me your story. You have one, don't you?"

Everyone had a story. She knew that too. She nodded slowly. "Yes, all right." She told him about the long journey in the coach to reach Vienna and her new life in her uncle's house. She explained how Milly had been sent away, and how she had no more news of the friends she'd made in the neighborhood, not even Lucas and Ruth. Now and again she paused for a mouthful of bread. "I think, if my uncle doesn't return soon, Dava and Herr Krauser will sell me to the gypsies." She seemed to be weighing the idea in her mind. "Do you think the gypsies will let me play the violin?"

Schmidt smiled. "Yes, that's probable. They're very good at that sort of thing."

The little girl seemed reassured, but Frederik clenched his big hands. The idea that this little fairy might end up out on the street was inconceivable. He'd been hearing rumors about the old vulture who'd taken advantage of Master Kurt's absence, assuming a position that didn't belong to him. "And your aunt?"

"She never comes out of her room, and I'm not allowed in. I think she's ill."

She said this with such despondence that it made his heart ache. She was as delicate as a doll. In the depths of a soul hardened by work and life's disappointments, Frederik felt something move. His hands might have been as strong as vices, but the bookbinder's ideas about beauty were no less so. He would never have been able to exercise his profession otherwise. And this little creature was far more than beautiful. There was a sort of light in her.

"What do you say you stay here for tonight?"

He was taking a risk, and he knew it, but he was ready to bet that the Krausers would not want to attract the attention of the authorities. One of the Vogels' remaining servants worked for him as well, and Frederik intended to question him the following day. If Clarice's aunt really was ill, and there was no news of Master Kurt, this girl was quite without protection.

Clarice's eyes widened. "Really?"

"Certainly. Unless you'd rather go to the gypsies." It was meant as a joke, but she replied seriously.

"Dava took my violin. Without it, I don't suppose the gypsies would be interested in me. So perhaps it's best if I stay with you. And anyway, I love books."

"Can you read?"

The child gave him a confused look. "Of course. You can too, can't you?"

Frederik smiled again. He made up a bed against the wall of the workshop. "You'll have to stay down here, though."

"Can I come and go tomorrow, as well, through the cellar?"

"Yes, whenever you want."

Clarice thought about it, then nodded. "You'll teach me to make books, won't you?"

She looked so hopeful that Frederik smiled. "We'll see. Now eat up."

CHAPTER FIVE

Be with me always—take any form—drive me mad! Only do not leave me in this abyss, where I cannot find you! Oh God! It is unutterable! I cannot live without my life! I cannot live without my soul!

—Emily Brontë, *Wuthering Heights*

The name was clear. Clarice Marianne von Harmel. That was what she said she was called.

Evening was falling, and Sofia felt a chill. She stood up to fetch a sweater, then crossed to the window. The city shone with light and promise. This was how she had always seen the sunset in Rome—painted orange and gold against a cobalt sky, the shades of blue showing a different side of the city, one you could only see if you knew where to look.

She turned to the book on the table, and her eyes fell on the sheet of paper. Then she averted her gaze, looking back to the sunset. She felt uncertain, confused.

When she'd decided to restore Fohr's book, she knew what she had in her hands. It was one of many copies, though an antique one, of a book she had read several times. She had studied it, discussed it with professors and colleagues. It held no secrets for her.

She'd been wrong.

This copy harbored another story, one that called everything into question.

A different perspective, she thought excitedly, her eyes still on the sky as the light faded.

It was all so strange, so incredible. Her head was churning with questions. At that moment, Sofia knew something had changed. This woman had written a letter, her testimony, using the book as a bottle thrown into the sea of time, and Sofia had been the one to find it. It was as though, as she read, the words became threads tying one woman to the other.

"What do you want from me?" She whispered the words softly. All of a sudden, she could feel the weight, the responsibility of her discovery.

"Who are you, Clarice?"

She opened the book again and quickly skimmed the notes written in the margins. The book had been printed in Stuttgart by Cotta, a well-known publisher of those times. She examined every page, all the folds in the leaves and inside the endpapers, looking for a clue to the woman's identity.

She turned on her laptop and anxiously searched for the name of the mysterious woman.

"Clarice, Fohr. Come on, come on . . . ," she said out loud.

Nothing, not a word about any Clarice Marianne von Harmel.

What Sofia did know was that Fohr's book had been published in three volumes. It was a utopian vision of the world, a place that cradled the soul and all that nurtured it. The first, *Discourse on Nature*, was a sort of celebration, with a wealth of suggestions on how to respect and protect Nature, the source of all emotions. The second, *Discourse on Humankind*, considered the role that each individual played, thanks to the gift of intelligence, and extended the concept of equality; it encouraged everyone to give their best to society. *Discourse on Thought* focused on the wonders of genius and human expression found in music, literature, and art.

At a time when humankind was trying to find relief and respite from its torments, Fohr had revealed an alternative, a different society, and gained honor and fame with this single work.

She stretched out her hand to the sheet of paper and reread it again. Clarice spoke of a secret, something that might bring her harm, something that must come out. "What are you talking about, Clarice? Why hide your confession in a book?"

Her eyes shifted to the computer screen, then she stood up and began to pace. Suddenly, she raised her head. The bookseller—he must know something about where the volume came from.

The telephone rang, making her jump. "Yes?"

"It's me. I just wanted to remind you I'll be back tomorrow."

"Right."

"Have you thought about what I said? Where do you want to go?"

She pursed her lips, eyes closed. "Why do you keep insisting? I already told you that a vacation won't change anything."

"We'll talk about it tomorrow."

"If you want."

She put the phone down. Tomorrow she'd think about what to say to Alberto. How to end a marriage? What was the right way to break off something you'd cared so much about for so long? The only way was to put it all behind you, move forward with your life. But whenever she tried talking to him, she could never bring it to an end.

She picked up the letter once again and held it in her hands, pushing away thoughts of Alberto. She dove into the words the woman had written, surrounded by candles on a night suspended somewhere in time. They were a sort of shelter for her, a place to hide.

She knew she had to find out Clarice's secret. It was the thing that would allow her to become Sofia Bauer, a whole person, again.

Glancing at the clock, she realized the bookshop must be closed. So instead, she tidied up her tools, then lay down on the bed with the book in her hands and the letter by her side. "Who was Fohr to you, Clarice?" She opened the first page of the book and started to read.

The next morning, it wasn't the sun on her face that woke her. Sofia blinked as the contours of her world began to take shape. Then she bolted upright in fear, her hands clutching the sheets.

"Alberto, what are you doing here? When did you get here?"

Leaning against the doorpost, her husband was staring at her, a cup of coffee in his hand. There was a cold light in his eyes, one Sofia had learned to recognize.

"I've been watching you for a while. How come you're still in bed?"

She looked for the alarm clock, her eyes still filled with the dream she'd been having. She knew that it would soon be a mere sensation, so she let it slip away. "I was up late last night."

"Is that so? And where were you? Or rather, who were you with?"

Sofia closed her eyes in irritation. She was not a woman who made the mistake of confusing jealousy with love. As far as she was concerned, her husband's words were just further proof of his lack of respect. She pointed to the book on the bed. "With him, a nineteenth-century writer."

Alberto finished his coffee and lowered his gaze.

At least he still had the decency to feel ashamed, thought Sofia.

"I'm sorry." He came up and sat on the bed, a tense, downcast expression on his face. When he took her hand, Sofia tried to withdraw it, but he held tight. "Listen to me, please."

It was a scene that had been repeated regularly over the past years—his way of apologizing, of regaining ground. She would've liked to get up, push him off, but she lacked the strength. So she resigned herself to listening in impassive silence. It was like traveling a path she already knew so well, she could follow it with her eyes shut. She knew perfectly well that her husband was setting up a truce, and she knew where that would lead them.

"Let's try again, Sofia. We can't give up."

She'd correctly predicted each and every word. They echoed in her mind, making her feel trapped. In that moment she decided she couldn't keep everything shut up inside anymore. She'd tried to be what he wanted, and it hadn't worked.

"It's not that easy," she said without looking at him. She knew if she did, she wouldn't have the strength to go on. "I don't know who I am anymore. I'm lost, Alberto. It's not just about us, as a couple, but about me. You have your work. You know who you are and what you want. Now, look at me and tell me: apart from being your wife, who am I?" She'd had so many passions, but she set them aside one at a time until there was nothing left.

He went on stroking her hand. "Is there something you'd like to do?"

This, too, was something Sofia had already heard: in these moments, her husband was ready to promise her the world, the moon above, and the heavens too. It was just words, and she knew it. But she didn't know what else to do, so she pointed at the book.

"I'd like to go back to work. Yesterday I bought everything I need for restoration. Perhaps I could do a refresher course."

"That might be an idea."

Encouraged, she went on talking. "When I took the book apart, I found a sheet of paper hidden inside. The story of a woman. It's fascinating . . ."

But as she was speaking, something in Alberto's expression changed. He changed. He wasn't listening to her anymore.

"I've got a better idea." He drew closer, passing his hands through her hair. "I think what you really need is a baby."

A baby? She looked up at him in amazement.

As Alberto took off his shoes and his shirt without taking his eyes off her, she was flooded with an anger she'd never experienced before. "A child to keep me occupied, a child as a sort of job or hobby—is that what you mean?"

He smiled. "I think the moment's come to start a family. A child would help calm you down."

Help calm you down. Nausea churned inside her. It was all too unbearable, absurd. She threw off the bedcovers and stood up. "You haven't listened to a word I've said."

"Of course I have. And if you really want to know, I'd be more than willing to go forward without a child, but you need something to do."

"It's not a child I need. I need a purposeful life!"

"Isn't that what children are for?"

Something cracked inside her. "The children born out of love can give their parents' lives new purpose, yes. They're brought up by both parents equally, together, and with love. Do you get it? It's love that makes everything possible, that—"

"Stop shouting."

She fell silent. There he was—her husband, the real Alberto. Stiff, with his arms at his sides, an annoyed, empty expression. The stranger she'd been living with.

"Children aren't for patching up a marriage that's over, don't you see?"

She dried her tears with her hand, and when he came toward her, she turned her back and left the bedroom. How could he dare suggest such a thing? She was so indignant her hands were trembling. She wanted to tell him what she really thought of him. Then, suddenly, everything was quite clear. There was nothing more between them; the very last thread had broken.

Surprise and an absence of pain. Sofia rode waves of anger and disgust, but then an immense calm fell over her.

In that moment, Joice's words came back to her—some things happen because they are supposed to give rise to others. Without this last indecency of her husband's, she might not have found the strength to leave him. Her anger turned into determination. When she heard him storm out of the bedroom, she slipped back in and threw a few things into a little suitcase. Then she went to fetch her tools from the study.

"What the hell are you up to?" Alberto came in, his voice sharp and threatening.

"It's over, Alberto. Enough. As far as I'm concerned, it's gone on far too long already."

He stood in silence, a dark, glowering presence.

Sofia finished packing, then put Fohr's book into a cardboard box together with the letter. "I'll be back soon for the rest."

He just stood there, incredulous. Apparently, he'd never really considered the possibility of her leaving him.

"You're just a spoiled child. Are you seriously giving up and running away as soon as things get hard? You selfish woman."

Selfish? The accusation was so offensive it took her breath away. She would have left things as they were, walked politely toward the door. But now, everything she'd been harboring inside for years demanded to be let out.

"You're wrong, Alberto. I have never been selfish, and I deeply regret it. I tried to be exactly what you wanted." She paused. "But once I was, you no longer knew what to do with me. And neither did I." She walked out the door without a look back.

As she hurried down the stairs with a suitcase containing the remnants of her life, Sofia felt more tired than she'd ever been, and she was afraid. She wouldn't be out on the streets; the keys to her grandparents' apartment were in her pocket, and she had a little money in an account Alberto couldn't reach. Practical questions started to flood her mind, and yet, with every step, she shed more of the weight she'd been carrying around for so long—the fear of pursuing her desires, her passions, and herself.

She loaded the luggage into her car, and when she got to Coppedè, she was trembling so much that it took her two attempts to park. She sat there, bent over the steering wheel, tears pouring from her eyes. Yet, not out of desperation. No, this was a sort of liberation, or purification.

She went up to her grandparents' apartment after making Felipe promise not to call a doctor. "Don't worry," she'd told him, "it's only a headache. I'll be staying here for a few days."

"Of course you'll stay here. And we'll look after you. You'll see, everything will turn out all right."

She'd forgotten how kindness can weaken you sometimes, stealing your strength and leaving you paralyzed by emotion. "Thank you." She couldn't say any more. She shut the door behind her and took refuge in the little bedroom that had always been hers during those long periods when her parents were abroad. She looked at the suitcase, uncertain whether to unpack. She wouldn't be staying long. She should call her grandparents to tell them. She knew they'd be happy.

As for her parents, she'd tell them later. She realized she'd been avoiding talking to them, as though they were a nuisance. And really, they were. Not because she didn't love them, that was impossible. She loved them deeply, but the truth was Sofia felt ashamed.

CHAPTER SIX

So in her bosom even now; the strongest qualities she possessed, long turned upon themselves, became a heap of obduracy, that rose against a friend.

—Charles Dickens, *Hard Times*

Vienna, 1805

Kurt Vogel's arrival in the middle of a snowstorm surprised everyone. They were less surprised when he burst into his house like a fury and put an end to the Krausers' fraudulent presence. All the neighbors, to varying degrees, approved of the unceremonious way he kicked the preacher and his relative out of the house. As they were led away, a chorus of voices and laughter added to the couple's disgrace.

When Kurt started looking for Clarice, he was told she was in the cellar, but there was no sign of her there. Finally, the servant who also worked for Schmidt told him where the child really was.

When the merchant crossed the secret threshold, calling loudly for the master, everyone trembled. Kurt scanned the workshop, but did not see the child.

That's because Clarice was in a special room, perched on a stool Frederik had brought down for her, her eyes following his every move.

Soon, the heated punch would melt the gold powder and the egg white would fix it to the leather. She knew this because she'd watched the procedure dozens of times, and her little hands itched to try it. The contrast between the darkened leather and the splendor of the writing, its motif in gold relief, captivated her. Finishing a book this way was one of the most important and delicate operations for the binder, one that established how skilled he truly was. Once it was set, it could not be corrected.

When Clarice had arrived in Vienna, she'd had to adapt to a new life. Without her amme to explain things, she had to rely on herself alone. Now, with Frederik, she was happy again. She always knew what was expected of her. He gave orders, and she carried them out. There were times when he was so pleased with the way his pupil had sewn the sheets, he started whistling, and warmth spread through her chest.

Clarice loved the books, their stories, the feeling of the paper beneath her fingers, the leather, even the fabric. If she went on working hard, then after three years of apprenticeship and three of practice, she would become a full-fledged bookbinder. In the workshop, there were only men and boys. Perhaps she would be the first woman.

It was a nice thought, and it made her smile. Three years and then another three, that was how long it took to learn, Frederik told her. So she would finish her training when she was sixteen!

"Sir, Master Vogel is asking for you."

Clarice's head swung around. Her uncle was back? She looked at Frederik, but he didn't seem to have heard the workman, who had only half opened the door to tell him the news. The bookbinder's concentration was unbroken.

The worktable sat against the wall, as did the frames and the various presses, all lit by a big fire that warmed this secret room where the bookbinder carried out his most delicate operations. It was here, in a safe, where the gold powders and precious stones used to decorate the bindings were kept. Few people were allowed inside, and never when the girl was there.

Clarice was seized by great agitation and had to force herself to keep still. Her uncle was back; her life was about to change again. She knew the bookbinder must never be distracted from his work, but she couldn't help herself.

"Will you speak to him?" she whispered, trying to keep her voice steady.

The man who had saved her was now examining the volume he had just finished, looking for any defects.

Frederik knew many fine stories and liked to tell her about the books and how he bound them. When he addressed her, he did so kindly and never with condescension. When she was with him, Clarice almost felt like she had her father beside her once more. While the two men were very different, their love of art was equally contagious.

She went on looking at Frederik as he stroked the book, his head bent, the fire reflecting off the hair so fair, it seemed white. After a long pause, he nodded.

"Didn't I promise I would? Now, my little sparrow, keep quiet and let me do the talking. In fact, it's best if you don't move from your seat."

Clarice heaved a deep sigh of relief. She bent her head and let her feet dangle. Frederik would take care of everything. He had a way of understanding what needed to be done. He'd bought Clarice new shoes—and a dress too. The apron he'd had made to her exact measurements was lightweight so it wouldn't hinder her movements as she worked.

"Clarice, come here immediately!"

She looked up, her mouth wide with surprise. Her uncle was standing at the door. In his fur coat, he looked like an angry bear. Clarice looked at Frederik. "Uncle, you're back."

"Just in time, by the looks of it. What on earth are you wearing?"

The child stood up. "It's my apprentice outfit."

Kurt's eyes widened, and he uttered a sort of groan. "What the devil has gotten into you, Schmidt? Do you know who this child is? She shouldn't even have set eyes on a place like this."

Frederik pressed his lips together. "You're probably right, Vogel. If I hadn't found her in the cellar half-dead from hunger and dressed in rags, I imagine I would've thought the same."

Her uncle's face became red. "I owe you a debt of gratitude, Schmidt, for what you've done. But I'm sure you, too, will understand that all this"—he gestured with his hand—"is out of the question. My niece is a von Harmel, and the very idea of making her into an apprentice is an insult to the memory of her parents."

Then he took Clarice's hand tightly, but she pulled it away.

"I like it here, Uncle. I want to go on working."

Kurt seized her arms and picked her up.

"Let me go, I want to stay here. I must learn how to make books. Let me go, I said." She tried to break loose from the man's grip. That was when he shook her violently, taking her breath away.

"That's enough. I will not allow you to make me look ridiculous. Schmidt, rest assured I shall find a way to repay you, but for now, you will keep away from my niece." He strode fiercely back through the workshop, the bookbinder a few steps behind.

Once the panel was back in place, a workman broke the silence. "They say you have to be wary of that man."

Frederik was pale and tense. "If he harms the child, he's the one who'll have to beware."

"I don't want to contradict you, sir, but—"

Frederik knew that his workers had been against his interest in Clarice from the beginning. "Don't then. And the same goes for all of you. I don't want to hear another word on the subject."

Kurt Vogel climbed the cellar stairs to the house, his niece in his arms. As soon as they were inside, he put her down.

"Go straight to your aunt. She'll look after you."

The child winced and ran off. He watched her go, then rubbed his face with both hands. He should have wrung Krauser's neck. What a fool his wife had been, not only continuing to let Krauser into their home, but taking in a relative of his too. They'd almost killed Marta, giving her that tincture of opium. Luckily, his assets were safe in the bank. Yes, they had stolen and sold a few trinkets, but nothing that couldn't be replaced.

It was the deceit he could not tolerate, the insult to his person and to his authority. What would people think of him? Devil take those two Krausers! He crossed the hall in search of something to drink, but there was nothing left in the sideboard, not one bottle. The kitchen, too, looked ghostly, cold and gray. He flung open the door and went out onto the street. "You there!" he called to one of the servants looking after the horses, "Do you know Milly, the cook?"

"Yes, sir, of course, sir."

"Do you know where she lives?"

The man pointed behind him. "Round the back of the church."

He threw the man a coin. "Go and bring her to me. Tell her Vogel is back and wants her at the house."

How could all this have happened? An honest man, a merchant with his status, robbed during his absence. It was all Marta's fault. By trusting those swindlers, she'd put his fortune at risk.

When his brother and sister-in-law and their eldest son had died, leaving Clarice alone, Vogel and his wife had rushed to Munich and, as her only relatives, brought the child to Vienna. The bankers who managed the von Harmel patrimony were concerned for the little heiress's future, but Kurt had managed to convince them that it was best for her to live with family.

The thought of what might happen if the story of the child's mistreatment became public weighed like a brick in his stomach. It was the bankers he really feared, and how they'd use the accusation of negligence to remove her from his control. He would fight tooth and nail before he'd give up control of his niece's inheritance. From that moment on, he'd make sure everything went as it should. He couldn't trust Marta anymore, poisoned as she was by the opium. He'd smelled it the moment he set foot in the house; it took hours and a bath in ice-cold water to bring her around.

"It wasn't my fault; forgive me, I beg you," she said over and over.

God preserve him from this woman's whining.

Such a thing must never happen again. He himself would choose a maid and a housekeeper and a tutor for the child. Personally, he believed that the farther away women were kept from books, the better for everyone, but he'd seen his niece's face and didn't want to run the risk of her disobeying him. So he would keep her busy. From now on, she would stay in the house, where he could keep an eye on her.

He fell into an armchair. When the maid arrived, he pointed to his boots. "Get them off and then prepare a bath."

Clarice knew that crying wouldn't change anything, but she couldn't help it. She'd curled up in a corner of her new room, head on her knees. She didn't know why they'd moved her to the first floor, next to her aunt and uncle's room, but at least her things were back, including the violin and her mother's mirror. She should have been happy, but if there was anything she'd learned in her short life, it was that she couldn't trust anyone. She felt like a leaf tossed by the wind.

"That's no help. You'll only feel worse."

At the door was a girl she'd never seen before, smiling at her. She was young and stocky with long white arms and red cheeks. Her hair was tied in two fat blond braids that wrapped around her head. She wasn't dressed like Dava or Aunt Marta but wore a short-sleeved white blouse, a red bodice, and a blue skirt.

"What do you want?" Clarice snapped. She bit her lip, her breathing staccato between tears. "Sorry," she then murmured. She wiped her face with her hands.

When the girl sat down on the floor next to her, crossing her legs beneath her skirt, Clarice's eyes widened in surprise. No one had ever done anything like that, not even her amme.

"My name's Charlotte, but you can call me Lotte. And from now on, we two will always be together."

"Are you my new amme?" Clarice couldn't have been more surprised.

"Yes, in a way."

Lotte told her about her life up in the mountains and the five younger siblings she'd left behind. As she described the blue sky above her house, and how, from the roof of the wood cabin you only had to reach out to touch the stars, Clarice forgot how sad she'd been a moment ago. She let Lotte help her get changed. And over the next few days, she made an effort to adapt to her new situation.

No more walks and her uncle even forbade her going to church with Marta, but at least her aunt started smiling again. She'd even asked Clarice to play the violin for her. A dressmaker made her some new dresses, though it seemed strange to Clarice that her uncle, instead of her aunt, chose the materials and colors. Milly, while she had returned to work and called Clarice down to the kitchen every day for meals, never pointed to the kitchen door again. It was chained shut.

Some mornings, her uncle called for her. Lotte would take her to the library and then leave them alone. Clarice didn't like his company, so she'd just sit silently in the depths of the armchair he pointed to. She learned to observe people and see what they expected of her. She learned that people say a lot of things they don't mean with their mouths, but the eyes do not lie. Her friend Frederik had taught her how to tell if someone was lying by looking deep into their eyes.

One night, Clarice decided to return to the workshop. She snuck down the steps, her heart in her throat. It was dark, but candlelight flicked under the little door.

"I'm here, master," she whispered.

A muffled exclamation, and then Frederik flung open the door. He had a glint in his eyes and a wide smile.

"It took you a long time, my little sparrow. I thought you'd forgotten me and the books."

"Never. That will never happen. I swear."

They established fixed days and times to meet, mostly at night, when everyone in the house was asleep and no one would notice footsteps on the stone stairs or the rustle of a dress. They were cautious and very quiet in their work. And as Clarice grew up, age-old knowledge passed from man to girl. She learned how to stretch the skin, spread the egg white, and create gold decorations. She became skilled at painting the fabrics and deciding on formats, making paper from rags, fixing the filigree that she would use for the octavos and sextodecimos. As she worked, she learned the importance of silence and prudence. The books became her companions, the ones who knew her secrets.

No one, apart from Frederik and Clarice, knew anything about this continued friendship, sealed during the long nights of stolen time. And then, suddenly, the violent wind that had calmed, allowing her to live a relatively tranquil life, started to pick up once again.

Kurt Vogel had not had any trouble from the lawyers and bankers who guarded his niece's inheritance. But now that she was sixteen years old and a woman, he knew things could change from one moment to the next. When she married, control of her assets would pass into her husband's hands—at least until she was of age.

An impending marriage worried him, and it was not only a matter of the bankers. He wondered how Clarice would react. Kurt worried he had overindulged her—the music teachers, the painting instructors, even a dancing master. And then there were the books, the paints, and those paintings of hers that Marta hung in every available space. Clarice had wanted her own library, and in the end, he had given in. He'd made the girl too independent.

What he could do was choose a suitable husband himself. Someone he could maneuver, who wasn't too old, someone Clarice could accept. Ludwig von Roth's son, for example, was a corporation councillor, not a baron, but he did possess a title. Neither the bankers nor the authorities would make too much fuss, especially if Clarice became pregnant shortly after the marriage. That shouldn't be a problem for the boy, Vogel thought, given the rumors about all the maids that Ludwig had had to silence.

The young Johann was a complete idiot—big as a barrel, with little ox eyes and a hungry expression. Kurt had seen him recently at a reception and he just sat there, gaping at Clarice the entire time, attracting laughter and comments from many of the guests.

Yes, von Roth's son would be an excellent choice. Kurt would have no difficulty controlling Johann, and Johann could deal with keeping the girl occupied.

Kurt still feared, in the back of his mind, that Clarice would escape from him. Though she obeyed him, he hadn't quite managed to break her will, and he knew it was only a matter of time when, one day, his niece would find the door open and fly away. He couldn't have that. The mere thought of it was an insult to all he had done for her over the past years. He hadn't worked so hard only to be robbed of his rightful share.

He walked along, his head bent, and his walking stick sinking into the piles of snow at the sides of the road. Just a block from his house, he saw a silvery glint, then felt a blade go through his arm. As he fell, an instant before hitting his head violently on the pavement, he managed to pull his pistol from the pocket of his overcoat and fire it. And there, in the flare of the shot, he met Krauser's demented eyes. He managed not to lose consciousness. Knowing that his life depended on it, he bit his lip until it bled, and the pain kept him awake. His heart hammering in his chest, he hoped he'd hit the man. The toothless mouth above him was like the rest of Krauser—terrifying. When it twisted into a sort of smile, he realized he'd missed.

"I'm going to kill you."

Kurt had forgotten the bitter taste of fear. He was lost. He couldn't reach his stick, and his arm felt like it had been set on fire. Krauser hit him with a clenched fist, making him scream.

"I should have killed you with my own hands," Kurt spat.

"You couldn't," Krauser said coolly. "God protects me. You are a demon, and I shall kill you. Then I'll go to your house and finish what I started: first your wife and then that cursed girl."

The blade flashed in the darkness before descending one last time. As Kurt raised his good arm in an attempt to shield himself, a shot lit up the night, and then another. The last thing he felt before losing consciousness was a pair of hands pulling him upright. A group of people came running and the world dissolved.

CHAPTER SEVEN

Sentiment is everything;
the name is sound and smoke,
clouding the burning sky

—Johann Wolfgang von Goethe, *Faust, Part One*

The Antico Caffè Greco on Via dei Condotti was one of those unique places where layers of history nestled atop one another. Landscape paintings of Rome covered the walls of the meeting place for penniless poets and painters. Their passionate descriptions, ballads, and dreams lingered on the walls, on the furniture, in frames, in yellowed and tattered photographs. Guests stood around observing the mysterious, enchanting scene, taking it all in, finding themselves with new questions instead of answers. Sofia knew the place well, yet every time she went, she seemed to come across another detail that had escaped her before.

"I'm so sorry." Ilaria's voice was kind, her hand firm on top of Sofia's. She had called her friend earlier that day to postpone the dinner they'd planned—she wasn't ready to see her old friends yet.

"Thank you, but you know, I can't say I'm not happy." She fell silent. Put like that, it was superficial, wrong. Sofia tried again. "I feel as though a part of me is suddenly missing, and at the same time I feel relieved." There was something else too, something so deep inside her that she couldn't talk about it to anyone.

Ilaria's expression changed. Profound sadness clouded her face. "Sometimes I wonder if there are any clear boundaries in life."

Sofia nodded in agreement.

"Things are always complicated where emotion's involved," continued Ilaria. "Everything takes on a less definite shape. There's no black or white, just shades of gray. Anyway, I think it's normal to feel confused in a moment like this. It's not easy to stop loving someone. In the end, I don't think that's what happens, exactly. The relationship changes, evolves, or fades."

"It's always been so easy to talk to you." Sofia smiled. She could have told Ilaria more about her relationship with Alberto, about what was going on inside her and what had happened, but she didn't want to. There were things that must remain private.

They went on talking amid the tempting aromas of hot chocolate and pastries. The afternoon passed pleasantly, and their initial stiffness fell away as they bonded over trifles and gossip. They were laughing when the alarm rang on Ilaria's cell phone; after a quick glance, she stood up. "I have to go and pick up Alessandro from kindergarten. I'll call you tomorrow, OK?"

"Of course. Thanks. I wasn't feeling much like going out, but I've really enjoyed this. Give your little boy a hug from me. I'd like to meet him."

Ilaria nodded thoughtfully. "Take care and keep your spirits up. Next time, I want to hear more about Clarice." She put on her coat and waved goodbye.

Sofia watched her go, a smile on her lips that faded as soon as her friend disappeared into the crowd.

And now? What should she do now?

The sense of panic that'd been with her every single moment in those difficult few days resurfaced.

It wasn't a question about the long term, which had begun to take shape in her mind. What she didn't know, and what alarmed her, was the here and now, the moment after the one she was experiencing, the present tense.

She sat still, watching everything and nothing as people shuffled in—young couples holding hands, elegantly dressed ladies out for a stroll, parents with their children jumping up and down in front of the pastries in the window, demanding to order something sweet. Then her gaze wandered over the frescoes on the walls and the other people who had stopped to look at them.

Her eyes settled on one figure in particular. It was a tall man in a white shirt and no jacket despite the chilly, late-afternoon air. He had broad shoulders and short dark hair. He moved confidently, paying no attention to the people around him, and suddenly he lifted a hand to touch something in front of him on the wall. He continued to move slowly, immersed in a world of his own.

Slowly, Sofia realized there was something familiar about him.

Just then, the man turned around, and his eyes met hers. He didn't smile, just looked. Then he moved toward her.

"The lady of peace and stars." He stopped in front of her, one hand on the back of a chair. "I didn't think we'd see one another again."

"Neither did I, actually." It really was the man she had met at the Galileo Society event. In the light, he looked younger than she'd imagined, but his expression was the same, intense and penetrating. She smiled at him. "This time I've found you in the midst of other people. Did you get tired of solitude?"

His expression softened, and a corner of his mouth turned up. "And yet a crowd guarantees something very similar, don't you think? We decide not to see, not to hear. It's a game of willpower."

It was true. She'd felt it herself. To be alone, it was enough to talk without understanding one another, to proceed in directions that only seemed to be the same.

"What you say is so melancholy, but you don't seem like a sad person. In fact, I get the impression you enjoy yourself very much."

The man looked around before turning to her again. "It's amazing." He was smiling openly at her now.

"Sorry?" Sofia waited for him to explain, but he just waved a hand.

"One day, perhaps we'll talk about it. My name's Tomaso Leoni. And you are . . . ?"

"Sofia Bauer." She offered him her hand, and he took it, bowing slightly. The elegant, old-fashioned gesture surprised her.

"Would you like to sit down?" she asked, pointing to the chair in front of her. It was just out of politeness. She didn't really feel like—she didn't even know what.

He seemed to think about it for a moment. "Better not. I get the impression this isn't a good moment for you. Have a nice evening, Signora Bauer."

Before Sofia could reply, he kissed her hand and walked away. It all happened very quickly. One moment he was there in front of her, and the next he was gone. She looked at her hand where he'd kissed it. What an odd character, Tomaso Leoni, with that inquisitive look of his. She realized that she was afraid of him.

Not afraid he would harm her—no, not that. She was afraid he could see through her, that he'd find her pathetic, as she found herself. She ran a hand over her face, trying to regain control of her emotions. He was just a stranger. Why should his judgment matter to her?

She tried to concentrate on the pleasant part of the conversation. He had called her the lady of peace and stars, and that felt good. But there was no attempt at seduction, just conversation. How could words be so sweet, even those of a stranger? Perhaps that's just what made them precious; they would never be crushed by the pitiless ballad of life. The words would be preserved by the unique quality of those few fleeting moments.

She stood up after a few seconds and called the waiter. "Would you bring me the check, please?"

"It's been taken care of, signora. Have a good evening. We hope to see you again soon."

Sofia blinked. "There must be some mistake."

The boy gave her a broad smile. "It's all settled. *A presto.*"

She left the café bewildered. Had Ilaria paid her bill? Or was it Tomaso Leoni? But why? They hardly knew each other.

She should have felt offended by the gesture; she was perfectly capable of paying for herself. And then she remembered the slight bow and the way he'd kissed her hand. An old-fashioned type of guy. As she walked through the crowd, Sofia turned up the collar of her jacket. The wind had picked up; she shivered and quickened her pace.

Tomaso Leoni entered his office and left the notebook on the oak table. The setting sun reflected on the marble floor and, through the large windows, the roofs of the buildings seemed like copies of the drawings he'd just seen at the Antico Caffè Greco. He loosened the knot of his tie and sank into the armchair, exhausted and angry. How the devil had Frank managed to get them into this mess? He'd thought about it all afternoon, rechecking the documents until there was no longer any doubt in his mind. The signature on the will, which his agency for forensic document reports had the task of examining, was not authentic. It was obvious. Yet his stepfather and business partner, Frank Hobart, had declared that it was.

He got up and started pacing back and forth across the spacious office. Then he stopped and stared out the windows, his hands deep in his pockets. He'd gone down to the café to calm himself and think things over. And there he'd met that woman again, Sofia Bauer. He let his thoughts linger on her for a moment, then he put them briskly out of his mind.

He crossed the corridor to Frank's office. He knocked loudly on the door.

The secretary hurried out. "You see if you can get him to see reason. I give up."

His eyes narrowed in concern, and he let Carla pass.

"What's going on?"

Frank didn't answer. "Where did you go, Tomaso?"

"It doesn't matter." He stepped into the room, closing the door behind him. Behind a Louis XIV desk on a thick Persian carpet, an American man of about sixty with a jovial expression was smiling at him.

"Why did you confirm the signature on the Baldini will?"

Frank poured himself a drink and gulped it down. "Because that's what we do in this office?"

Tomaso went up and placed his hands on the desk, leaning toward his stepfather. "Rubbish. It's false, a fake, and you know it."

"You've always been like this, an arrogant kid. You need to moderate your language, my boy, and calm down." He shook a finger at him. "And in any case, I did all the tests and comparisons. You're wrong. I'm certain." He paused. "Fairly certain."

Frank's hesitation and the slight trembling of his fingers confirmed the warning signs Tomaso had so obstinately been ignoring. His stepfather had been behaving strangely for some time now, and in the same moment that Tomaso recognized the gravity of the situation, he felt like laughing. His mother always said that he hated being right, and now he understood what she meant; he would have given anything to be wrong.

"Withdraw it, make an appointment, call the judge—do what you want, but withdraw the report."

Frank's jaw dropped. "Don't you think you're overdoing it?"

Tomaso showed him the sheet of paper he was holding. "This is Armando Baldini's signature taken from his ID, and this is the one you approved." He paused. They were so absolutely identical that it was not only improbable but impossible for the signature to be authentic. Tomaso would have bet anything that it'd been stamped onto the will with the aid of some mechanical device, probably a pantograph. "What's going on with you? Why didn't you ask for an expert opinion from the mechanical engineer?"

Frank looked at him, puzzled. "Are you checking up on me, Tommy?" A shadow of sweat glistened on his forehead. He looked redder than ever.

"Don't call me that, Frank."

Of course he was checking up; it was what he did best. Incongruences and irregularities had always stood out like sore thumbs to him. It wasn't often pleasant to possess this skill of visual hypersensitivity, causing Tomaso to recall images with absolute precision, but he'd decided to use it to his advantage. His passion for handwriting and calligraphy had accounted for the rest. He became a forensic graphoanalyst, taking his father's place at the agency he'd founded with Frank. But his was not simple handwriting analysis; it was interpretation. Comparing graphic elements was not enough; it was a scheme and a pattern that he sought. He was looking for significance.

Tomaso's attention now moved to a pair of glasses that had fallen under the armchair. Since when did Frank wear glasses? "Do you have eye problems I'm not aware of?"

"What?" Frank followed Tomaso's gaze, then bent down to pick up the glasses and place them on the desk. "No, nothing." The man sank back into his chair and closed his eyes.

"You're lying. What on earth is happening to you, Frank?" As he approached his stepfather, his face was lined with worry.

"Leave me alone." Frank jumped up and staggered.

Tomaso reached out and caught his arm. "I'll take you to the hospital."

"It's nothing, I promise."

"I'd prefer to hear that from a doctor." Worried, he called for Carla. "I'm taking Frank to see a doctor."

She was there immediately, flinging open the door. As Tomaso went out, she whispered something to him. He turned around in surprise. "When did this happen?"

"Yesterday. He said it was just a dizzy spell."

Tomaso felt his stomach tighten. "You should have told me."

"I ordered her not to," muttered Frank, wiping his forehead.

"Why?" Tomaso was dumbfounded.

He looked away. "It's none of your business."

Frank was caught off guard for a few seconds, but then he recovered rapidly. The pain was like a flame, and when the first burning sensation was over, you could ignore all the rest. That was how you kept on your feet and got on with things.

"Can you walk?"

"Yes."

She wasn't sure they'd allow her into the archives. Even though Sofia had worked at the Bibliotheca Hertziana, the rules were very strict. Still, she had to try. Without a few objective references, she wouldn't be able to get any research done, and it'd be as if Clarice never even existed.

A sympathetic former colleague granted her an hour in the archives, so Sofia rushed to look through the books on bookbinding at the time and consulted volumes on the history of Vienna, looking for news of the family. Still, she found nothing, not a single trace of a female book-binder. It was then that Sofia had an idea. She looked for material on Fohr, especially anything autobiographical, and photocopied what she found.

On leaving the library, she knew where she had to go to talk to someone about Clarice, the book, and all the rest. The bookshop was open. She rushed in, letting the door slam. "Signor Vinci!" She hurried breathlessly to the counter.

A smile appeared on his wrinkled face. "Sofia, what a surprise! I didn't think I'd see you again so soon."

"I've already been back twice, but you were closed."

Vinci sighed. "At my age, Sofia, my dear, some days are worse than others." He spread out his arms in a gesture of resignation. "I caught a cold." He smiled mildly. "But you look troubled. Has something happened?"

She grinned. "The book you gave me was no ordinary one. There's another story inside it."

The bookseller took off his glasses, picked up a cloth, and cleaned them slowly. "I'm certain I'm not the first to tell you that books dream." He stopped, clearing his throat. "'A book is the only inanimate object that can have dreams.' Ennio Flaiano said that. And frankly, I've always thought he was right. And so, my dear, who does Fohr's book dream about?"

Sofia's heart was thumping in her chest. "A woman. Her name is Clarice Marianne von Harmel. She entrusted her story and secret to that book."

CHAPTER EIGHT

The dawn has a mysterious greatness of its own, made up
of the traces of dreaming and the beginning of thought.

—Victor Hugo

"What did you say?" The smile had disappeared from the bookseller's
face. Slowly, he stacked the volumes lying on the counter. On top was
the one he'd been reading when Sofia arrived, with a sheet of paper
slipped into it, on which he had noted down quotations. "You found
a message from a woman amongst the margin notes in Fohr's book?"

She shook her head. "It's more complicated than that." For a second, Sofia toyed with running back to her grandparents' place for the
letter. Then something made her change her mind. "While I was examining the book, I found a sort of pocket in the endpaper. That's where
someone hid the letter. I think it must have been the same woman who
wrote it, but I'm not sure."

It took the bookseller a few moments to respond. "That's an incredible story. Tell me everything. What exactly did it say?" He was about
to add something, but suddenly broke off. Glancing around to make
sure they were alone, he came out from behind the counter and locked
the shop door. He turned, his eyes shining with interest. "Let's go and
sit over there. We'll be more comfortable."

Andrea Vinci was moving with difficulty, so Sofia offered him her arm. "Lean on me."

He smiled at her, bending his head slightly. "It's just a touch of arthritis." He lowered himself into an armchair. "Now, Sofia, would you start from the beginning, please?" he said, addressing her as *tu* for the first time. "Excuse me taking liberties, but I find it hard to express my emotions properly in formal language. And identifying emotionally with a text is fundamental to understanding it."

She understood perfectly. She'd always been guided by her emotions. They allowed her to enter into the story, to go beyond the words. "It's a message from Clarice about her life. She was born into a rich, aristocratic family who loved her, and then something happened that caused everything to change. What I'm most afraid of is that the truth will be lost."

"What truth?"

"It's not clear. It's as though this letter were only the first part of the story." She paused. As she spoke, her ideas seemed to expand—everything was becoming clearer. "I think the first question is why Clarice chose Fohr's book." She paused again. "Why did she hide her message in the binding of this book, a place few people would have access to?"

"What sort of people?"

"A book expert, sometime in the future. The idea of that gave her confidence," Sofia said.

"What makes you think that?" The bookseller's question was curt, and the look he gave her was demanding.

"By hiding her message this way, she intended it to be found by someone like her."

The bookseller nodded. "That makes sense."

Up until then, the mysterious woman had been just a vague image in Sofia's mind. But as she spoke, the words so elegantly inscribed on the page seemed to rise up and take on the shape of a face, a figure. Clarice was an attractive woman, strong, capable of facing difficulties and overcoming them. She had experienced great pain, had managed to survive, and had learned an art. Her sense of justice was intact, and it encouraged her to do what was best. In those few lines, she'd mentioned that her actions might put her family in danger, and yet, despite everything, she'd forged ahead. Her eyes were blue, a dark blue that almost seemed black, like those of many aristocratic women in that part of the world. She had brown hair, worn in the long style of the period. She loved books and, as a bookbinder, had a deep knowledge of them. In those days, that meant being highly educated.

Andrea's voice roused Sofia from her reverie. "It sounds like she didn't trust her contemporaries. And there was something that couldn't be uncovered immediately, but couldn't be lost, either." His hands were joined, and he rested his chin on them.

"Yes, but she says the secret isn't hers; she *knows* it. And then she talks about something that was done and must be handed down." Sofia fell silent as the words came back to her. *What is Nature without humankind and its thought?* Her eyes flew open. "There's a sentence at the bottom of the letter. 'What is Nature without humankind and thought?' Nature is the theme of the first volume, humankind of the second, and thought concludes the work. It's as though Clarice was telling us to check the other books in the trilogy!"

She turned around and ran her eyes over the shelves. "The rest of her story must be inside the other two books; they should have the same binding." She stood up. "Do you have them here?"

The old man's eyes flashed, then dimmed again. "I don't have them. It was alone when I—found it. There were no other volumes."

How could that be? "Isn't there any chance of finding them? It's a first edition by the Cotta publishing house in Stuttgart, 1816. A cover in red morocco leather . . ." She uttered the words distinctly, trying to persuade the bookseller. She couldn't give up.

When he made no reply, she began pacing. "Bookshop catalogs, libraries—everything's digital now. Don't you think we could . . . ?" Her voice faded. The volumes could be anywhere in the world.

"There's always been something all books share." The bookseller's voice was low, reflective.

Sofia shook her head. It couldn't end like this.

"They're made of paper," he continued. "They burn or get wet. There may not be anything else to find."

A heavy silence fell, and then suddenly, Andrea smiled. "My dear girl, I remember clearly that the book had notes written in the margin. Comments on the text. In the light of this new information, they may help us to understand Clarice's letter better." He stopped for an instant, his forefinger tapping his chin. "Have you read them, yet?"

Sofia brightened a little. "Only very superficially. I haven't had a lot of time." So he'd noticed too? He hadn't mentioned the notes before. "They're in German, like Clarice's message, and in very similar handwriting." She paused, thoughtfully. "But I can't establish with any certainty whether they were written by Clarice. If they were, it would make all the difference."

The old man went behind the counter, took out a notebook, and opened it. His gnarled fingers flipped through the pages as Sofia waited with bated breath. "Here we go: Frank Hobart and Tomaso Leoni. They're expert graphoanalysts. They'll be able to give you some answers." He wrote the details on a piece of paper and gave it to Sofia.

"Graphoanalysts?"

"Yes, they have an agency that deals with forensic document examination, for legal purposes or for evaluations by antique dealers. Those men have the ability to make or break people's fortunes." He glanced at Sofia, then he closed the notebook with a smile and a deep sigh. "I must apologize, my dear. I can see from your face that I've overdone it."

"What? I don't understand."

He stretched out a hand. "You're obviously upset. I'm sorry, I didn't mean to insist on you investigating." He laughed softly, then shrugged his shoulders. "It's just that it's all so mysterious. A woman who lived two centuries ago hides a message in a book. I give the book to you, and you manage to find it . . . I'm afraid I got carried away."

Sofia smiled at him. "It's not that at all—I was thinking of Tomaso Leoni. I know the man."

It was the bookseller's turn to be surprised. "Really? What a coincidence."

For a moment, she agreed. But if she really thought about it, their meetings could be traced back to their common interests. She had met Tomaso at the Goethe presentation, then at the Caffè Greco, a place that had always attracted writers and art lovers. Now she'd discovered his remarkable profession. You'd have to be very perceptive to analyze handwriting. No, she decided, it was no coincidence. They were both part of a small world.

"He made an excellent impression on me. I'll ask him for a consultation."

She said goodbye to the bookseller. On the piece of paper, Andrea had added his own contact information too. She slipped it into her pocket and left with a smile on her face at the idea that she could continue with her research.

As she walked, she reflected that Vinci didn't even know how much her life had changed since he'd given her the *Discourse on Nature*. It was as though Clarice, through her letter, had obliged Sofia to look inside herself and grasp something she'd been searching for. Was it possible that this was all it took? One day something happens, and everything takes on a new meaning?

Then she shook her head. No, that sequence of events had begun a long time before, like a chain made of many links. For a moment, her thoughts wandered to Alberto. Her husband's telephone calls had become less frequent until they'd stopped altogether. That silence left her in peace.

Felipe greeted her at the door. "You're looking much, much better today, signorina."

"Thank you. I feel better." She returned his warm smile.

Once inside the apartment, she started to get dinner ready, weighing what her next steps would be. She'd already told her parents about leaving her husband, though they hadn't talked for long. They were both very practical people, used to solving any problems they came across. The fact that they'd never been close to Alberto was a help. With her grandparents, things would be different.

Sofia didn't want them to know how much the situation had drained her. Although she knew objectively it wasn't just her fault, that the failure of her marriage was something they had both been responsible for, she couldn't shake the guilt. She looked at her cell phone. Tomorrow, she thought. She'd call them tomorrow. For now, she'd concentrate on pleasant things.

"Tomaso Leoni," she said softly. "Who would have thought?" She smiled and sat down, the piece of paper on her lap, the phone in her hands. She dialed the number and waited.

"Hello?"

"Good evening. I'd like to speak with Tomaso Leoni, please."

"That's me. How can I help you?"

And now? How should she proceed? "I need to make an appointment."

His voice was just as she remembered it, deep and kind. "Could I have a few more details?"

"Well, it's rather complicated."

There was a silence, during which Sofia could almost see that strange smile of his.

"Try starting with your name. Then we'll get to the rest."

She took a deep breath. The situation amused her, but also frightened her a little. She had no idea why the man had this strange effect on her, but she tried not to give it too much thought. Vinci had recommended Tomaso, and Clarice's story was too important not to pursue. "Actually, we know each other."

A moment's silence. "Sofia?"

CHAPTER NINE

It would lack that element which characterizes great passion: the immensity of the difficulty to be overcome and the black uncertainty of events.

—Stendhal, *The Red and the Black*

Tomaso waited as the CCTV camera turned to focus on him, his fingers drumming impatiently on the steering wheel. The automatic gate opened slowly. He shifted into gear, and the car entered the lot. As he drove down the wide avenue, he forced himself to take deep breaths.

He didn't like this house, but more than anything, he didn't like being obliged to do things. He parked in his usual place, beneath the great elm tree, all the while growing more irritated and uneasy.

The villa in front of him was framed by a series of archways leading to a portico and surrounded by small groupings of red geraniums, illuminated by a soft light. The three-story structure rose high toward the sky, but despite its classic style, it wasn't actually old. Nonetheless, the objective of patrician grandeur had been fully achieved.

Tomaso was ten the first time he saw it. They had to drag him inside, and he didn't stop struggling until he saw his mother.

His thoughts shifted back to the present when he saw the small, slight woman in uniform who was waiting at the open door. Despite her age, her eyes were bright and her smile sincere. "Good evening, sir. How are you?"

"Very well, thank you, Scilla. And you?" He didn't give her his jacket but went toward the closet hidden behind an oak panel and hung it up himself.

The housekeeper watched him in amusement. "Now that you're here, very well. Have they told you lately how handsome you've become?"

He returned a smile and then bent down to give her a kiss on the cheek. "The last person to do that was you. But your opinion doesn't count."

"The fact that I bandaged your skinned knees when you were still in short pants doesn't mean I'm blind." The housekeeper clucked disapprovingly. "What's wrong with the women in this country? In my day, a man like you would have been snatched up long ago. You'll be thirty-six next month; you should bear that in mind."

Muttering, Scilla led him into the large sitting room.

Tomaso followed in silence, an amused smile on his lips. He'd forgotten how tiring, and yet pleasant, it could be to have someone fuss over you. He'd never really formed deep ties with anyone. The women he'd shared periods of his life with were like him, interested in making their mark in their professions. And that meant keeping a certain distance.

He'd left his stepfather's house as soon as he turned eighteen and only went back to visit; building a career had absorbed all his energy, and he found it easier to interact with Frank if they kept things on a purely professional level. Yet Scilla's concern made him wonder if the limits he had established for his life had deprived him of something important. But that was just sentimentality. He made sure to bring his thoughts back under control.

"Your mother's in the living room. I'll leave you alone. And don't you dare go without saying goodbye," she threatened.

"OK, but you have to promise you'll come out with me one of these evenings."

Scilla stopped in the doorway. "Do you remember when you asked me to marry you?"

"Of course I do. Your refusal broke my heart. At eleven, some things hurt like hell."

The housekeeper's smile broadened. "I gave you some advice then, and I think now the time's come to follow it." She disappeared behind the door with a last wave of her hand.

In his early days at the villa, it was Scilla who had taken care of him. She was the one who covered for him so he could escape to his father's library. That was his shelter, the safe place where he could be alone. Afterward, when the building was rented out, Scilla had arranged for the volumes to be moved to a storehouse. Every now and then, she'd take him there so he could see that what was left of Massimo Leoni was safe and preserved for him.

The vast darkened windows of the storehouse seemed like walls of black velvet. Tomaso would stare vacantly toward them, a doorway into the past. As the years passed, he found he couldn't remember his father's face, and that filled him with desperation. They had bonded over their shared love of words, so he decided to take up his father's profession. Tomaso left Italy for New York and showed up at his mother's brother's home with a letter in his hand. His uncle had given him a pat on the back and a roof over his head and helped him to find a job so that he could pay his way through college. There, Tomaso had become a man.

"There you are at last!" He turned in the direction of the voice. "What took you so long?" Luisanna Leoni Hobart approached, offering him her cheek. Before bending toward his mother, Tomaso half closed his eyes. He gave her a slight hug instead of a kiss and, with a flash of concern, realized how thin she had become.

"The traffic on the ring road is getting worse. Next time, I'll have to leave a day early to get here in time for dinner. Be sure to give me plenty of notice."

Luisanna shook a finger at him. "You insolent boy. You know very well you don't need an invitation to eat at your own home."

Tomaso saw a shadow in her eyes, but there was nothing he could do about that, just as he could do nothing to change what he thought about this place—Frank's home, not his. In the end, it was enough that his mother was sincere.

He took her hand and kissed the back of it before finding a reply both truthful and kind. "I apologize, Mother. You know what I'm like."

A flash of emotion crossed the woman's face, immediately replaced by a grimace. A tense silence descended between them. Luisanna was about to say something, but stopped herself. A forced smile appeared on her face. "Come upstairs. Your father—I don't know what to do with him anymore. He doesn't listen to me, but I hope he will to you."

Tomaso's jaw tightened, and for a moment he regretted having accepted the dinner invitation. Why did his mother feel the need to bring up his stepfather in a moment that belonged to them alone? He hated that. Her efforts to make him accept Frank as his father were the reason they'd grown apart. Still, he felt compassion for her.

"What were you going to say to me before?" He took her hand. He could feel her tension, the trembling of her delicate fingers.

Luisanna looked at him over her shoulder. "Not now," she begged.

"I just want to know what you were going to say to me." He had seen a crack appear in that smooth surface before she had closed it, shutting him out.

Her beautiful eyes had dark circles under them. "Can't you guess? Do you really need me to say it?"

What a strange question, he thought. Luisanna had the kind of beauty that doesn't fade with time but is transformed into charm and elegance. Her smooth black hair was done up on top of her head, above the pale, oval Madonna face with a melancholy smile that mirrored her eyes. He didn't take after her in the least. He was tall and broad, with large, strong hands. No one would ever have guessed they were mother and son.

Luisanna bent her head, and when she raised it, her eyes were glistening. "You're the spitting image of Massimo. He would be so proud of you."

A knot rose in his throat. He'd lost his father unexpectedly, and although over twenty years had passed since then, Tomaso missed him every day. "Thank you," he whispered.

He was ashamed of having lost his patience. His mother never spoke of her first husband, but it had taken Tomaso years to understand that this was not because of indifference. However often she might bring up Frank, Massimo Leoni was still in her thoughts.

Luisanna smiled and took his arm. "I need you, and so does Frank. If you hadn't made him go to the hospital, he would have died. I don't know how to thank you, my dear."

He didn't want her thanks. And he didn't want his mother to feel she had to be so formal with him. "Getting himself discharged early doesn't seem like the best way to stay alive."

"I've tried to persuade him to go to a clinic, but he doesn't want to hear it. He keeps downplaying his symptoms. But I—I've never seen him like this."

"What do you mean?"

She lowered her voice even more. "Confused, absent. He can't see, you know? I came upon him groping around with his hands. It happens suddenly, and then everything goes back to normal. I don't know what to do."

His mother half opened the bedroom door. "Frank, darling, can we come in? Tomaso's here. You wanted to talk to him, remember?" She fell silent, alarmed to see her husband slumped on the pillows. "What's wrong? Do you feel OK?" She rushed to his side.

"I was just resting my eyes." His voice was hoarse, and his breathing seemed painful. "I'd like my tea, please. Would you make it for me, my dear? Don't let Scilla do it; I don't like hers."

"Of course. I'll be right back." Luisanna went out, leaving the two men alone.

Frank tried to pull himself up, only to fall back heavily on the bed.

Tomaso was at his side in an instant. "Leave it to me." He supported the man and helped to make him comfortable. In the few days that had passed, his stepfather seemed to have aged ten years. "You shouldn't tire yourself out."

The man broke into a laugh, which ended abruptly in a racking cough. He pointed to the door his wife had just gone through. "You know, I've never understood why she agreed to marry me. After your father died, it was as though she'd gone with him." He fell silent for a moment. "In any case, thank heavens she did."

Tomaso remained stone-faced.

A grimace, a bitter smile. "I understand, Tommy. You were right to hate me back then. And, between you and me, you weren't exactly my favorite, either. You were a quarrelsome little bastard." He paused. "You've improved with age, I must say. You Italians have it in your blood—elegance. But you still look too much like him."

He sighed, gazing into the distance. Then he shook a finger in Tomaso's direction. "It was like having Massimo constantly underfoot." Another bitter sigh and a long pause. "We only quarreled once, she and I, and it was about you. She even packed her bags. That was the day I finally understood that, if I didn't find a way to love you, I would lose her. So when you took your father's place at the agency, I supported you and gave you free rein. As for your mother—God help me, I did everything that was necessary to give her all she deserved."

Not for an instant did Tomaso mistake his stepfather's words for an apology. It was Frank's way of putting him on his guard. Worry surged inside him. "What exactly did you do, Frank?"

His stepfather looked away, staring at the door again. "What I had to. Now it's up to you, my boy. Look after her. Your mother is going to need you."

For a brief moment, Tomaso imagined shaking Frank until he spat out the truth. Instead, he took a deep breath. "What did the doctor say?"

"The usual things." He wiped his mouth with the back of his hand. "The truth is that I could do with a new heart. This one's had it."

Not until then did Tomaso notice the paleness around his stepfather's lips. Before he could find out any more, Luisanna came back into the room. "Here I am, darling. You've talked for long enough now—time to rest."

Tomaso took the tray out of her hands and placed it on the bedside table. "I'll wait for you outside."

He went into the corridor and downstairs, Frank's cryptic words replaying in his head. It had been a long time since he used to let off steam with his fists, yet Tomaso felt his hands itching to punch the diabolical old man. As far as Tomaso was concerned, Frank Hobart and his bizarre sense of honor could go to hell.

CHAPTER TEN

Two roads diverged in a wood, and I—
I took the one less traveled by,
And that has made all the difference.

—Robert Frost, "The Road Not Taken"

Sofia sat inside her car, observing the entrance to the building where she'd lived for the last few years. She checked her watch for the hundredth time, still unable to make up her mind whether to go in. She doubted that Alberto was in the apartment, but she needed to be absolutely sure she didn't run into him.

She took a deep breath and tried to pluck up her courage. She'd written him a message to tell him that she would be swinging by to pick up some of her things, but he hadn't replied. "Not even common courtesy," she muttered.

The distance she had put between them helped her to see how stupid she'd been to let the marriage drag on, especially since it had shown signs of fragility from the very beginning. It was as though she'd spent years stubbornly searching for the sunny, amusing young man she fell in love with, inside a sullen, resentful stranger.

At the beginning of their relationship, Alberto had had such a zest for life. Yet after only a few months, nothing remained of it but a sort of greedy hunger and blind egoism. Something was growing in him that stopped him from enjoying his success—the little satisfactions, the beauty surrounding him. If a problem came up related to his work, it was because his colleagues hated him. There was always someone in the legal office trying to defeat, humiliate, or take advantage of him. That, in a nutshell, was his philosophy on life.

She hated that way of thinking; it was poisonous. And even though she now woke up alone at night gripped by fear, it was an enormous relief to have that poison out of her life.

A knock on the window made her jump. "My God, Joice, you scared me. What are you doing here?"

"I saw you out the window. Come on up for a chat. Your husband came to see me the other evening."

Sofia wondered why. Joice had never approved of him. "Do you know if he's home?"

Her friend shook her head. "I passed him in the hall this morning, and he was leaving in a hurry."

Sofia got out of the car, and they walked toward the building together. As she approached, the familiar sensation of oppression returned. She still felt too close to it all.

She put her key into the lock and tried to open the door. "I can't believe it," she said. "He changed the locks."

"The day after you left." On Joice's face there was an expression of compassion mixed with amusement. "Don't make that face. If I were you, I'd be happy."

"But all my things are still in there." As she spoke, she realized how silly it was. Her things could go to the devil for all she cared—that wasn't the point. She and Alberto were mere strangers now. She was determined not to see him or hear from him.

Joice shrugged. "You can always get in from the patio. But first, tell me: What did you leave behind that's so important you'd go back into the wolf's den?"

Sofia gave her a dark look. "Wolf's den? Aren't you overdoing it?"

"Not at all." Joice opened the door to her own apartment. "You always see the best in everyone. Even him."

"What did he want from you, anyway?" asked Sofia.

"How am I supposed to know?"

"Didn't you say he came to see you?"

"I didn't let him in. I just watched through the peephole."

It took less than a minute to get over the wall separating their patios, something she'd done dozens of times when she still lived there. "Let's hope he hasn't locked the sliding doors." As she turned the handle, the panes slid apart. The two friends exchanged a look.

"It isn't breaking and entering, technically, because you're still married. And this is your marital home."

Sofia went straight to her bedroom closet, but it was empty. The shoe rack in the studio was empty too. Nothing. Nothing in any of the rooms in the house. Every object that belonged to her had disappeared. Clothes, books, photographs. Sofia realized he must have thrown it all out, as though he wanted to stop her from regaining possession of her life.

"I guess this would be a good moment for a few tasteful curses. Something to do with Alberto's ancestors, perhaps." Joice sighed. "I'm sorry to tell you, Sofia, but your husband has severe problems in relating to others."

"He isn't my husband. He hasn't been for some time."

She turned down Joice's invitation to stay for coffee and rushed back to her car. As she was starting the engine, she saw Alberto. He was crossing the street. For an instant, she thought of stopping the car in the middle of the road and telling him what she thought of him and his deplorable behavior, but she changed her mind. The idea of looking him in the face after what he'd done made her feel sick. Then a sort of calm washed over her.

After her appointment with Leoni, she'd call Ilaria. Perhaps her friend knew a good divorce lawyer. The sooner she got rid of Alberto De Santis, the better.

He should have known what Frank was up to. He knew the smell of betrayal, but he'd ignored it out of consideration for his mother and the promise he'd made her to try and get along with his stepfather.

Tomaso was sitting on the floor with his shoulders against the wall, and his face showed every trace of the night he'd spent checking documents and registers. Now they all lay piled at his feet.

Frank had kept two sets of books. For every transaction he completed, he kept a percentage for himself. It had been some time since he'd properly paid the suppliers or covered the expensive consultations with chemical engineers and mechanics. He hadn't even paid the researchers in full. Now, although there was no shortage of work coming in, the agency was in trouble. He covered his face with his hands for a moment, then stood up. What a fool he'd been. But what the devil had made the man do something like this?

He left the office and opened the main door just as Carla was coming in.

"Ciao, Tomaso, good morning."

He didn't reply, merely nodded, a dark expression on his face.

Carla's broad smile faded. "Is Frank worse?"

"No, but we need to talk." He gave her a cold look. His stepfather couldn't have managed to trick him without help, and it was Carla who dealt with the accounting.

He stepped aside to let her pass, and as she carefully hung up her coat, he seemed to see her for the first time. In her early fifties, she was still an attractive woman, although pale at that moment, with trembling lips.

"How long have you and I been working together?"

She blinked. "What makes you ask that?" She went to her desk and sat down, her head held high, her shoulders straight. She began moving things from one side of the desk to the other, a drawn expression on her face.

"Is there something you want to tell me?"

Carla flinched, but remained silent, her eyes on the wall, as though the wallpaper might suggest an answer.

A flash of anger made him turn his back on her. He strode back to his own office, aware that if he didn't leave immediately, he would say or do something he regretted. "I want your notice on my desk immediately."

He slammed the door and then knelt down on the floor. As he gathered up the files, he heard the door behind him open slowly.

"I warned him you'd find him out, that you'd find us out. But he wouldn't listen to me. He said that if anyone was capable of understanding what he'd done, it was you."

Tomaso was incredulous, his heart hammering inside him. He placed his hands on the floor and turned toward Carla. "What on earth do you mean? Understand? What is it I should understand? Tell me! No, don't. I don't want to hear another word." He turned his back on her again. "I should report you both to the police. Fraud, embezzlement, forgery. Is that enough, or should I go on?"

"It's not what you think."

He wanted to scream. As he gathered what remained of his agency from the floor, he realized how stupid he'd been. For some time, he'd had a feeling that something wasn't quite right, but he decided to ignore it. And now he was paying the price.

"Go away, Carla—get out of here."

She stepped back.

When Tomaso saw the fear on the face of the woman he'd always considered a friend, he stood up and moved away from her toward the window. "I trusted you."

"Listen, it isn't how you think it is."

"No? How is it, then?" He went on looking out the window, his hands bunched up in the curtains. He was tired and wanted Carla to leave him alone. He had to find a solution, and he couldn't do that if she insisted on staying.

"Don't judge Frank before you know all the facts."

"What the hell are you talking about?"

"Your stepfather lost everything in the Lehman crash. He tried to recover it, but it reached a point where there was nothing more he could do. There was nothing left."

"He had the agency, his work."

"Let me finish." She remained silent for a moment, thinking. "He'd built his fortune thanks to his ability as a broker, you know that."

"He played the stock market, using the agency's money?"

"No, he invested it. That's different."

"Do you think I'm an idiot? In any case, the money didn't belong to him, and he had no right to use it that way."

"He was obsessed. He wanted your mother to be able to go on living as she was accustomed. He spent nothing on himself, and if you think he did it for me, you're very wrong."

It was all too much. While Tomaso understood that Carla couldn't have stopped Frank, she hadn't even tried to warn him. Now he had rising suspicions about the secretary's relationship with Frank. The thought made his stomach turn.

"Leave my mother out of this."

Carla shook her head. "I can't. I—let me show you something." She went back into the other room.

Tomaso heard her opening and shutting drawers. He followed, furious, propelled to demand an explanation of what she was hinting at. She and Frank had imperiled everything he'd built up over the years, all his hard work. The agency could collapse from one moment to the next. He didn't even want to think about his mother. The idea that his stepfather might have betrayed her was intolerable.

Carla handed him a stack of files.

"These are the mortgage bills for your mother's house, and these," she said, laying one hand on a file, "are the payments. You can check them yourself. The figures correspond exactly to the irregularities you discovered. And here's a record of expenses related to the upkeep of the villa. These are the shares he bought. One day, they'll rebound and Luisanna will be a rich woman."

As Tomaso flipped through the pages, he raised his eyes to look at Carla now and again. It all seemed to check out. "OK. Let's agree that Frank stole the money he needed from the firm to pay my mother's and his personal expenses. So then, how do you come into this?"

Carla moistened her lips and perched on her desk, her hands on the polished wood surface. "Your stepfather is my representative. I'm your business partner, not him."

"What?"

She crossed her arms. "A few months ago I bought Frank's shares from him. He used the money to pay off his bank debts. As you can see, if there's anyone who has confidence in you, to the extent of investing all their money in your work, it's me."

"But why?" Tomaso exclaimed. "You knew everything; why would you have done something like that?"

Carla remained silent for a moment, then she cleared her throat. "I've spent ten years of my life in this office. I have no family." She spread her arms. "The agency is everything to me. I'm not young enough to look for another job—to start again." She looked away and took a deep breath. "Before I came to you, I sold pharmaceutical products. I had to learn everything from scratch, and believe me, Tomaso, I couldn't do that again. I can't start over, and I don't want to because I like what I do, what we do. The research, the inquiries. It's right to make sure a signature is authentic, isn't it? And so few things are nowadays."

She held up a hand for him to let her finish. "I know I should have stopped Frank and found a way to warn you, but I couldn't. He was so convincing, and deep down his motives were good." She paused. "Have you ever done anything crazy for love, Tomaso? No one's ever done anything like that for me. Never. I—"

She laid a hand on his shoulder. "I've been trying to find a way to tell you for weeks now, and I can't tell you how sorry I am. I know it's wrong, and Frank should have talked to you about his problems, but I understand him too." She paused again, choked up. "He couldn't. He didn't have the courage, and I think, in the end, all of this caused his heart attack. He became obsessed with the idea that your mother might lose the villa and that he would no longer be able to support her. You know what he's like."

Tomaso's head was spinning. "I would have taken care of her."

She laughed bitterly. "But you're his wife's son. For a man like your stepfather, that would have meant absolute failure. Don't you see? He would have lost face. He would have had nothing left at all."

"If my mother found out about this, do you think she'd take it well?"

Carla sighed. "And who would go and tell her, Tomaso? Frank? Not even on his deathbed. As for me, I can assure you I don't have the slightest intention of telling Luisanna anything. That leaves you. Are you going to take revenge on Frank? Are you going to destroy the idea your mother has of her husband?"

In that instant, something inside Tomaso snapped. He felt like laughing. He felt trapped and lonely as he never had before. That's what secrets do: they separate people from others, launching them onto a path they have to travel on their own, or at best, with accomplices.

"I have confidence in you, and I know you'll set things right."

Idiot. "Spare me the optimism, Carla. I don't want your stupid confidence. I've got no use for it."

Tomaso felt as though he were drowning. He fell silently into the closest chair. The world he knew seemed to have capsized completely.

CHAPTER ELEVEN

Sofia stood in the hallway, not wanting to ring the bell yet. She glanced at her watch to make sure she wasn't too early and looked around. From the outside, it had seemed the usual anonymous office building, but now she could see the frescoed walls and the original lines of the double staircase. The little building had the character and charm of an ancient home. She took a breath and pressed the button.

"You must be Signora Bauer," said a smiling woman with short snow-white hair. "Do come in. I'm Carla Bertini."

Sofia returned her smile. "Thank you."

The waiting room was elegantly furnished. She settled onto the divan, the bag containing Fohr's book comfortably nestled on her lap. She gazed slowly around, taking in the natural stone walls, pale oak floors, and antique furniture. A faint flower perfume suffused the room.

"Would you like something to drink?"

"No, thanks, I'm fine." Where was Tomaso?

"May I ask you the reason for your visit?"

"I need an expert opinion on handwriting in an old book." She said no more.

She shifted position nervously, hoping she hadn't made a mistake. When she heard a door open, she stood up.

"Good evening, Sofia." Tomaso approached, holding out his hand.

"Thank you for seeing me." She smiled at him, but he didn't smile back. He was polite, but cold. She felt her courage waning.

"You said it was very urgent."

Over the phone, Sofia had insisted on making an appointment as soon as possible. He clearly hadn't appreciated it.

"Yes, that's right."

She felt embarrassed to realize she'd expected a different welcome. She looked longingly at the exit, wondering if it wasn't too late to make a run for it. And what then? She would never know who Clarice had been. It would be the hundredth lost opportunity, another part of her life she'd allowed to get away.

"Would you care to step into my office? Perhaps you'll feel more at ease when I've explained the way I work."

Sofia met his eyes, and Tomaso's expression softened. She had the sensation that he was once again the kind man she'd met. Perhaps he had noticed her unease and was trying to remedy the situation. "Yes, thank you."

The office was spacious and full of light. Sofia stopped in front of the massive desk at the center of the room.

"Come, let's sit down." Tomaso pointed to a pair of armchairs near the window. "First, I want to ask you how you knew my profession."

"You were recommended to me by an acquaintance of mine, a bookseller. I recognized your name."

"And you need help with a handwriting identification," said Tomaso, looking straight at her.

"Yes." She opened her bag and took out Fohr's book, holding it in her hands for a moment before handing it to him. "There are notes written in the margins. Not on all the pages, as you can see. They're comments on the text."

Tomaso lingered on the frontispiece. Then he started to browse through the pages. He turned them over carefully, slowly. His face showed complete concentration, as though only he and the book existed. And he knew German. Sofia would have bet on that. In that very instant, he was reading the notes on freedom and love. After the bookseller's suggestion that the margin notes might provide a clue, she'd learned them all by heart:

> *And in truth I ask myself whether there really is any justice in the common morals that impose decency, like a veil thrown over truth that must never transpire. And so true sentiments are sacrificed to the golden lie of respectability, because they are too difficult to accept. In the end, this is merely the celebration of hypocrisy. It is none other than the denial of the soul.*
>
> *It is by sharing thought that the soul is enriched, grows, and prospers.*
>
> *Love is the only truth we know. It is the mirror in which we reflect ourselves, the one that shows us who we are, without any indulgence.*

"The notes weren't all written by the same person. I would say, with some margin of doubt, that some come from a female hand and some from a male one." He closed the book and handed it back to her.

Sofia took it and held it on her lap. "How wide is the margin of doubt?"

For the first time since she'd entered, Tomaso smiled. But not at her, more as if he had remembered something amusing. "One or two percent. If you want a more precise analysis," he went on, speaking slowly, as if he wanted to make sure she understood, "an official analysis, let's say, it will take a little longer. But if it's purely a matter of personal interest and not a legal one, I can tell you that we're talking mid-1800s; the print is compatible with the pens and ink used at the time and, judging by what I can see, there's absolutely nothing odd about the notes. People have always made very different uses of books. From family births and deaths being recorded in Bibles to diaries kept on blank pages."

Sofia wasn't listening anymore. She was still thinking about what he'd said: two different people wrote the notes.

"What's necessary for an identification?" she asked, her face tense.

Tomaso frowned. "You want to know who wrote in the book? Know the identity of the writers, is that it?"

"Yes, precisely." An idea was taking shape in her mind, something so big she hardly dared to think it through: Clarice and Christian—it was the answer to her initial question. Why had the woman chosen to hide her story in *that* book? Perhaps because she knew the author?

She remembered something she'd read once: "If it's white liquid and it comes in a bottle, it's almost certainly milk." It was a way of saying that the most obvious answer is often the right one. Clarice had chosen Christian's book because she knew him. Sofia was more and more convinced of it.

"I'll need documents, letters, anything written personally by whomever you believe might have been the author—authors—of the notes. The more material I have, the quicker the identification will be."

She had documents: Clarice's letter and the documents by Fohr she'd photocopied from the library. Sofia was euphoric. Once more, she felt that something truly special had come into her life.

"Let's say it's possible that I can provide you several such documents. How long would it take you to do the analysis?" Her face was flushed, making her eyes shine and highlighting her features.

Tomaso could see there was something very important to Sofia about the book. He took a better look at her without making it obvious; the woman was an enigma. At times she seemed quite ordinary and might easily go unnoticed, but at others, she seemed to transform into another person. Her bearing, the determined expression on her face, her passion—she was attractive in a way that forced you to look at her. With a flash, he realized that Sofia Bauer wore a mask. *Who is she?* he wondered, but immediately put the thought aside. He must concentrate on the question she'd just asked. How long did he need to compare the handwriting samples?

He didn't give her an immediate reply, or rather not in the terms she'd imagined. It wasn't a good thing for his clients to know that he was capable of making an identification almost instantly. That was something he'd learned to keep to himself. He'd grown up in his father's agency and learned the art of calligraphy from him. Handwriting had always been a family passion. After graduating from Columbia University in New York, he decided to perfect his abilities. He took various courses and specialized at La Trobe in Melbourne, Australia. That was how he had become a forensic graphoanalyst. But what made him truly excellent at his job was his photographic memory, along with the merciless logic that he applied to each project.

"Time isn't important. There's a different question . . ."

If she'd seemed anxious in the waiting room, she now looked as though she were ready to start shaking. He had to proceed with caution, and quickly, if he wanted to learn more about this story that had whet his curiosity.

"Let's take it one step at a time," he continued. "What can you tell me about the book's history?"

"It was beautifully bound," she started. "Red morocco leather, gold leaf and powder in the engraving. I was the one to remove the cover. It was damaged and practically crumbled in my hands."

"You did keep it, didn't you?"

"What do you take me for? Of course I did."

Tomaso cursed his misstep. Sofia Bauer was extraordinary, and he'd known it from the first moment he set eyes on her. She was a woman who'd leave a party to recover the sense of things by looking at the stars; she liked peace and silence. And she knew about antique books. If he wanted to pull her out of the place where she was hiding and find out more about her and the book, he had to be cautious.

The thought led him back to the discussion he'd had with Carla before Sofia had arrived. If only he'd been more direct with Frank . . . A stab of bitterness shot through his stomach. Why hadn't his stepfather told him about the trouble he'd been in? He would have done everything in his power to lend a hand. How did Frank not understand that about him?

He brought himself back to reality, to the woman in front of him, whom he'd so thoughtlessly offended.

"My apologies, but isn't it plausible that someone who didn't know the book's history might simply get rid of something in such a deteriorated state?"

Tomaso was perplexed. She must be an expert, and yet he'd never seen her before in the small world of booksellers, librarians, collectors, and calligraphers, except for that one evening at the Galileo Society. He would have remembered her; he was sure of that.

"I was a librarian, and I have a passion for bookbinding."

Tomaso stared. "Of course, I'm so sorry."

"It's all right. You couldn't have known."

She smiled, and the tension between them eased.

"Let's try starting over. You have the original cover of this book with the handwriting inside it, right?"

"Yes, that's right. It was definitely the original binding."

"Good. Now let's concentrate on the notes that occur throughout the volume. We've established that they belong to two different people. You want to know the identity of the people who wrote them, and you have handwritten texts by the presumed authors."

"Exactly."

"May I ask why? Are you doing research? A study of the writer?" Before she could answer, he decided to explain himself better. "It's not just curiosity on my part. I need to focus my attention in a specific direction, or I won't be able to find what you're looking for."

While Sofia had initially been irritated by Tomaso's questions, now she looked at the analyst in a new light and felt she could trust him. Honestly, she wanted to trust him. She needed to recover her faith in other people. She didn't want to let Alberto drag her down into a world of suspicion and resentment; that wasn't who she was, even if lately she'd been starting to slip into those habits. She'd shut herself away in her own little world, even excluding the people she loved and who loved her. First her friends, then her family.

Her new willpower swept away all her remaining reticence. She opened her bag. The envelope containing Clarice's letter was inside. She handed it to Tomaso.

"This was hidden under the endpaper. It is extremely important to me to know if this was the woman who wrote the notes."

Tomaso examined the sheet of paper. "How do you know it's a woman?"

"She signed the letter. Her name is Clarice Marianne von Harmel."

He looked closely at Sofia. "Is she an ancestor of yours?"

"Why do you ask?"

"You talk as if you knew her."

She shook her head. "No, I came across the book completely by chance. It was given to me by a bookseller who wanted to have it restored. That's all."

Tomaso didn't seem to be convinced by her explanation, but something on the paper caught his attention. It was the same symbol he'd noticed on his first examination of the book, a circle with two wings inside. It was stamped onto the thin paper of the manuscript and appeared in the form of a filigree on the boards. Then he lost himself, completely absorbed in reading the letter.

Suddenly, he stood up, taking the book and the letter with him. He placed the paper carefully onto the photocopier, which lit up as the page was copied. There was complete silence. Sofia went to Tomaso and he met her eyes, beckoning her to come closer.

"Some of the notes were written by the same person who wrote the letter. Clarice. There are slight variations, probably evolutions as the author aged."

She knew it! A sense of euphoria swept over her. In that moment, smiling at Tomaso, she felt even more certain of who had written the rest of the notes. She was so convinced of her theory that she didn't want to consider any others. It had to be Clarice and Christian. Now she'd have to uncover the story of their connection. Her heart was beating fast, and she felt happy, electrified.

"Judging from your expression, I'd say that was good news."

She had to stop herself from embracing him. "Wonderful!"

Her enthusiasm was contagious, and Tomaso found himself beaming back at her. "I somehow have the impression you know whom the other handwriting belongs to."

"I have a theory," she replied.

Tomaso studied her for a moment, resisting the temptation to ask. "How strange that of all books in the world you've brought me one of my favorites."

"You know Fohr?"

"Yes. I studied German, and I have a passion for the Romantics. Personally, I find his prose poetic and his ideas illuminating."

That was the very term she'd have used to describe Christian's writing—*illuminating*. They exchanged another smile, embarrassed by the intensity of their emotions.

"Is that all you wanted to know, or can I do something else for you?" He handed her the book, the letter on top.

"Do you have any idea where I might find the other volumes?"

"Naturally. Any self-respecting library has at least one copy of Fohr's complete works. But you don't want just any old copy, do you?"

"No, that wouldn't be any use."

He squinted, observing her carefully. "Why don't you explain exactly what it is you're looking for?"

Tomaso marveled as Sofia Bauer opened up. He saw fear, hope, and then something that made him hold his breath: faith. Total, blind faith. It was so strong that he immediately wanted to put her on guard again. She mustn't trust him. She mustn't trust anyone like that.

"I think the rest of the story is hidden in the other volumes of this edition. But I don't have them."

They sat in silence for a moment, taking it in.

"This isn't just an antiquarian's puzzle, is it? You really want to know what secret Clarice is referring to, but just how far are you prepared to go for the answer?"

The expression on Sofia's face was so perplexed, it made Tomaso smile. "You must excuse my choice of words. I'm not usually so clumsy. You came to me, which means you're not able to carry out this search alone. And it's not something for amateurs, if you'll excuse the term."

Suddenly, he seemed withdrawn. His tone was formal and detached.

"I want to find the truth," she replied, "to know Clarice's story, discover why she chose to hide her secret in Fohr's book, and why she wrote that sentence alluding to the two following volumes, as if it were a clue, a sort of path to follow."

Tomaso nodded. "Let's imagine I provide that part of the story. Would you be willing to sell me the book, the letter, and anything else we find?"

"No!" exclaimed Sofia. "Why on earth should I do that?"

"The usual reason, the one that makes the world go round?"

However much she might need money, Sofia would never sell that book. Never. The fact that he hadn't understood that disappointed her. She hugged the book to her and shook her head. "Thanks for the offer, but no."

"Of course. I understand."

No. He did not understand. All the joy and connection she'd felt vanished abruptly. Sofia couldn't wait to get out of there. It had been a mistake to contact Tomaso Leoni. She should have gone to another expert, someone she didn't know and wouldn't have cared about in the least. "Shall I pay the lady at reception?"

"You don't owe me anything. It was a pleasure to help you. Let me show you out."

"Thank you."

Tomaso shut the office door, his hands in his pockets, a pensive look on his face.

"When are you starting?"

"What?"

Carla handed him some sheets of paper. He looked at them, then at her. "Why did you print out the scan of the documents? I was just doing an analysis of the text. This is something that requires the client's consent." Tomaso's voice was icy.

"Why do you think I did it?"

"You listened to the whole conversation," he accused her.

Carla shrugged. "Actually, it was quite boring. But when you suggested she sell you the book, I realized there must be something important underneath it all. I didn't get everything," she complained, pointing at the documents, "but I got quite a lot. If you wanted that volume, it means you saw something special in it."

"Perhaps you didn't hear the part where the woman refused my offer."

Carla huffed. "There's one thing I've always admired about you, Tomaso."

He raised his eyebrows.

"You've never treated me like an idiot. If you continue doing that, we'll continue getting along. You realized that letter is a path that leads somewhere. Perhaps to a precious antique."

Tomaso shouldn't have been surprised. Carla knew how he thought and how he set up his investigations. While the agency relied on his work as a forensic graphoanalyst, his true passion was searching for mysterious and untraceable books.

"It may well be, but the legitimate owner of the volume has no intention of selling, so we're out of the game."

Carla banged a fist on the desk. "We aren't interested in what Sofia Bauer wants or doesn't want. If the secret were a precious one, and you managed to discover it, our agency would no longer have any problems.

We could pay off our debts and the PR boost could be tremendous," she concluded.

"It was a consultation. What Signora Bauer and I said in there is strictly confidential."

"Do you think I intend on telling anyone?"

"The answer's still no." He left her standing there, returned to his office, picked up his jacket, and went out. "Close the office, please. I'm going home."

He was almost on the threshold when he stopped. "I want to be quite clear about something, Carla. There are things I don't accept, but I can understand. However wrong it was, what you and Frank did together is among those things. I don't know if I'll be able to get us out of the mess you made; it'll depend on a whole series of things, some of which are out of my hands. As for the rest, I'll try my best."

He fell silent for a moment, then fixed her with a piercing stare. "But do not, by any means, push me when it comes to the ethics of the agency, who I am, or what I represent. There are things I'm not ready to ignore." His voice was deep and calm. "Throw away everything you have on Sofia Bauer. The matter doesn't interest us any longer."

As he walked out the door, they both knew: even if he managed to save the agency from bankruptcy, nothing would ever be the same between them.

Carla stared at the documents, shaken. Tomaso had never spoken to her like that before. Why couldn't he accept that the solution to their problems was trapped inside those documents? She raised her eyes to the door he'd shut behind him. What if—but she knew what the consequences would be if she deceived him again.

With a sigh, she put the documents into the shredder and watched them reduced to tiny strips. She put on her overcoat, switched on the alarm, and left.

CHAPTER TWELVE

In this world, shipmates, sin that pays its way can travel
freely, and without a passport; whereas Virtue, if a pauper,
is stopped at all frontiers.

—Herman Melville, *Moby-Dick*

Vienna, 1812

It was the screams that woke her. Clarice tried to hold on to her dream
for a little longer. She clenched her teeth, but nothing could bring it
back. The dream was like time; it kept moving forward.

She rubbed her eyes and sat up in bed. The embers of the fire that
Lotte had lit for her the evening before were still glowing dimly in the
darkness. Barefoot and shivering, she went to the door, slid back the
bolt, and pulled it open. A shout made her jump back. She slammed
the door and leaned against it, gasping. What was going on? She cocked
an ear—terrified. From downstairs came other noises, furniture being
moved, suppressed crying. She ran to the window. People were crowd-
ing around the front door.

Her thoughts flew to her aunt. Over the last few days, she hadn't
been well and had been mumbling strange things to her about the
future. Clarice flung open the door and flew down the dark stairs, her

heart in her throat. She came to the last step and made her way forward, staying close to the wall. When she saw her aunt kneeling in a corner of the hallway, she ran and put her arms around her.

"What's happening?" she whispered, pushing her aunt's hair out of her eyes.

Marta didn't reply, shaken by silent sobs, her hands covering her mouth.

"Light—for God's sake, bring candles!" A towering man of about thirty, in a heavy fur coat, seemed to have taken charge of the situation. His abrupt order sent the servants running.

Clarice took advantage of the space that opened up to draw closer. Her eyes widened. On the ground lay her uncle. There was blood covering his face and chest. Kurt stirred, moving his head, and Clarice was filled with relief. He wasn't dead. She must reassure her aunt.

The strange man squinted at Clarice, looking her up and down, his eyes straying to her nightgown. "What are you doing here? This is no place for you." He seized one of the servants by the arm. "Get the women away from here."

"Don't you touch me." Clarice glared at the servant. "As for you," she went on, turning to the man, "who are you, and what has happened to my uncle?"

In reply, the man took off his fur coat and walked toward her. Clarice had to raise her head to look into his eyes. But she did not retreat, holding the stranger's impenetrable gaze.

"He was injured by a criminal. Don't worry, he'll recover." He placed the coat around her shoulders. "I am August von Kirchberg, a distant relative of your uncle."

She had never heard of the man, but this was of little importance at the moment. "We owe you our thanks, Herr von Kirchberg." She took off the coat and gave it back to him, then helped her aunt to her feet. Clarice didn't notice the looks following her, or know that the candlelight had made her nightgown transparent as a veil. "Come, Aunt, let me take you back to your room."

August followed them to the foot of the stairs and waited until the two women had reached the upper floor. As he retraced his steps, he heard a servant comment about how pretty the girl was. Grabbing the unfortunate man by his collar, he hissed, "Get out of here," pushing him over the threshold. When he turned around, all the other servants were gaping at him. He clenched his big hands. "Until my cousin recovers, you will obey my orders. Any more comments?" No one dared protest.

He returned to Kurt. The bleeding had stopped, but behind his beard, the man's face was deathly pale. August whispered something to the doctor who had arrived to examine the wounded man.

"Get him into his bed," ordered the doctor. "Fetch a blanket."

Later, once Vogel was resting in silence, August entered the bedroom. "Just in time, eh, Kurt?"

Vogel's eyelids fluttered, and he slowly opened his eyes. It took him a moment to focus on the figure leaning over him. "You?"

"Why, aren't you pleased to see me?"

Kurt tried to sit up as his senses returned to him. "And Krauser?"

A cruel smile appeared on the younger man's face. "If you're referring to the man who was about to cut your throat, he got what he deserved."

"But how—why were you there?"

Of course, if Kurt was in a better state, he would have understood right away, thought August. He'd been keeping an eye on Kurt for days, waiting for the right moment. Vogel was in his debt, and he was there to get his money back. As for the family relationship he'd mentioned, it was almost true. Once, the two men had almost been brothers-in-law.

"What do you want, August?" Kurt's voice was hoarse and weak.

The man came to his side. "Vienna is a fine city. I think I'll stay. Naturally, I'll earn my keep." He paused and smiled. "I've told everyone I'm a relative of yours, so see to it that you remember that."

"Whyever should I?"

August bent down so that their eyes were on the same level. "You'll see that it's in your best interest. At the moment, you need all the friends you can find." He didn't even wait for a reply; the threat was clear. He was already at the door when Kurt called him back. He stopped without turning around.

"I'm sorry about Else. I never wanted things to go like that."

August nodded, hatred burning within him. "Of course," he murmured.

August left the room and strode to the end of the corridor. As he passed one of the bedrooms, he heard the door shut quickly. A slow smile crossed his lips. He was ready to bet the girl slept there. He looked around and then turned back. The room next to Clarice von Harmel's would do just fine.

When he'd arrived in town and heard that Kurt had taken in a niece, he'd imagined a child. But the girl who'd come downstairs, showing herself to everyone without the slightest sense of shame, was a woman—a very young one, but a woman nonetheless.

Over the following weeks, Kurt Vogel fought hard. He accepted all the treatment he was subjected to, but the wounds caused by Krauser's filthy knife became infected. Consumed by fever, he hung between life and death for a long time. When he finally came around, he found his wife beside him.

"It's a miracle," he heard her whisper. Marta was thanking God for saving him, and he was ashamed of himself and of the scarce love he had felt for the woman.

"I'm hungry," he whispered, a moment before he slipped away into sleep.

From then on, his recovery was quick, but Kurt never returned to the man he was before. He spent a lot of time in his room in front of the fire, staring at the flames. Marta smothered him with attention, which he accepted without protest, just as he accepted the presence of August von Kirchberg in his home. The man now managed Kurt's house and his business. He kept his wife and niece company at supper and accompanied them when they went out for a walk or to church. And Kurt could do nothing about it.

Every time he looked at him, the thought of Else overcame him. August had the same large, bright brown eyes as his sister—the woman Kurt had abandoned a lifetime ago.

He leaned back in his armchair, letting his head fall back, his eyes fixed on the ceiling. He closed them, and she was with him. "There was nothing I could do," he whispered. He still had a precise memory of the day he left her, his promise that he'd return. She had believed him for a while until she caught wind of his engagement to Marta and killed herself. For Kurt, Marta meant the city, a career, and a different life.

He rang the bell he kept on his desk. A moment later, the servant knocked. It was a new boy, someone August had hired. For a moment, Kurt thought of giving him his notice, then shook his head. He must stop acting like that. He had even grown suspicious of Marta. "Take this letter to von Roth and wait for the answer. Make haste."

The boy disappeared as rapidly and silently as he had entered.

Kurt got up and went to the window, pulling aside the curtain and following the young servant with his eyes. Then he returned to his table. His hands were shaking. He had no choice, he told himself, suddenly troubled by second thoughts. He would never give up his niece's inheritance, and the only way to keep control of it was through her future husband, Johann von Roth.

He had to act before von Harmel's bankers did.

August entered the courtyard, unsaddled his horses, and tethered them. He gave instructions to a stable boy and sat down in the darkness, looking out into the night. No one was expecting him—his return was scheduled for the week after. With a little help, he had managed to settle Vogel's affairs.

Gradually, he'd grown comfortable, taking advantage of Kurt's negligence. In the past, the merchant had been shrewd, but illness had weakened him. Now, it was just a matter of time, thought August. He just had to be patient for a little while longer, and everything would go to him and Clarice.

The thought sent a shiver of desire through him. He rubbed a hand over his forehead, a smile playing on his lips. Would she still be up or already in her room? He wanted to see her; he liked the way she listened to his stories, how she hung on each word, imagining the world that was forbidden to her. He had promised to take her on a journey one day, but Clarice didn't seem to believe him.

There was a strange, astute streak in her too. Something that made him uneasy. Perhaps it was the way she considered his words, or how she watched him with those careful, pensive eyes.

He spied her windows. They were closed, no light showing. A parked carriage indicated visitors were at the house. He wondered what the young woman was wearing. He liked her clothes, the way she played the violin, the way her neck bent as the bow touched the strings. He liked her. One day he would have her. And there was a certain pleasure in waiting. He entered the kitchen, yawning. He'd have something to eat and go straight to bed.

"Good evening, Milly."

"Welcome back, sir."

August shook his head. He and Milly were more or less the same build, absurd for a woman. He took off his tailcoat and, after relaxing his shoulder muscles, looked for the remains of supper on the stove. As he sat down to eat, he realized that the cook was scowling and thumping dough as if it had wronged her.

"Has something happened?"

The woman grunted a reply, her elbows white with flour, a menacing look on her face.

"Tell me what's going on, would you?" He was starting to lose his patience.

For a few seconds Milly was quiet, then she swore out loud, pointing at the door. "Weren't you informed? Clarice is getting married."

He paused, his spoon in midair. Then, slowly, August started eating again. But now the soup had lost all its flavor. He pushed away his bowl. The maid who had just come in hastened to take it away. August went to the door. "And who is the lucky man?"

"Johann von Roth."

August frowned. "There must be some mistake. The young man is an idiot."

Milly sniffed. "No mistake." She wiped her face. "As if she hasn't suffered enough already, the poor child. To marry her to someone like that . . ."

He didn't bother to reply, just rushed toward the library. A glance inside was enough to confirm Milly's claim. Ludwig von Roth was sitting opposite Vogel, and Marta, motionless in a corner of the room, looked ready to faint. There was no sign of either Johann or Clarice.

What really bothered August was the fact that he'd assumed Vogel had the girl's best interests at heart, seeing how he tracked her activities even from his room. And yet, no one with an ounce of good sense would force even a servant of his to marry this Roth.

What had he missed?

August went upstairs, one step at a time, lost in thought. The corridor was lit by a single flickering candle. He was almost at the end of the hall when a noise stopped him. His hand flew to his dagger. He turned slowly. Clarice's door stood ajar. That sound again. August stiffened.

Fury exploded inside him. It was a moan. A woman moaning. He flung open the door, almost knocking over the girl. Surprised, he seized her arm, preventing her from falling. "What the devil do you think you're doing?" he barked at her.

The girl was as surprised as he, but immediately regained control of herself. She was wearing a heavy overcoat, and at her feet was the bag that had just fallen to the floor. "I'm going. Get out of my way."

"Where to?"

"It's of no importance." Her eyes were red, her face swollen. "They're forcing me to marry. I'm just an object to them."

August's head spun with desire; he needed her.

He recalled that his nurse used to tell him of women who were capable of bewitching anyone they wished. This Clarice was an enchantress, he knew. Even bent over her embroidery or deep in a book, she knew how to captivate everyone around her. August could read it in the eyes of every man who entered the house, in the sighs that filled him with anger.

"It's the fate of every woman. What's wrong with marrying and bringing children into the world?"

He had never felt so shaken before. At that moment, he would have been capable of killing Roth—and Vogel as well—without the least bit of regret. He took both of her hands and pressed them to his breast; he wanted to feel them on his body. He averted his eyes from the mouth that tempted him with its quivering, her supposed fragility. She was a witch, a cursed sorceress.

"Anyway, there's nowhere for you to go. Your uncle will find you."

He would too. She would never get away from him, but this he kept to himself. He needed to dominate her. It was the only way he could regain control.

Clarice tried to pull away, but August held on tightly. "You know yourself that it will be your fate, so why do you oppose it?" He wanted to torment her, wound her. He wanted her to tremble.

Clarice lifted her chin, a determined expression on her face. He hadn't frightened her, August realized. Her pride was still there.

"Answer." He shook her, burning to do something quite different.

"I'm a person. I have the right to choose for myself." Her voice was clear and resolute.

August was fascinated by that passion, the beauty of those proud and delicate features. The thought of bending it to his will set his blood on fire.

"I will talk to my cousin. I'll help you."

Clarice sized him up for a long moment. She wasn't stupid; he would have to act shrewdly to persuade her and win her confidence.

"You must trust me."

She stared at him, a tired light in her eyes. "Will you really talk to Uncle Kurt?"

Her tone was skeptical, but August grasped a thread of hope and hung on to it with all his might. That was her weak point: like all women, she believed what she wanted to believe. He squeezed her hands again, pressing them to his lips, then letting go. "I promise. Now go to bed."

Clarice moved away and nodded. She reached for the bag, but he was quicker. He frowned at the weight.

"What the devil have you got in here? Vogel's silverware?" He opened it, puzzled. "Did you think you could survive out there on books?"

The thought amused him and bolstered his self-confidence, which he had doubted only a moment before.

"They're mine."

"No doubt, but believe me, Clarice, they wouldn't have been any use for buying your freedom." He laughed softly and handed her the bag. He felt calmer now. In the end, she was just a foolish little girl.

He was already at the door when he stopped. "I expect you to be grateful for what I'm about to do. I'm your friend, Clarice. Don't forget that."

It took a little time, but she finally answered. "I have no doubt."

The next few weeks were a nightmare for Clarice. Her uncle relaxed his surveillance, but the price she had to pay for those few moments of freedom, when she went out with Marta to parties or the theater, was extremely high. Johann von Roth came to see her every evening with gifts of all sorts, and she was obliged to receive him.

Lotte tried to persuade her to accept her fate and so did her aunt. Both women made every effort they could to help her, but there was very little they could do. The engagement had now been announced, and the wedding was imminent. The needlewomen were working hard on her trousseau. The dress, too, had been sewn. The only thing left was to be practical and accept her fate; it was a means to survival.

"Resisting will make things worse. You have to pretend to be docile and obedient. When you get pregnant, things will be better, you'll see. Men are always sensitive to the arrival of an heir."

But Clarice felt like her life was ending. How could they talk so frankly about such a terrible fate? Johann, who hung around with a vacant look in his eyes and a hungry expression on his face, frightened her.

August remained her only hope. He had promised to help. She just had to be patient. She was sure he'd be back soon from the latest journey he'd undertaken for her uncle. When he returned, August would speak to Kurt and it would all be over. There would be no wedding. He'd promised.

Clarice knew that August was fond of her. And yet, when he smiled at her, told her about his adventures, or surprised her in a corner of the house with his jokes, she felt happy and troubled at the same time. The shivers she felt were strange and made her desire things she couldn't even put a name to.

One evening, while Clarice was waiting for Johann's visit, August burst in.

"Go and change, Clarice. I hope you've got something suitable for the occasion."

"What do you mean?"

"Johann von Roth is dead. I believe he fell from his horse."

Lotte stood up, and her embroidery tumbled to the carpet. "I'll go and call the mistress." She rushed out, leaving Clarice alone with August.

"It's terrible," Clarice whispered. Yet she couldn't ignore a sense of deep relief. How could she be so coldhearted?

August smiled, a slow stretching of his lips. "Aren't you pleased?"

"No! I didn't want to marry him, but it's terrible that he's dead."

"Don't worry. Now everything will fall into place."

August didn't tell her that a wedding would still be celebrated; instead of Johann, whom he had dispatched with surprising ease, August would stand in his place.

He'd already come to an agreement with Vogel. Once he'd discovered Kurt's interest in the girl's inheritance, negotiating an agreeable plan was child's play. August had already chosen a house where he and Clarice would live. He'd even written to his sister Maud, asking her to come and help organize the wedding.

He smiled to himself and pressed his lips to Clarice's brow. "You'll see. From now on, things will be perfect."

CHAPTER THIRTEEN

> We do not succeed in changing things according to our
> desire, but gradually our desire changes . . . We have not
> managed to surmount the obstacle, as we were absolutely
> determined to do, but life has taken us round it, led us past
> it, and then if we turn round to gaze at the remote past, we
> can barely catch sight of it, so imperceptible has it become.

—Marcel Proust, *The Sweet Cheat Gone*

At that time of evening, the steps to Trinità dei Monti were crowded
with tourists. Families with children were replaced by groups of teenag-
ers, solo travelers, couples, all in search of special moments. Later, they
would pull out the memory and relive it all over again. Rome would
have become the background to an unforgettable kiss, a confession, a
chance meeting that changed everything.

The luckiest of them would exchange mischievous looks as they
told the story of that night when, in the streets of that wonderful old
city, their life had taken an unexpected turn. They would laugh about it
together. Others would sit in bittersweet silence. The worst fate would
rest with those who thought back with regret, distraught at the thought
of what they hadn't had the courage to do.

Sofia wove through the crowd, a tired look on her face, Clarice's book hugged to her breast. Her sadness was a solid presence by her side.

Too many things had happened over the last few days, she thought, and she'd clung to Clarice's story like a life preserver. But she knew that life wasn't like that; nothing could keep a drowning person miraculously afloat without their own willpower.

And no one knew this better than she did. In the past, she had carefully avoided change, afraid to lose what she'd convinced herself she had. Not until now had she fully realized this. Everything she'd experienced, everything she'd thought she wanted, appeared so clearly to her that it took her breath away. How could she have been so stupid? What had she done to herself? What had she allowed others to do to her?

It was all too much. The desperation was so profound that, for a moment, she was afraid she might burst into tears right in the middle of Via Condotti.

She looked around, perplexed. How was she still on the Via Condotti?

It seemed she'd gone a long way around only to return to her point of departure. She blinked. The window of the Caffè Greco was in front of her. Sofia approached slowly, her eyes stinging. *One minute,* she thought. That was all she needed to recover her composure. But everything behind the glass looked hazy.

The place was crowded, buzzing. Yet it wasn't an unpleasant sensation. It was like being alone, really. And she was used to that.

"I'm sorry, there's nowhere to sit." A waitress smiled apologetically. "Would you mind waiting a few minutes?"

Sofia would have happily sat on the floor. "That'll be fine."

The girl smiled again. "Wait here a moment. I'll be right back."

The waitress then led her to a corner with high stools, like those in a normal bar, only better designed. Sofia leaned on one, and her eyes fell on the table she had occupied a few days before. She should call

Ilaria; she had so much to tell her. But it wasn't really her friend she was thinking of.

She forced herself to look away, but her thoughts stubbornly stayed on Tomaso. He had been direct, brutal. He wanted Clarice's book. No, not Clarice's, Fohr's.

Why had Tomaso Leoni asked her to sell him the book?

As though her thoughts had the power to summon him, she saw Tomaso enter the café. He didn't notice her. He didn't seem to notice anyone, as though he were in a dimension of his own, to which others were not invited.

The same waitress who had greeted Sofia hurried up to him. They said hello as if they knew one another and exchanged a few words. The girl noted something on her pad, nodding her head. Sofia looked at him again, sure she hadn't been seen. He seemed distracted, tense. His hair fell over his forehead; he'd loosened the knot in his tie and unbuttoned his shirt. He took off his jacket and scarf and hung them on a coat hook. As he made for the corner with the high stools, Sofia quickly turned her back.

She realized how childish she was being. Tomaso hadn't done her any harm, and his request to buy the book was perfectly reasonable. The fact that she was disappointed because she had imagined he was different and because she was so wrapped up in Clarice's story—that was her own problem.

The waitress returned. "There's a table free now. Right this way. What can I get you?"

"A salad will be fine. And some tea."

The waitress jotted down the order. "I'll be right back."

Sofia's table was on the far side of the room. From there, she could no longer see Tomaso. All the better, she decided, since she was merely wasting time instead of tackling her real problems.

She had to look for a good divorce lawyer, a decent place to live, and a job. And then there was the offer from her parents, who wanted her to go and live in France. They had a house in Camargue and a small apartment in Paris, an efficiency. Sofia had always liked Montparnasse, but she didn't know if she was ready to leave Italy. Of course, moving would mean a clean break with the past.

She ate her salad and left the café without saying a word to Tomaso.

As she walked along beneath the streetlights, she thought of how warm she felt in Rome. It was home to her, where she belonged. She would miss everything about the city—the trees and paths in Villa Borghese, the palazzi, and what remained of the ancient temples. She liked the decadent aura of the capitals and pillars, loved the old city center. And she had an authentic passion for Coppedè and its bizarre asymmetrical architecture. She loved the mixture of ancient and modern, its strange harmony, impossible to repeat anywhere else.

As she climbed the steps of Trinità dei Monti, her thoughts turned to the woman who had called out to her from the past, entrusting her with her story. Under her breath, she whispered, "Clarice, I would have so loved to know more about you. I especially would have liked to help you." She felt as if she'd abandoned her, failed to do everything in her power, and it was a very intense sensation. Tomaso had noticed. Hadn't he asked her if they were related?

She was almost at the top when she decided to continue toward the Pincio. It was one of the most fascinating neighborhoods in Rome. On reaching the summit, she stopped for breath. From there, Rome was like a painting, shining in thousands of little glimmers.

Her throat tightened. What was happening to her? She'd always had nerves of steel, and now practically anything could move her to tears.

She stayed to admire the view a moment longer; the sensation of peace was addicting. She could see it on the faces of all the people around her. She liked that because it meant she wasn't so strange after all, that others appreciated the beauty of the place. She breathed in the cold air deeply, holding her breath for a moment before blowing it on the tips of her fingers. The walk served her well. She'd shaken off the worst of the anguish. A little sadness remained, but nothing she couldn't deal with. She moved to find a better spot.

That was when she saw him.

Again? Was it really Tomaso Leoni, leaning his elbows on the parapet? She didn't fully believe until her eyes met his.

"You are the most disconcerting woman I've ever met."

"I just wanted—" She fell silent.

"What. What did you want, Sofia?" His voice was low and deep.

Now they were side by side, shoulder to shoulder.

Sofia moistened her lips. "I saw you earlier, at the Caffè Greco."

He nodded, still looking out at the piazza. He turned slowly toward her. "I know."

His gaze was so calm that Sofia decided to ask the question that'd been tormenting her. "Why did you want to buy my book?"

"I think you know that."

Once again, she had the profound sensation that she had always known Tomaso well, better than anyone. Could you possibly feel such a connection with someone you'd only just met?

But she had already made the mistake of assuming too much about him.

"Give me a clear answer, please."

"Very well." He pointed to the avenue. "Let's take a stroll."

She agreed. It seemed like a good idea to keep moving; it would get rid of the chill she felt.

"How broad is your knowledge of antique books?"

"I have a degree in the conservation of cultural heritage, with a specialization in library science."

Tomaso nodded. "And how did you come to be a bookbinder?"

"I took courses, but that was a while ago."

Tomaso gave her a long look. "Just as you have a passion for bookbinding, I have a passion for lost books. I'm a book hunter."

"Like the mythical Corso?"

He chuckled. "Frankly, I'm not sure I appreciate the comparison. Anyway, I hope you're referring to the original *The Club Dumas* by Pérez-Reverte."

"You don't mean the film version? *The Ninth Gate*, starring Johnny Depp as Corso, if I'm not mistaken."

"You're not." Tomaso shot her an exaggerated, menacing look.

Sofia was surprised to find herself having fun. "Don't make that face. It wasn't all bad!" She felt lighter.

Tomaso took off his scarf and wound it around her neck. "If you go on shivering like that, I'll start feeling cold too."

She tried to ignore the gesture, his look, the smell of him that she now had on her body. It meant nothing, she told herself. She still had questions to ask. "So you saw more in that book than you told me, didn't you? That's why you wanted to buy it."

Tomaso nodded. "There are many legends about lost books. According to the history of literature, Christian Philipp Fohr wrote only a single work in three volumes."

"I'm well aware." Her voice trembled as she pulled her jacket tighter, her breath turning to steam.

"But that's not necessarily how it is. Books have something special about them. By their very nature, they contain answers to all sorts of potential questions. Lost books are doubly fascinating, because we all project our hopes onto them. A human being's imagination is an extraordinary driving force. It makes you undertake the most daring enterprises." He kicked at a stone and watched it roll away. "Every book hunter knows the rumors about a book may well turn out to be true. Books disappear and reappear continuously. It's as though they had a life of their own."

"But I studied Fohr extensively and never came across any reference to an unpublished work."

Tomaso raised an eyebrow. "Stories like these are rarely written down. We only know about it from the oral accounts of Fohr's contemporaries."

"And you think that's the secret Clarice was alluding to?"

"On its own, the letter would be nothing more than a fascinating account from the distant past. But her choice to hide the letter in Fohr's book was no coincidence. Fohr, who wrote something so powerful that it forever remained in the memory of those few friends he showed it to."

"Do you know anything else about it?"

It took him a while to reply, and when he did, Sofia had already decided that if Tomaso Leoni helped her in her search, she would be eternally grateful.

"It's believed that his second work was written right here in Rome. He spent several years in the city and died here, as I'm sure you know, but no one ever managed to find the manuscript. Perhaps, because of his sudden death, his villa was left without a caretaker, and the text was stolen. Or perhaps it was taken by the family."

"But then why wouldn't they have published it? He was one of the greatest writers of his time."

Tomaso shook his head. "Lord Byron's friends decided to destroy an unpublished work of his; and after her death, Sylvia Plath's husband prevented the publication of her unpublished works. There are many books we'll never see because of an heir's decisions. The same thing may have happened in the case of Christian Fohr."

They looked at one another for a while. They'd arrived on the opposite side of Villa Borghese. The street was deserted. "I'll walk you home."

"No."

He raised a hand. "Then let's say you'll walk me home."

Sofia shook her head. "I was referring to Fohr. Clarice's letter promises to reveal a secret and implies that all three books should be kept together. What if she hid the instructions for finding Fohr's unpublished work inside the other volumes? We must find them, Tomaso."

"We?"

"That's right. I won't sell you the book, but we'll find the others together. I'll contribute the idea, Clarice's letter, Fohr's book, and you'll help me with the search. Is it a deal?"

Tomaso fell silent, reflecting calmly. "I accept. But tomorrow we'll set down the terms in black-and-white. If you change your mind before then, I'll understand." He offered her his hand, and she shook it.

His jaw dropped. "You're frozen." He pulled her to him and put an arm around her shoulders. "Don't get any ideas. I'm just looking after my investment."

Sofia laughed again. She was elated, and as they walked together in search of a taxi, she wondered where the story of Clarice and Christian would lead them.

CHAPTER FOURTEEN

Today is only one day in all the days that will ever be. But what will happen in all the other days that ever come can depend on what you do today.

—Ernest Hemingway, *For Whom the Bell Tolls*

Although the greenhouse was equipped with modern devices for controlling the temperature and humidity, it looked like a Victorian winter garden, with long glass windows in wrought-iron frames and a domed ceiling.

It had always been part of Sofia's world, because Max took her there often when she was a child. There, her little fingers stroked the first buds of the moth orchids, *Phalaenopsis*; she learned to recognize the scent emanating from the *Dendrobium* flowers and observed the many different shades in the petals of the *Vanda* plants hanging from the ceiling by their long silver roots.

Max had passed his love for those exotic plants to her, along with a love of books and reading.

"There's nothing that makes you feel freer than a book." He had told her that when she was a child and had to stay at home, immobile, after a skating accident. Her parents had been in the United States at the time. While she'd cried and then remained obstinately silent all morning, Max soon coaxed her out from under the sheets with the story of the March sisters. That was how, on a hot summer afternoon, Jo, Meg, Beth, and Amy had invited her into their lives.

Sofia enjoyed the idea that books were places, but she also thought of them like the mirrors that her grandmother collected. It was up to you in the end, whether you managed to immerse yourself in the pages so deeply you found yourself reflected in them, as in a mirror.

The morning after her surprising evening with Tomaso, Sofia took refuge in the silence of Max's greenhouse. Her thoughts were falling into place, and slowly, as she watered, cleaned, and repotted the orchids, her reflections seemed to dissolve, giving her some breathing space.

That day, she and Tomaso were to fix the terms of their agreement and, although the formalities made her a little anxious, she couldn't wait. She looked around her. The scent of flowers at that temperature was strong and enveloped her in a bubble of well-being. She took off her gloves and placed them on the tool shelf. After checking the thermostat and the vaporizer one more time, she stepped outside, closing the door carefully behind her.

There was one more thing she had to do before meeting Tomaso. She had an appointment with a lawyer. The thought of Alberto throwing away her personal belongings made her feel ill. How could he have gone so far? Her face clouded. After an initial, instinctive fear of facing him, she had returned to what had been their apartment. When he opened the door, she hadn't gone in. There, on the landing, she had told him what she thought of him and how she now felt ashamed to have married him. It had only taken a few minutes. Alberto, caught off guard, had tried to protest, but Sofia had cut him off.

"You threw away my things—things that didn't belong to you—because you wanted to hurt me. Stop putting the blame for your own mean actions on other people. Do yourself a favor and get help."

Joice, who'd been listening behind her front door, had offered her cake and admiration. "I'm proud of you, Sofia. I was afraid you'd let him get away with it again."

She wanted no more to do with him. Her marriage had been a mistake, and she had no intention of wasting any more time on that man; as far as she was concerned, she'd wasted enough already.

She finished tidying up. On her way to the front door, a glance in the mirror brought her to a halt. She looked at herself. She'd lost weight, and she was pale. Her hair fell lankly around her shoulders, and she had dark circles under her eyes, although they were bright. She decided it was time to make a few changes. For starters, she would get her hair cut shorter. Then she would sort through her clothes. She didn't like the dress she was wearing; it was too traditional, like all her outfits. Sofia was changing, and she was fully aware of it—scared, but aware.

The lawyer was a very pleasant man, and Sofia didn't have to go into too much detail. She merely said that there was no chance of reconciliation; she told him what Alberto had done but refused the proposal of economic compensation. "I don't want anything. All I'm interested in is for everything to be settled as quickly as possible."

"In that case, and in view of the fact that there are no children involved, the process will be very brief."

After leaving the lawyer's office, she parked along the river. She needed to take a stroll. With tearful eyes, she walked the streets of the old Jewish Quarter, her steps as heavy as her heart. She got something to eat, then followed the flow of pedestrians, stopping every now and then in front of a shop window. Antiques caught her attention: a heavy gold necklace, a sewing box, a wall ornament. Whom had they belonged to? What stories did they hold?

She came to the heart of the neighborhood, where the smell of fried artichokes, fish, and kosher bakeries filled the air, combined with laughter and exclamations of people saying hello to one another. In one of the street markets, she found a blue-and-golden-yellow dress. Then a pair of high-heeled shoes. When she got back to the car, she felt lighter and more confident. There was no longer any trace of the pain that had unexpectedly seized her. It was normal, she told herself. She couldn't just amputate something without feeling a sense of loss, but it would pass. *It's the new opportunities that ferry you toward the future,* she thought. Hope is what really gives you the strength to change.

Once home, she changed quickly. She had a little time before seeing Tomaso, and she wanted to have a chat with her grandparents. On the second ring, Max answered the phone.

"Liebling! I was wondering when you'd remember your old grandfather."

Sofia smiled. "What if I told you I've been thinking of you every day?"

A long, satisfied sigh and then a chuckle. "I'd believe you, light of my eyes. Tell me, then, was it very hard?"

"Yes."

"You've just changed the course of your existence, and you're starting on a new adventure. Every step you take from now on will carry you further and further."

She was silent for a moment, reflecting on her grandfather's words. "Perhaps I'll go and live in France."

"Really? And why's that? I always thought you loved Rome."

"It's complicated. I have nowhere to live, I don't have a job, and at the moment, I'm fairly confused."

"What do you mean, nowhere to live?" Max didn't wait for Sofia to reply. "Your grandmother has something to tell you—listen to her! Liebling, you're always in my heart."

"You're in mine too." Her grandmother wanted to talk to her? Therese hated the telephone. She only used it when she absolutely had to. She preferred to stand next to Max and let him do the talking.

"Sofia, darling! Have you eaten? Are you sleeping enough? You've got a good lawyer, I hope. But first of all, how are you?"

She didn't lie; her grandmother would know. "It's hard, Grandma. But I'm getting better every day. It's a strange feeling. The more time that passes, the more clearly I can see how stupid I've been."

"No, don't say that. You're shaking off difficult thoughts and situations, some of which never belonged to you and never fully convinced you. That's why you can see everything more clearly now. It's normal; that's what freedom is."

Freedom. A question of choices, awareness, extreme courage. Few are capable of attaining true freedom. Most people prefer to move around within the boundaries established by others. She had created her own personal prison, molding to Alberto's demands. But then Clarice came into her life, setting off a chain of events that had led her to this moment, standing in her grandparents' apartment, waiting for a man who was to help her dive deeper into the life of that woman who'd lived centuries before and uncover her secret.

"I like making my own decisions. As for the rest, we'll see what happens. I couldn't go on like that, Grandma. I tried, and it was a mistake."

Therese sighed. "I would so much have liked Alberto to be the right person for you. The fact is there just wasn't enough love between you two."

"I thought the rest would be enough." She knew her grandmother understood. It had always been like that between them.

"I have to tell you something, darling, and I hope you can help."

"Of course, Grandma. What's going on?"

"It wasn't easy to persuade your grandfather to return to Munich. Then, one morning, I don't know what got into him, he packed and there we were at the airport. So you see, I'd like to take advantage of this sudden urge of his to travel, and see Vienna too. After that, I want to go on to France. I promised your mother I'd visit. Can you take care of the apartment for a little longer?"

Sofia was overcome with relief. For a moment, she'd feared that something bad had happened to her grandparents. "Of course. This way, I'll have more time to decide what I'm going to do." She was about to tell Therese about Tomaso, but changed her mind. "I've started a project too. As soon as I know more, I'll tell you all about it."

"Take care of yourself, Liebling. Your grandfather sends you a big hug and leaves you in charge of his little ones."

"Give him a kiss from me. I'll send him photos of the orchids; the *Vandas* have flowered. Tell him to check his e-mail." She hung up and smiled.

When the apartment buzzer sounded, Sofia jumped. She looked at her watch. It must be Tomaso.

"Yes, Felipe?"

"There's a gentleman asking for you."

"Thank you. Send him up, please."

She opened the front door and went back into the library, where she had arranged her bookbinding tools on the table. The *Discourse on Nature* was at the center, and next to the book were the boards, the spine, and every single scrap of thread she'd removed, all of which she'd cataloged and photographed before pausing to follow Clarice's story.

"Good afternoon, Sofia." Tomaso's voice took her by surprise.

"I'm sorry, I was distracted." She smiled, beckoning him to come in.

He continued to look around him admiringly. Going up to the table, he pointed to the book. "May I?"

"Of course. Please do."

She opened the shutters, and the room was flooded with bright light, revealing the high walls covered with bookshelves. "This is the kingdom of my grandfather, Max Bauer."

"It's a splendid library."

Sofia nodded. "Yes. He says his books are made up of places where you can find yourself."

"And what do you think?"

Tomaso continued to surprise her. She liked him more all the time. She looked away. "Books possess great power. They set fire to what you have inside you, like sparks. They take what already exists and allow it to grow and develop."

As Tomaso pulled on the rubber gloves, a slight smile softened his features. "I wonder if that goes for everything."

"I don't understand."

He pointed to the table. "Clarice and her letter. What does it mean to you?"

"A fresh start." She immediately regretted saying something so personal. They barely knew each other. "What do you say if we get down to business?"

Tomaso squinted at her. "Of course."

Sofia returned to the table, a notepad in her hand, watching as he examined the pieces of the book, one at a time.

"This mark—it might help us trace the other volumes." Tomaso touched the paper delicately.

"It's a filigree. On handmade paper."

"Exactly. We see it on the endpapers and the spine."

He leaned forward, focusing on the curious symbol. "They're wings, a pair of wings." One of the symbols of freedom.

They remained silent for an instant.

"What do you say we sum up what we've got before moving on?" Tomaso's voice was even, but his eyes betrayed his impatience.

"All right."

"You start, please." Tomaso sat down, Fohr's book in his hands, his eyes moving back and forth between Sofia and the book.

It took her a minute to decide where to start. She had to detach herself from Clarice and her story and be as objective as possible.

"An autobiographical letter hidden inside a book promises to reveal something about a secret that cannot be lost. The text is in German, and both the paper and the ink can be traced back to the first half of the 1800s. It's probable that the person who wrote the letter also did the binding of the book and hid the letter in the cover."

Tomaso nodded. "What do we know about the woman who wrote it?"

"She learned the art of bookbinding as a child. She came from a noble background, but went through a very difficult period. When she wrote the letter, she was afraid of the consequences of revealing this secret. Nevertheless, she had to let it out because the truth must not be lost."

He signaled her to go on. "What do you think of it all?"

"Clarice was well aware of what she was doing. She hid her message in a place where it would only be found by a book expert, someone who could understand her." She stopped for a moment. "Hiding the letter in the first volume of the work by Christian Philipp Fohr, perhaps the greatest writer of her time, wasn't a coincidence. She and Fohr lived in the same period and same area. Some of the notes in the margins were handwritten by her." She stopped. The time had come to give Tomaso more evidence of her trust. "Can I show you something?"

"Certainly!"

Breathing softly, Sofia opened a drawer and extracted a few sheets of paper. "These are examples of Fohr's handwriting." She handed him the digital copies of the handwritten fragments she'd found in the library, among which was a signature.

Tomaso glanced at them, then moved quickly to the table.

The time he spent bending over the book seemed endless, at least to Sofia. She decided to go into the kitchen and make some coffee to give her something to do besides hold her breath.

The afternoon sun poured through the big windows, making the dust twinkle. In the library, there was total silence. Immersed in his task, Tomaso's eyes raced between the book and the papers Sofia had given him.

He didn't need an extensive analysis to know the unidentified notes were written in the same hand as Fohr's. After a few minutes double-checking and a few more reflecting on the implications, he waited for Sofia to come back. "It's him. This is his handwriting. Christian and Clarice wrote the notes."

"I knew it. I knew it!" Sofia walked into the room in the grip of irrepressible happiness. Then she stopped. Tomaso was staring at the book, a somber expression on his face.

She went up to him cautiously. "Is something wrong?"

He shook his head. "Some of the notes in the margin are the work of a single hand. They belong to either one or the other. But these," he said, pointing to one page, "are written as though the two authors were sharing the page. It happens again here, and here too."

Sofia didn't have the courage to speak. What Tomaso had just given her was the confirmation of her own suppositions.

"What do you think of that?"

She was breathless with emotion. "They knew each other."

"It appears they did." Tomaso pointed at the book. "Sofia, this is a historical document of immense value. The nature of the notes implies it was Fohr's personal copy. He continued his reflections in it."

"And Clarice? She didn't merely do the binding . . ."

"What we know for certain is that it was in her possession for a while. We need the other two volumes if we want to be sure of anything else."

"How will you find them?"

Tomaso looked at her. "I have contacts. I'll put the word out. As soon as I know something, I'll let you know."

There was something in Tomaso's expression that alarmed her. "If you go searching for the books, I'm coming with you." She had no intention of staying home, waiting by the phone. "My proposal is a fifty-fifty agreement. Equal risks, equal advantages. Together."

He rubbed his forehead. "Listen, I have no intention of cutting you out. But you must be clear about one thing. It's essential to make snap decisions; I won't have time to confer with you about every detail. We have something enormous in our hands. The success or failure of the search will depend on how convincing and swift I am, and God knows what else."

"That seems reasonable."

The comment took him by surprise. He'd expected further protests. A flash of admiration appeared on Tomaso's face. He knew Sofia was perceptive. What struck him about her was the direction of her thoughts; it was as though they looked at things through the same lens. He would have to take that into account, he decided. But it didn't alter the situation. He had no idea what he'd have to do to procure the missing volumes. She could be a hindrance to his process.

She'd gone to look out the window, but now she turned back to Tomaso. "But I want to know everything. Every single thing. As you said yourself, you are not to cut me out."

"We agree, then. Carla will draft an agreement. Can you come by tomorrow afternoon to sign it?"

"Yes, of course."

He put on the jacket he'd left in the hallway. Standing in the doorway, he stopped and turned to her.

"What's wrong?" Sofia felt uneasy. She'd expected something different from their meeting, but Tomaso seemed satisfied, even amused.

"Nothing. I'll start my investigation immediately. See you tomorrow at the agency."

She watched him leave, wondering what it was he hadn't said.

CHAPTER FIFTEEN

Love and reason are two travelers who never stay in the
same hotel together: when one arrives, the other departs.

—Pagnon and Callet, *Allan Caméron*

It was already nine o'clock when Tomaso left the office. He stretched his neck, relaxed his shoulder muscles, and yawned. He'd worked straight through without a break, exhausting the search engines, scanning online catalogs, and making a series of phone calls. He'd stirred things up. Now all that remained was to sit back and wait.

Once home, as he was getting dinner ready, his thoughts strayed from Sofia to Frank. He'd made an appointment with the lawyers of the Baldini heirs and the counterparty. He had no idea how to undo his stepfather's mistake and would have to improvise. One thing he was quite certain of, though, was that he couldn't allow any more injustices. The signature on the will was not authentic, however much it might seem to be.

He ate slowly, in a bad mood. There was no question of discrediting Frank. It was the quickest way out of the mess, but he'd have to find another way. His stepfather's condition had improved slightly, but not enough for any confrontations. Still pressing was the question of the deficit in the company's accounts. How could Frank do such a thing?

Tomaso pushed his plate away and stared into the void for a moment. He was trapped. In whichever direction he looked, he saw barricades. He cleaned up the kitchen and took a long shower. Wrapping a silk robe around himself, he returned, barefoot, to the living room.

His apartment was located in a late eighteenth-century building in the old center of Rome. An ancient stone wall separated it from the street, giving him privacy and a barrier against the noise of the city. When he'd decided to restore the home that had belonged to his father's family, Luisanna had tried to change his mind.

"The past must remain in the past. Look to the future, forget, free yourself of everything."

But Tomaso wanted to take care of his patrimony. It was a matter of duty, tradition, and continuity; something his mother appeared to have lost all interest in.

Tomaso hadn't made many changes to the layout. The rooms were large with enormous windows that had been designed to let in as much light as possible. They made him feel comfortable, at home. The place was his refuge, something that belonged to him alone. He'd never brought anyone home.

He had made sure to furnish the room in a simple, classic manner— solid wood furniture with smooth and linear surfaces, pale oak floors, clean white walls. In one corner of the lounge, next to a tall window, he'd placed an antique writing desk. It was an original piece with a built-in seat and a writing surface that could be inclined with slots for inkpots. No one knew whom it had belonged to. Tomaso had come across it on the upper floor, where his grandmother had lived years ago.

He'd never met Ludovica Devoto Leoni; he just knew that she had been an unusual woman, free and strong. She was widowed at a very young age and never remarried. Since no one told Tomaso much about her, he had formed his own view. It was the decor of the rooms, the clothes left inside the wardrobes, still bearing traces of a delicate, flowery perfume, and the grand piano at the center of the living room that told her story. It was the paintings, sketches, notebooks, and albums that held her memory. Ludovica had been an artist. In those rooms, which his father, Massimiliano, had conserved without changing a single detail, the woman's essence was preserved. Tomaso had been careful to leave it, even as he adapted the place for his own use.

Tomaso wondered, with dismay, if he would end up having to sell everything to cover the debts. And then he'd had enough thinking for the moment. He needed to relax, and only one thing would do the trick. He pulled the curtains in the living room and turned on Chopin's nocturnes. The writing desk was ready.

First he set out the paper, thick and handmade. He had it sent especially from Fabriano. He chose the pen and the ink—black, like his mood. As he started to trace the characters he so loved, the only thing he heard was the sound of metal brushing against paper. A melody of gestures, an exact expression of himself. His concentration grew with each character until there was nothing else. His hand and his mind became one. Around him, everything was in turmoil, but on the desk, the words, traced so precisely, dissolved all tension and doubt. When he stood up later, he was calm. He stretched out on the bed, his arms beneath his head, his eyes on the ceiling, where the light filtering through the shutters went on writing, just as he had a moment earlier.

Dawn would soon be breaking; he closed his eyes. His breathing became more regular, allowing him to slip into a deep sleep.

Sofia had never been an impatient person, but since signing the contract with Tomaso, she hadn't seen or heard from him, and she didn't like it at all. She didn't know what to expect. She had no idea how these things proceeded and had no measure to judge them by. On one hand, she felt she could trust him and wanted to, but on the other, she'd experienced too much unpleasantness to be confident. Perhaps, if she'd known him better—but she wasn't sure that was the right path, either.

There was certainly something between them; she could feel it: a physical sensation more than anything, something that happened in his presence that sparked tension and expectation in her.

She picked up speed, venturing farther into the park along a rough path. She'd taken up her morning run again, to help fill those days made up of so many hours. To take her mind off things, she had even accepted an invitation for an evening out organized by Ilaria.

"I won't take no for an answer. So get yourself ready, and you'll see how happy everyone will be to see you again."

And that's just how it had been. The dinner with her university friends the night before had surprised her. They had all changed, and yet they were all still the people they had been. It was easy to reconnect, to exchange confessions and advice, as though the years-long separation had been just a short pause. The familiarity made her feel good, though it also reminded her how much she'd lost by making poor decisions along the way.

She dodged the branch of a tree and recovered her balance. When she came out into a clearing, she slowed down, then stopped, her hands on her legs, breathing hard. The air was cold and clear, as it often was on autumn mornings. In front of her, the little lake was a mirror, reflecting the white clouds. She observed it for a long time, thoughts whirling around in her head. She was tired of being afraid, of tiptoeing around. She wanted to reach her goals, and no one could do that for her.

On the way home, the thought became more urgent. She was alone. She must start taking care of herself; she'd had time to think things over, and now she must act. She owed it to herself and to Clarice. A smile slowly stretched across her face; the idea that the woman was relying on her came to mind more and more frequently in those days, and she was intent on upholding her promise. She would not let her down.

She hadn't been home long when Felipe called her on the intercom. "There's a letter for you, signorina; I'll bring it up."

"Thank you, but don't trouble yourself, Felipe. I'm just going out again. I'll come down and pick it up."

I wonder what it is. Apart from her family and a couple of other people, no one knew she was staying in Coppedè. She got ready quickly. Passing through the hall of mirrors—as she had started to call her grandmother's collection—she allowed herself a brief, apprehensive glance at her reflection. Then she took the stairs down to see Felipe.

"Good morning. Here you are. It was only delivered a few moments ago."

"Thank you."

She exchanged a couple of words with Felipe and left. As she walked, Sofia clutched the envelope in her hand. There weren't many people who still wrote real letters nowadays—and closed with a seal, no less! She turned the envelope over and was stunned by the handwritten address. It was spectacular—elegant italics with character. Who on earth could still be writing like that? She broke the seal with the tip of a finger and pulled out the letter. Her eyes followed the writing, full of excitement. Tomaso?

But her excitement was replaced by anxiety.

> *Dear Sofia,*
> *Thank you for the opportunity of this new adventure.*
> *However, there are things that must be done in a certain way, and I have to do them alone. I'm sure the final result will more than make up for this. I'm just asking you to have confidence in me and in my experience.*

Overcome with confusion and a feeling of being justified in her initial doubts, she went to get her car. Once inside, she put down the envelope and dialed the man's number on her cell. "Come on, answer!" She tried and tried again. No luck. She looked straight ahead for a moment and then started the engine. Quickly, she calculated how long it would take her to get to the agency. At that hour, many offices closed for lunch. She thought of calling Carla, but then she changed her mind; she'd better not. There was something about Carla that made her uneasy, though she couldn't quite put her finger on it.

It took her longer than she'd imagined to get to the agency. She crossed Via dei Condotti quickly, and just as she was about to ring the bell, the door burst open.

"Sofia, good morning. Can I help you?" Carla closed the door behind her.

"I need to talk to Tomaso."

She shrugged. "I'm afraid that's impossible."

"Why? I don't understand."

"He left this morning. Didn't he tell you?"

For a moment, Sofia was speechless. He'd asked her to trust him, he'd thanked her for the opportunity she'd given him, but he hadn't mentioned a journey. "When will he be back?"

"When he manages to find what he's looking for, I imagine." Carla turned up the collar of her jacket and smiled again. "Well, if that's all, I'll wish you a pleasant day."

Sofia stood there in confusion for several long moments. Why hadn't Tomaso told her he was on the trail of the books? She looked up.

Carla had just turned the corner. *No.* This time Sofia had to do things her way. She'd had enough of watching life go by, being a spectator. She ran after the woman and caught her arm.

"What—"

"I'm sorry, but I need to know where Tomaso is. I have to talk to him."

Carla half closed her eyes. "If and when he thinks it's the right time to contact you, he will. And now, if you'll excuse me, I have a lunch meeting."

"No."

"I'm sorry?"

Sofia didn't back down. "He's cutting me out, and it isn't right. You know the terms of our agreement. He should have kept me up to date. I will not stay here, doing nothing until he gets back. Tell me where he is. I have the right to know."

Something in Carla's irritated expression changed. "Munich, Platzl Hotel. Make sure it's worth it."

"What do you mean?"

Carla seized her up with her eyes, but this time her expression was affable. "You wanted to know where he is, and I told you, breaking a few key rules. Bear that in mind. Now, let's see what you do with the information."

The challenge was not only in her words but in her eyes too. Sofia had the sensation that the woman was testing her. She'd told her where Tomaso was, but she didn't think Sofia was capable of taking action.

Carla had gone only a few steps when she turned around. "Take something warm with you. Autumn in Munich isn't like it is in Rome."

Tomaso had always liked Munich, with its plump, domed towers. The city had never bowed its head and had reacted with dignity and grace to all the blows it had been dealt. It had been rebuilt many times, never sacrificing beauty.

He glanced admiringly at the buildings and promised himself he'd be back again soon.

As he crossed Marienplatz, he wondered if Sofia had received his letter. He had the impression she wouldn't take his departure well, and that was why, to make up for his silence, he'd written only that there were things he had to do on his own. But everything had happened so quickly.

Paul Vagar, one of the agents he dealt with, had suggested, indeed strongly advised, he take part in a private auction. Several copies of Fohr's work were in the catalog that the auctioneers Smith & Sofitel had put together. It had been a long time since Tomaso had attended a sale organized by them, and he didn't have positive memories of them. But this was undeniably a rich collection, perhaps the most complete, dealing with Romantic authors over the past few years. In any case, he couldn't risk missing the occasion. He'd had nothing but one disappointment after the other in the last few days. There were still many extant copies of the Cotta first edition of Fohr's work, but none of them bore the unmistakable signs found in Clarice's. This auction could easily be an expensive flop. But it was the only trace Paul had come up with, and Tomaso knew his agent must think there was a decent chance of success.

Vagar was waiting for him beneath one of the porticos of the town hall, tall and thin as a reed, wearing an old raincoat. Tomaso was happy to see him. And even happier that he'd decided to accompany him.

"There are several buyers, so it won't be simple, but they say there are some special items that are not in the official catalog. We'll go for those."

It was typical of him to skip the niceties. Tomaso knew him well enough not to take offense.

Paul didn't ask why he was so urgently searching for the second and third volume of that specific edition of Fohr's work. His discretion was rare in their field, which fed on the tiniest snippets of news. Information was a precious commodity for antique book hunters.

"The owners?"

Paul grimaced. "The usual story: the grandchildren are managing everything." He paused. "That's life. You leave everything. What we possess, even the things dearest to us, are on loan; then inevitably it's all lost."

Tomaso didn't see it the same way. For him, the past was a point of departure and so were antique books, but he had no intention of arguing with Paul.

As the rain slowed, the clock tower's carillon started up, filling the air with festive music.

Sofia flipped through the magazine full of useless images, faces, and advertisements. It was just a way of keeping occupied, calming the trembling in her fingers and her heart. Immobile in a corner of the lobby in the hotel where Tomaso Leoni was staying, she was faking a feeling of serenity. Every now and then, she'd glance toward the reception desk. The hotel was practically full. She'd spun the receptionist a story, and now she was waiting for them to find her a room.

"Frau Bauer?"

Sofia felt her stomach tighten. *Here we go.*

"A room has just become vacant. We've managed to put you on the same floor as your fiancé. I hope you'll understand; if Mr. Leoni had left instructions, there would have been no problem at all in allowing you to share suite 202."

She was overcome with relief. "Thank you, it'll be fine like this."

She followed the porter, her heart in her throat. She'd never done anything like this before. If they hadn't said there were no rooms available when she arrived, she never would have considered spinning a lie about a last-minute surprise for her fiancé. She'd placed all her bets on the city's famed courtesy and, fortunately, things went exactly as she wished. She thanked the porter and looked at her watch. She had no idea where Tomaso was; his phone was always off. She sat down on the bed, her eyes following the rain on the roofs outside. What was the sense of all this? *At least you didn't just stay in Rome waiting around for him,* she thought to herself, *but what exactly are you doing here?*

She stood up, her heart heavy. Were her grandparents still in Munich, or had they already left for Vienna? In any case, she couldn't get them involved in this affair. She sighed and went to take a long shower. She wouldn't stay in the hotel room, tormented by doubts. She was in Munich, and she was going to make the most of it.

She opened her suitcase and put on a fancy suit. Tying back her hair, she put on some makeup. When she went out, it'd stopped raining and a mist had formed, making way for the afternoon sunlight. She pulled her overcoat closer around her, Carla's words echoing in her head.

At that time of the afternoon, the city was full of life, tourists mingling with residents. She smiled at a child staring at her from beneath a wool hat, his cheeks shiny and red. A sense of anguish suddenly seized her. It wasn't just the child, but the parents, who looked about her age. The man was pushing the stroller and joking with his partner. It was a simple, ordinary scene. Sofia walked on with a sense of emptiness inside her, something she'd never felt before, thinking of what she'd never had.

The town hall with its twin towers rose above Marienplatz. The neo-Gothic stonework and gargoyles were embroidered in golden light. Although Sofia was familiar with them, she was spellbound. Walking a little faster, she made her way to the porticos. She liked the sensation of being alone in a foreign place; it made her feel free. She could decide what to do with herself. The magic of Munich was starting to get a grip on her; the shop windows sparkled, and there were already Christmas lights up. She stopped in front of a bookshop; she wanted to be in the company of books.

Despite being small, the shop was bright and lovely, with high bookcases and a rolling ladder for reaching the topmost books. There were a lot of people browsing. She thought she would do the same, so she looked for a modern edition of Fohr's trilogy on the shelves.

"You're interested in Christian Fohr?" A shopgirl had come up to her as she was paging through the volume.

"Yes, I'm a great admirer of his. Although I prefer the antique editions of his work."

The girl nodded. "Excuse me for asking, but he's an author I adore, and unfortunately he's so little known nowadays. Brilliant, don't you agree? The idea of such a just world, free from abuse . . . What a dreamer. I'd have loved to meet him. I'd have been head over heels for someone like that." A colleague called the girl by name. "Sorry, I'll be right back."

"No problem."

The girl's words troubled her. *I'd have been head over heels for someone like that.* Was that what had happened to Clarice too? Sofia was about to leave the shop when the girl returned.

"As it happens, there's a private auction of antique books today." She passed Sofia a card. "If you're interested, I'd be glad to let you have my invitation. I wanted to go, but they need me here. Let me know if you find anything interesting!"

She walked off with a wave and a smile that cheered Sofia up. She scanned the invitation. The venue wasn't too far away. Outside the bookshop, she looked around and sighted a string of taxis. Getting into one, she gave the driver the address. "Bayerstrasse."

Not her favorite part of Munich, but it was a safe city. She wouldn't be in any danger. Sofia relaxed her shoulders, realizing just how tense she was. Tomaso was mistaken if he thought she'd let him do just as he wanted. It was her story. She'd promised not to get in his way, but she had no intention of standing aside.

"You're sure this is the place?" asked the taxi driver as he pulled over. The building was in pitiful condition, with the plaster flaking off and iron bars over the windows. "If you like, I can wait for you," he said with worry in his voice.

"Thank you, that won't be necessary."

Inside, she went up some stairs and came to a hall opening into two large rooms. In one of them, the auction itself was being held, but it had already begun, and she was told it was no longer possible to go inside. *How unlucky,* thought Sofia, moving to the room next door, where an employee pointed out the less precious books that weren't up for auction: odd volumes, slightly damaged ones, and the like. They had been placed haphazardly on a table, octavos together with sextodecimos and even big atlases. The covers were fine but badly worn. There were various reprints of Flaubert, Tolstoy, Hugo, Balzac, and a few Wildes and Joyces. Sofia went through the volumes slowly, wondering if just maybe—

And then she saw it at the center of the table. It was in red morocco leather, the same size, and she had the burning sensation it was just what she was looking for.

Sofia drew nearer, stretched out an arm, and grasped it. Fohr's *In Praise of Perfection*, the second volume. It was the right one! She was ecstatic. She looked at the pile of books and again at the one she was holding. With trembling fingers, she opened it. Immediately, her smile vanished. The endleaf was of marbled paper, no filigree. She checked the edition. With a sigh, she put it back onto the table.

"Find what you were looking for?" The man working there was smiling at her.

Sofia shook her head. "Unfortunately not."

He ran his eyes over the table, then pointed to a shelf. "Try taking a look up there."

Sofia thanked him, made her way through the crowd of buyers and, to her great surprise, realized that there, too, were two books with red morocco leather covers. She took one, flicked through it, and put it down again, her spirits sinking. She reached for the other volume, and as she held it in her hand, something felt different. The weight, the grain of the leather, the size . . . Her heart started beating out of her chest. She opened the cover, and when she saw the circle with the two wings inside, she almost yelped. It was her book; it was Clarice's book! There were no notes in the margins this time, but that didn't mean it wasn't the right one. She'd found it, and the price wasn't even too high. If she'd had to, she would have given all her savings, down to the last cent, to have it.

CHAPTER SIXTEEN

Fortune loves those that have least wit and most confidence and such as like that saying of Caesar, "The die is thrown."

—Erasmus of Rotterdam, *In Praise of Folly*

The auction seemed interminable. The auctioneer had moved on to the more valuable items, reciting their qualities, but Tomaso had no interest. Two editions of Fohr had attracted his attention, but neither corresponded to Clarice's binding.

Tomaso knew it would take incredible luck to locate Clarice's volumes among all the copies still in circulation. The Cotta printing works in Stuttgart had produced multiple editions of Fohr's work that same year, and it wasn't easy to distinguish which volumes were the first editions and which were merely bound the same way as the book Sofia had found.

Tomaso headed back to the hotel and found it full of life, with guests constantly coming and going. Munich was a lively city at night. He stopped at the front desk, exchanged a few words with the receptionist, and went upstairs. Once in his room, he freed himself of his overcoat and jacket. He ordered a light dinner and finished undressing. A long, hot shower washed away the rain and fatigue. He was starving.

"Here's hoping room service is quick," he muttered.

He pulled on his bathrobe and lay down on the bed. Looking up at the ceiling, his thoughts turned to the day's events. If he wanted to have any chance of finding the two volumes, he needed a better plan.

His phone started vibrating. He glanced at the display and closed his eyes. A fitting end to the day. "Ciao, Sofia."

"Are you at the hotel?"

Surprised, he pulled himself up into a sitting position. *How did she know?* "Yes." He heard her sigh with relief.

"I'm on my way."

"What?" But she had ended the call. Tomaso's eyes widened.

What on earth was going on? He didn't have the chance to wonder any further. There was someone at the door and, judging by the way they were knocking, he doubted it was room service. He flung it open and stood there, stunned. "What the devil are you doing here?" He sounded harsher than he meant to be, but he was floored. But how—and when—had she arrived?

"We'll talk about that later. Come with me." She grabbed the sleeve of his bathrobe, pulling him out of his room.

Tomaso resisted. All he needed now was someone to see him like that in the corridor. "Wait a minute."

But she was already unlocking a door just down the hall. "I've got something you absolutely must see."

She was anxious and pale, yet there was a light in her eyes and an urgency that troubled Tomaso. He blinked, and a thought started to take shape in his mind. *It couldn't be.*

"You found the second book."

But how the hell had she done it? This woman truly was special. The sense of triumph was mixed with something deeper. A shiver, a powerful physical sensation. He crossed the hall to Sofia, stretched out an arm, and closed his hand around her delicate wrist. He held it tight, skin to skin. He felt her pulse beating beneath the palm of his hand. Then he let go.

"Let's go in."

Fortunately, it was a large room with a little lounge area and armchairs. Plenty of space. This was a complex situation, and his desire to touch her complicated it further. He moved away, putting as much distance as possible between them.

"So, how did you do it?"

"By chance. When I got to Munich to look for you, I went into a bookshop—"

"I imagine I have Carla to thank for the pleasure of this surprise," he interrupted her.

Sofia looked away. "Don't blame her."

"Very generous on your part."

"I don't want to talk about that now."

Tomaso marveled. What had happened to the calm, reflective woman he'd met? Was she this force of nature he found in front of him now? *Yes*, he thought, it was the same Sofia. With a little added self-possession.

"Are you listening to me?"

"Every word, I swear."

Sofia told him about the girl from the bookstore and her invitation. "I went, of course. It was an incredible coincidence, and if you had answered your phone, you'd know all of this already." She paused.

She had a couple of other things to say on that account. A glance at Tomaso's face, however, persuaded her to put them off for another time. "I didn't manage to get into the main auction, but I found Clarice's book among the other damaged volumes on sale. It sounds incredible, doesn't it?"

Tomaso's gaze moved from the book she was holding in her hands and fixed on her eyes. It was the second time Sofia had come into contact with Clarice, and both times the circumstances had been unusual, to say the least. Sofia didn't seem to realize how exceptional this occurrence truly was. She was more energized than he'd ever seen her, full of life and so beautiful. He sighed and sat down on the divan. He stretched out a hand in her direction.

"Incredible," he murmured. "Can I see?"

She went up to him, but instead of handing him the book, she sat down beside him. "Look, the endleaves are the same and so are the symbols on the filigree. It's one of Clarice's books, there's no doubt."

It wasn't easy to ignore the warmth of her body through her clothes or her delicate perfume. Tomaso had trouble concentrating on the pages she was showing him.

"Now, all that's left is to see if our friend has left a letter here too."

"Of course." Sofia looked around. "All I've got is my manicure set, but it should work."

Taking advantage of a corner that had come unstuck, she slipped a nail file between the front board and its endleaf.

"Let me give you a little light." He moved one of the lamps. Sofia placed the book on the smooth surface of the table. "Wait, I'll help you," he said. He held the cover firm with his fingers, allowing her to proceed more safely. They worked together, in unison, and their natural synchronization aided the operation; they found themselves in an intimate whirlwind of gestures and emotions.

Sofia proceeded with exasperating caution, complicated by the electricity between them. The silence was complete, hardly broken by their breathing and the sound of the paper coming away under the pressure of the nail file she was using as a blade. "Here it is," she whispered. She finished lifting the sheet of paper, and her eyes filled with tears. Tomaso took her hand in his. Both of them stared. Out of a little pocket, identical to the one in the previous volume, peeped a sheet of rice paper.

It was true. It was all true. A knot formed in her throat. Sofia had hoped that the woman from the past had left another message for her, but she couldn't be certain of that. Now everything made sense.

"Ciao, Clarice," whispered Sofia.

Tomaso lifted her face, using the palms of his hands to dry the tears that had started to flow. "You've been great."

At that moment, Sofia knew that, whatever the future held for them, the moment they had just shared would always remain with them. "We must never forget this."

Tomaso looked at her with a strange expression on his face. "I like remembering lovely things."

There was no mistaking the look he gave her. They remained like that for a moment, in the grip of joy and emotion, and at the same time incapable of going any further.

Suddenly, Tomaso moved away from her. Disconcerted, Sofia's eyes followed. He went to the drink tray and filled two glasses with wine. He raised one in her direction. "To the most surprising woman I've ever met. And I'm not referring to Clarice."

Sofia accepted the wine. She needed it.

Not until finishing the glass did she focus on the book again. Slowly, she extracted Clarice's new message, unfolding it carefully on the table. She raised her head, her eyes on Tomaso opposite her.

"Read it, Sofia. Tell me about Clarice, and her secret."

I have already spoken of what happened at the beginning of my life. Regrettable circumstances changed a fate that had seemed preordained. I was incautious, imprudent. I mistook his torment for affection. I placed my trust in someone who did not deserve it, ignoring the voice in my heart that had tried to put me on my guard. I didn't know that what drove him to ask for my hand in marriage was my name and the inheritance bound to it, a treasure inaccessible to me. Women under guardianship are not allowed to dispose of their own wealth.

A woman is born a prisoner. She merely passes from one guardianship to the next. I thought he wished me well, just as I, at the beginning, wished him. I would have been content with very little: to walk among other people without a hand guiding my steps, to choose for myself the colors I wanted to wear. To paint what I wished, play the music I wished. Or simply sing, if I wanted to.

I was wrong. He was a pit of evil. My only excuse is that I was a mere girl. Yet I could not tolerate what he had done. I ran away. I escaped to Italy.

It is but a short distance from humankind to thought, and with this, you'll find the knowledge you are seeking.

CHAPTER SEVENTEEN

A lady's imagination is very rapid; it jumps from admiration to love, from love to matrimony, in a moment.

—Jane Austen, *Pride and Prejudice*

Vienna, 1813

She hadn't wanted anyone else to deal with her books. Clarice had personally arranged them in piles and, under Marta's doubtful gaze, wrapped them one by one in wool. She placed them in big wooden crates.

"Don't you think it'd be best to leave them here? Many husbands don't like their wives to be interested in that sort of thing. You could come back and read them whenever you wanted."

Her aunt was right and, in fact, Uncle Kurt didn't approve of his wife reading, but August was different. He knew how important books were to her. Although she still had some doubts about the marriage, Clarice couldn't help remembering the danger she had escaped, her first betrothal.

Luckily, all that was over now.

"Ah, there you are, I was looking for you."

Maud, August's sister, was a good-looking woman with red hair, arranged in braids around her head, and a proud expression. She always wore black, despite the fact that she was still unmarried. In the presence of her younger brother, she became gentle and docile, offering a thousand and one little kindnesses, all of which had persuaded Clarice to be patient with her authoritarian ways. Once the woman had become convinced of her devotion, she would surely become gentler with her too.

"Come in, Maud. We're just packing the last few things. Clarice's books will soon be ready to take to the new house."

The woman approached with a rustle of silk. She glanced at the crates, suppressing a laugh. "Haven't you explained to your niece that those," she pointed, "are not an appropriate dowry?"

Marta blushed. Clarice bit her tongue. Why did Maud speak as though she herself were not present? She would have posed the question herself if her aunt hadn't asked her to be patient.

"August will understand," said Marta. "He wants her to be happy."

"Really? What a silly idea."

Clarice stood up, brushing down her skirt. "Doesn't one get married in order to take care of the other person?"

Maud laughed out loud, a hand in front of her mouth. "You're very amusing, I'll give you that. Go on entertaining your illusions. That's what young girls do, isn't it?" She was already at the door when she stopped. A cold glance, a grimace. "I'm afraid your books will have to wait. There's no room in my carriage."

Clarice had no intention of acknowledging the woman's bad temper. She finished packing her things, though Maud's interruption had put her on edge. She wondered how they would manage to get along living in the same house. She would have to make an effort, she thought.

"I'm sorry." Marta's voice was as soft as a sigh.

"About what, Aunt?"

Marta knelt down beside her. "I'd have liked you to be older so that you could understand."

Clarice looked at her in perplexity.

Marta stroked her cheek. "You're so pretty, Liebling, so good. You are more and more like your mother. She was strong and happy. I wanted the same for you." She was about to add something, but then she bowed her head.

"Don't you think I will be?" Clarice asked gently. "August is a good man, and he loves me. He says he'll look after me, and we'll have a family."

Marta was pale, and she couldn't meet her niece's eyes. "He's still a man. I'll give you the same advice I gave you about Johann. Agree with him and don't rebel, and everything will be fine." She kissed the girl's forehead, tears filling her eyes, then stood up silently and left the room.

Clarice shivered. She tried to concentrate on what had to be done, but fear still hovered all around her. Although August gave the impression of being kind and considerate, there were moments when she caught him staring at her, something like fury in his eyes.

She went downstairs. Maud was taking her leave, and their eyes met for an instant; after a conniving smile, off she went, her future sister-in-law. Clarice continued down the stairs until she came to the cellar. She shut the door carefully and went to the old barrels. She waited until quiet fell, suggesting Frederik was alone, and knocked on the wooden boards in the corner.

"My little sparrow, how wonderful. I haven't seen you for so long. Why the long face?"

Clarice forced a smile. Her old friend had been ill, so she hadn't told him anything. She didn't want him to worry. "Next week I'm getting married, and I'll be leaving this house." She sniffed, her eyes running over that world of marvels that sheltered her for all those years.

Frederik's eyes hardened. "So I've heard. You're so young, my little sparrow, a mere girl. Wouldn't you rather wait?"

A long moment passed. Then Clarice stamped a smile on her face and ignored the little voice telling her to ask the bookbinder for shelter.

He wouldn't have been able to in any case, so there was nothing to do but marry. "I'm fine. I shall begin a new life, and I'm taking my books with me. August—he agreed to that."

"Really?" The bookbinder's voice was flat, expressionless, but Clarice could read his face, the disapproval there.

She bent her head and then searched his eyes again. "As soon as I can, I'll be back to visit you."

The bookbinder took her hand and pressed it to his heart. "Whatever you need, any time of the day or night, know that you have a friend you can ask anything of." He paused and lifted her chin with one finger. "And never forget, my little sparrow, that you hold my heart in your hand."

They looked at one another for a long moment, then Clarice embraced him.

"Thank you, Father."

The word paralyzed Frederik. When the girl left, he closed the door carefully, wondering when, if ever, the girl he considered his child would open it again. As he returned to the book he was working on, he had to stop and wipe his eyes. He wanted to believe her, wanted to hope that things would go just as his little Clarice had said. But he knew men like August. He was the sort that consumed himself and all those around him.

After the solemn wedding mass, Vogel wanted an elaborate reception. Clarice was a spectacle. Her hair piled up on her head, her blue eyes shining with emotion. With her delicate features and slender, elegant figure, Clarice had a special kind of beauty. August had been proud of this, but now that the woman finally belonged to him, all the attention his bride was attracting made him feel ill. By the end of the day, he was furious. As she was saying goodbye to the guests who had begun to take their leave, one man took her hand and kissed it. Clarice tried to withdraw it, but the man, who had been drinking, didn't let go. August pushed him away and dragged Clarice back by her arm.

"You're making me look ridiculous," he shouted. "Stop it at once."

Her mouth fell open. "I don't understand."

"Oh yes, you do. You will not bring shame upon me with your behavior."

A gloved hand came to rest on August's arm. "Everyone is watching, Brother."

He fell silent and raised his eyes. A tense silence reigned. He made an effort to regain control of himself, breathing deeply. Clarice, her eyes wide, was as pale as death.

The shock caused by his outburst gave way to whispers and ill-concealed contemptuous looks. He wasn't one of them, and no one in Vienna knew him; if it hadn't been for Kurt Vogel, they wouldn't have had him in their homes or even greeted him.

"Smile. Ask your wife to dance. This is a party, remember. You are in public."

"You're right, Maud. I'm sorry." Suddenly he bent down and brushed his bride's lips with a kiss. "Let's dance now." He smiled at her and lifted her hand to his lips, then pulled her onto the dance floor.

Clarice couldn't speak. Her mouth was dry, and terror gripped her. In her husband's eyes she read boundless anger, a violence that not even the uncouth Johann had demonstrated. Her steps faltered during the dance, but each time August lifted her, preventing her from falling. She felt no gratitude, just the deep, dark terror of having made a terrible mistake.

It was the custom for the women in a household to prepare the bride before her new husband came to her on the first night, but August shut them out. He was the one to let his wife's hair down. It was he who seized it in his fist, pulling as though it were a rope. He might have stopped if she had cried, if she had submitted, but Clarice remained silent.

She'd done it to punish him, August was certain, the same way she had allowed the guests to dance with her, touch her, and kiss her hand.

And that thought, which he had been nurturing all evening, exploded. All his good intentions of being gentle with her were swept away by anger. He told himself that, if he was rough, it was Clarice's fault.

When he awoke, hours later, the first thing August noticed was her absence. He pulled himself into a sitting position, and remembering what he had done to her, he felt scared.

He leapt to his feet, searching for her in the darkness. It wouldn't have been the first time a young bride had escaped or decided to put an end to it all. He found himself praying and imploring the heavens. He pulled on his trousers, his heart hammering against his ribs, and ran to the door. It was locked from the inside, as he had left it the previous evening. He turned around. His eyes, used to the darkness now, fell on her.

Clarice was curled up in a ball on the floor, her long hair acting as a pillow. He swallowed as the blood coursed through his veins again. With delicacy, he picked her up in his arms. She was cold. As he placed her on the mattress, she woke up. His wife's body, which had been so soft and yielding in sleep, became hard as stone.

"You will never leave the bed again without my permission."

Those were not the words he'd wanted to say, but she had withdrawn, turning her face away from him. The little fool thought she could hurt him. When Clarice hid her face in her hands, August realized she was afraid. "Next time things will go better." He covered her and lay down beside her, but when he found her lips, they were cold and stiff. Hard as he tried to soften them with kisses, delicate ones this time, they remained firmly pressed together.

In the end, frustrated and gripped by remorse, he let her go. She took refuge on the opposite side of the bed. But the emptiness August felt between them was so complete, it was as if she were on the other side of the world.

She had never experienced physical violence. However much Krauser had frightened and mistreated her as a child, nothing could have prepared Clarice for abuse as ferocious as August inflicted on her wedding night and the nights that followed. At the beginning, she tried to resist him, but her survival instinct eventually forced her to submit.

And so, day by day, Clarice became removed from everything. Enveloped in a torpor of pain and resignation, she took refuge inside herself. She cared nothing about what went on around her. Maud ran the house as if she didn't exist, no longer bothering to hide the hostility she felt toward her. She exercised her power by preventing Marta Vogel from visiting her niece. But when Vogel protested to August, her aunt was at last allowed in.

Clarice had become much thinner. Her drawn face and dull eyes reflected her suffering. Nothing remained of the light and joy that had always set her apart.

After a year of marriage, August had transformed Clarice into a pale, dull woman who trembled every time he approached.

Her uncle and aunt seemed to regret their role in the matter. They went to see her as often as possible and tried everything in their power to improve their niece's existence. They gave her jewels, clothes, sweets. They asked insistently for news of her health, but Clarice's pallor was not due to pregnancy, as they had hoped.

Marta advised her niece to be patient. "As soon as you're pregnant, your husband will behave better. You'll see. He'll leave you in peace."

Clarice didn't reply.

"Men become indulgent toward the mother of their children. A real transformation, believe me, my dear."

Kurt, too, frequently went to visit his niece. He'd summon August and warn him about the consequences should his behavior become too rough. He desperately wanted a grandchild, a family. He'd suddenly realized that everything he had would be lost after his death. But if Clarice had a child, he would love them.

The only things Clarice could cling to in those long months were her books. They offered her shelter, brought momentary solace, gave her hope. In that prison of hers, books offered a window to the world, the places she would travel to in her imagination. More and more, she shut herself in her room, reading and drawing the lake at her childhood home, the castle where she grew up, imagining a world where everyone was free to decide their own destiny.

Sometimes Maud would stare at her. They'd be embroidering together in the drawing room after dinner, and while brother and sister talked, Clarice remained silent, her eyes on the flames. In those moments, Maud would tell her brother what Clarice had been doing, if she'd lingered too long at the window or in the courtyard, and if anyone had visited her. Her sister-in-law always found something objectionable in her behavior. Clarice wondered where her hatred came from.

One day, she had asked the question outright. "An eye for an eye" was Maud's reply.

She thought perhaps her sister-in-law had gone mad. "But I haven't done a thing," she whispered.

Maud sneered. "And whoever said it was you?"

Clarice—who knew nothing about August and Maud's sister, Else, being abandoned by Kurt—had never asked again, but from then on she understood there was a deep vein of folly in the woman, which made her dangerous.

One evening, Clarice was late for dinner. Nausea had kept her in bed almost all day. She sat there with her head down, but just looking at the food on her plate made her feel worse.

"You should make her give you the attention you deserve," Maud said to August, who had just returned from one of his trips.

He was tired and agitated. He glanced at his wife and then back at his plate.

"I can't do it all on my own, Brother. Look at her. She doesn't even appreciate the food we put on her plate. She's ungrateful. You could have made a better choice. Any girl in Vienna would have jumped for joy to be in her place."

Generally, August liked being flattered by his sister, and in the beginning, he'd enjoyed the verbal abuse she showered on Clarice, but now the girl had stopped reacting. Her abject suffering had begun to make him feel bad. She let him take her body, but it was as if no one was there. August wondered how he could shake her out of it and manage to revive the vivacious girl he'd wanted so badly.

At dinner, Maud continued to pick at Clarice as August observed his young wife, her eyes lost in the distance. Was it possible there wasn't a scrap of courage left in her? Perhaps he should insist. So he nodded in his sister's direction, encouraging her to continue.

At every shiver Clarice gave, every tremor of those lips, August's heart accelerated. He would have done anything to have her back. Coiled like a spring, he spied on her, waiting for a reaction.

"You should check her room. I've tried, but she shut me out."

August's interest was aroused. "In what sense?"

Maud shrugged her shoulders. "She spends so much time in there that I wouldn't be surprised if she were hiding something."

Now both of them stared at Clarice: Maud with the intention of hurting her, August because he wanted to reach her again.

"Are you really hiding something in your room?" he mocked her gently.

He knew it was impossible. He entered the room almost every night and would have noticed if there was something in there that shouldn't be. Clarice shook her head, looking at her hands. But then, all of a sudden, she couldn't control herself. She jumped to her feet, threw her napkin on the tablecloth, and ran off.

Maud lifted an eyebrow. "What did I tell you?"

August jumped up. Could he have missed something? But the house was guarded, no one had ever even come close. When he flung open the door to Clarice's room, she was sitting at her writing desk, her back to him.

"What's all this about, then?"

Clarice did not reply. Her pen brushed the paper, and a cluster of candles illuminated her straight back, her skirt spread out like the petals of a flower. Surprised, August advanced on her. A glance at what his wife was drawing left him dumbfounded. It was a portrait of a woman, a man, and two children. Behind them was a mountain.

"Who are they?"

She didn't answer. It was as though he wasn't even in the room. She was looking at the drawing with such love that August understood. His wife was there, in that drawing. That was the place that had stolen her from him.

He looked around at the walls covered with books and thought of all the times he had seen her bending over one of them. Every time he set eyes on her, Clarice had a book in her hand. That was what was separating them: her damned books. Without them, there would be nothing left for her to seek refuge in but him.

A wave of anger crashed over him. He pushed her away from the desk, grabbed the drawing, and threw it into the fireplace amid the flames.

Clarice shrieked.

At last, August thought. Encouraged, he seized the first book he came across and threw it into the fire. "I'll burn them all."

"No, you will not!" Something cracked in Clarice's soul. He had taken everything else from her; he would not take the only thing that remained.

Although August had been looking for a reaction from his wife, he wasn't ready for the pure hatred in her eyes. That wasn't how it was supposed to have gone. She was supposed to beg him, not challenge him. Now Clarice stood in front of him, hissing with contempt.

"You will not touch my things, and you will not touch me, ever again."

He had never seen her like that. He imagined life without her, and the thought brought him to his knees. He grabbed her by an arm, but she screamed and dug her nails into his face, scratching until she drew blood. She went on hitting and scratching until August threw her on the bed and began to beat her.

Maud stood frozen in the doorway, watching the scene. Behind her were the servants. When a chorus of protests rose, she shook herself. She ran to her brother and shielded her sister-in-law's body with her own.

"Have you gone mad? Do you know what they do to murderers?"

August stopped. Clarice was covered in blood. The contrast with the white bedsheets brought a groan from him. He was overcome with horror. He seized the edge of a sheet and wiped her face. "Open your eyes, please, please—" He kept repeating the litany until his sister managed to pry him away.

"Stop. I'll take care of it now." Maud, stone-faced, could hardly breathe.

The past flooded back to her. The blood-soaked hair, the bruises, the lifted skirt. She'd seen them before, the day she found what remained of her little sister at the bottom of the gorge, where she'd thrown herself after Kurt Vogel left her behind.

A profound sense of desperation suddenly filled her. "It'll be all right. Don't be afraid, Else, I'm here."

But the girl was not Else, and at that moment Maud realized she'd been an accomplice and that a vendetta was a bitter fruit, too bitter. She couldn't dwell on that now; she must act quickly. She had to hurry.

"You," she shouted to one of the servants, "bring me hot water, immediately. And my medicine bag."

"We must call the doctor. She's not breathing," panted August.

Alarmed, Maud placed her hand on Clarice's camisole. Her heartbeat was weak, but it was there. "No doctors. They couldn't save Else. I'll take care of her myself."

Day and night, Maud took care of Clarice. She stopped the fever and pulled her, tooth and nail, from the claws of death, obliging her to drink, feeding her, washing her. She talked to her for hours, telling her all about August, Else, and herself when they were young, and how her little sister was a joy to them both. Neither of them had much liked Kurt, but they accepted and welcomed him due to their love of Else, until he betrayed them all. She asked Clarice's forgiveness and forced August to do the same.

One morning, Clarice opened her eyes, and when Maud thanked God, Clarice squeezed her hand before sinking back into sleep. At that moment, the woman swore she would do everything in her power to protect the girl. Maud kept her promise.

"A carriage will take you to your uncle's house. Vogel will protect you." Maud helped her downstairs.

In the hallway, a group of servants had gathered. Clarice felt lost. But one of them stood aside and another encouraged her. "Quickly, my lady. The carriage is waiting."

The journey to her uncle's house seemed never-ending. An acute whistling between her ears threatened to split her head in two, and her throat ached. When she got out of the carriage, Marta was waiting on the steps. She embraced her niece and took her upstairs to her old room.

"Your uncle will drum some sense into the head of that crazy husband of yours. Don't fear, my dear, things will change. From now on, August will treat you as you deserve." She ordered the maid to bring Clarice a cup of hot chocolate and stayed with her niece for a while longer. "Now you had better rest."

Clarice obeyed. She said nothing, but in her heart, she knew that both Maud and her aunt were deluding themselves. August would not stop, not until he killed her, but it didn't matter; nothing mattered anymore. She fell asleep.

The next morning Kurt summoned her to the library. Sitting in a corner of the room was August. His shirt was stained, his hair awry. There was a dazed look in his eyes.

"Come here, my dear. Your husband tells me that lately there have been misunderstandings between you. I think the time has come to deal with them together. What is making you so unhappy, my dear?"

Clarice raised her head and observed her uncle. The purple bruises on her skin provided a clear enough answer. He looked away and muttered something. The tension grew. Suddenly, August stood up and she raced for the door.

"Stay away from me!" she screamed before slamming the door behind her and running to her room.

It was just a matter of time before her aunt and uncle would have to give in. She was her husband's property. Her throat tightened bitterly. Her impotence drove her to consider some wild ideas.

Hours later, as she was looking out her window, knees drawn up to her chest, she saw a carriage pass by. Inside was a group of girls, and on top, trunks and cases were piled. There wasn't a single man among them. She had heard of the sort of trip that some young people from good families took after concluding their studies and before entering society. She wondered what it felt like to be so carefree and happy. She closed her eyes, laying her cheek on her skirt. She would have given anything to see the world her books described.

On that day in her uncle's home, Clarice von Harmel thought of death and of life. She could return to her husband, until one day he finally managed to kill her, or she could escape him and live.

She made up her mind.

She got up and packed a bag, carefully choosing what to take and what to leave.

Then she waited for the night to come.

It wasn't hard to get down to the cellar. The door behind the barrels was just as she had left it. And as before, a shaft of light revealed Frederik's presence. She knocked and waited, her heart in her throat. A moment later, a familiar hand opened the door.

"My little sparrow, what are you doing here at this time of night?"

The man's voice faded as he saw the signs of mistreatment on the girl's face. Clarice let him embrace her and wept for a long time. She didn't explain. It wasn't necessary.

"I can't stay. I must get as far away as possible."

Frederik dried her tears and then, after signaling her to keep quiet, he went upstairs. He reappeared after what seemed to Clarice an infinitely long time.

"There's a chance you can travel with a dear friend of mine. I have just sent a trusted messenger to her, and he says she's about to depart. She will take you far from Vienna."

He opened his safe and retrieved a little bag. He took out some gold coins and counted them thoughtfully before closing the bag. "You must always keep it on your person. Trust no one."

"I can't—"

"Hush, my little sparrow. We must make haste. It will be a long journey."

Dawn had not yet broken when the carriage left Vienna. Two soldiers were escorting the Baroness Margareta von Neumann and her ladies. The noblewoman intended to visit Italy and, who knew, perhaps she would go on to Egypt too. They spoke so well of the place and its rich history.

In a corner of the carriage, Clarice blessed the bookbinder. She owed him everything. He had taught her the power of books and had once more opened the door of her cage.

"Goodbye, little sparrow. Have a good flight," he had said to her, an instant before she got into the carriage under the watchful eye of the baroness.

"Don't worry, Frederik, I'll take care of her."

And so, another chapter in Clarice von Harmel's life ended as a new one began.

CHAPTER EIGHTEEN

When she put down her suitcase in the hall of the apartment in Coppedè, Sofia had an inkling that something was off. She looked around, but everything was as it should be, not a thing out of place.

As she took off her jacket, the events of the last few days filled her mind and demanded consideration. It was as though the new experiences and discoveries had influenced her very existence, and now change was urgent.

For the first time since leaving her husband, she felt the deep need to have a place of her own. Not necessarily a physical place, but something that represented her, that might act as a shelter but also a point of departure.

And she realized she didn't want to leave Italy.

Rome was her city, and it was here that she'd go on living. And she wanted to work with books. She had no idea what exactly she would do, but she was tired of making compromises.

Her thoughts flew to Tomaso too—the way he spoke to her and the way she felt when he looked at her. It was something eminently physical, but why not, after all? To feel, that was what she wanted. To be moved, to laugh, even cry. Anything was better than the vacuum she'd been in. God, how much time she'd wasted!

It was in the greenhouse, close to her grandfather's flowers, that slowly, very slowly, the tension relaxed its grip, and she managed to disentangle the threads of her thoughts.

The discovery of Clarice's second letter had shed new light on the entire story, and now Sofia was burning with curiosity. Clarice hadn't mentioned her secret this time, but the final sentence seemed to point them to the third volume of Fohr's work. Sofia and Tomaso were convinced that they would find the secret revealed there.

She couldn't stand being alone, but she didn't want to call Tomaso again. That left only one person to whom she could tell her theories about Clarice: Andrea Vinci.

When she got to the bookshop, he'd already turned on the lights and was deep in a book, as usual. Sofia stood on the threshold for a moment, breathing in the smell of old paper and leather while the ringing of the bell slowly came to a halt. Not until he had finished the page did Vinci look up. His eyes lit up with pleasure, and Sofia knew she had done the right thing by going to see him.

"Good evening, how are you?"

"Much better now that you're here, my dear. But tell me how you are. You look splendid."

Sofia let him embrace her. She was quivering with the desire to tell him about her progress. "I'm well; it's just that so many things have happened. You remember Clarice, the woman who hid a letter in Fohr's book?"

The old man pointed to the armchairs. "Come over here; let's sit down. Of course I remember. Tell me, are there new developments?" He leaned heavily on his walking stick.

Sofia didn't remember him having one before. His fingers seemed so thin they could hardly grasp it. Since she had last seen him, the bookseller seemed to have aged. "Are you feeling OK?"

"Come on, what else have you found out?"

For a moment, she didn't know where to start. "I've found the second volume!"

Andrea's eyes widened. "Marvelous. You're sure it's the right one?"

"Absolutely certain. Hidden in the cover was the same pocket as in the first volume and inside it a letter from Clarice."

He was dumbfounded, a slight smile on his lips. "What a wonderful adventure." Then he pulled himself up and stroked her hand. "And what does this second letter say?"

Sofia's smile faded. "Clarice had to escape to Italy. Her husband mistreated her; her life was hell."

"An unhappy fate for many girls, unfortunately." The bookseller sighed, but then his face lit up. "Of course"—the man's tone brightened— "Clarice came to Italy, and Fohr lived in Rome between 1814 and 1817, until he disappeared. Suppose they met in the city? That would explain a lot."

"There were a number of foreign intellectuals in Rome at the time," Sofia said softly. "They often moved in the same circles. Byron, Shelley, Goethe, Stendhal. Who knows how Christian and Clarice may have met? It seems she was an aristocrat, so perhaps they met at some ball or a salon, in view of their common interest in books."

They went on talking, and the more they exchanged ideas, the clearer the picture became.

Sofia was ecstatic. Clarice and Christian together in Rome! "Can you really not remember where you bought Fohr's first volume?"

The bookseller shrugged his shoulders. "Here in Rome. From a bookstall down in Trastevere. A traveling bookseller sold it to me. But I already told you that."

No, he hadn't; Sofia was more than certain of that. She started thinking aloud. "So the first book was found in Rome, where Clarice lived and probably met Christian. The second in Munich, where she was born—"

Suddenly, Sofia had a flash of intuition. She had to see Tomaso. Rome and Munich had been important cities for Clarice, but there was another place: Vienna.

"I must go now." She hugged the bookseller, and as he patted her shoulder, she felt a little of the weight on her heart fade.

"Promise you'll come back and see me, my dear. This is a very exciting story. I haven't enjoyed myself so much in years."

Tomaso went down the steps and crossed the lawn toward the villa. The soft grass was like a carpet beneath his shoes. The warmth of the autumn afternoon spread the intense perfume of plants all around him. Under one of the oak trees, Luisanna had had a gazebo put up. Sheltered from the sharp breeze, she and Frank were chatting—a content old couple. A light laugh joined a deeper one. Frank had improved a lot; he moved easily, laughing and chatting with his wife.

Tomaso halted, thinking. He had bad news. The meeting with the lawyers had gone poorly. The damage their clients had suffered because of Frank's report demanded compensation. He hadn't mentioned his stepfather's declining health. That information might have been of use in a court of law, but a trial would mean exposing Frank and the agency to public scrutiny. So he'd decided to negotiate. The heirs seemed more than ready to come to an agreement, though a very expensive one. Tomaso also needed to confront Frank at last about the embezzled money.

"Tomaso, what a surprise!" His mother rushed over, grasping his hands.

He took hers, bending to kiss them. "I was in the area, and I thought I'd come by and see how things were."

"Much better. The cardiologist says that the situation is still delicate, but he's strong. I'm sure that, soon, all this will just be a bad memory. But tell me about yourself. You look tired."

His mother's worried look was more than Tomaso could bear. He shook his head slightly, forcing himself to smile. "I'm well. A lot of work, a worry or two, that's all."

Luisanna nodded, but furrowed her brow. "Why don't you go and sit with your father? I'll pop back into the house and fetch you a shawl."

"I can do that."

"Of course. I know that. But there are things you only say to one another when you're alone." She stroked his face. "Mothers know a lot, even if their children obstinately pretend not to realize." She kissed him lightly on the cheek.

Tomaso waited for her to go and slowly walked toward Frank.

"Come and sit next to me, my boy. So, what's the news?"

It took him a second to decide. Finally, he shook the hand that the man he had never managed to consider a father was holding out to him. "Things are fine." He lied, fearing that the truth might disrupt the calm afternoon. He lied for his mother's sake, for the smile she had given him, for the look in her eyes.

"I'm glad, Tommy. I was sure everything would turn out all right."

He'd always envied his stepfather's optimism. Even in the worst of situations, the man showed an enviable ability to bounce back. Tomaso listened, distracted, to what Frank was saying, nodding every now and then, but his mind strayed to Sofia. Something good to think about. He wondered if they would be able to find Fohr's lost volume together, if it really did exist. It would be a huge stroke of luck and could save the agency. He also wondered if their ways would part at that point. He liked Sofia, but there was something in her that suggested he proceed with caution. And that's what he would do; he had no intention of frightening her.

He stayed with his mother and stepfather for a while longer, but all that idle talk, just to fill the silence, soon made him restless.

He said goodbye to them both, and when he shook Frank's hand, his stepfather held on a little too long, which annoyed him. He hadn't asked any questions, even though he knew the disaster he'd caused with his foolish behavior. Tomaso had the sense Frank was washing his hands of the matter, knowing that his stepson would make every effort to prevent a disaster. Anger boiled up inside him. He pulled his hand away, turning to his mother.

On leaving the villa, Tomaso's thoughts turned to Sofia again. The smell of the food that Scilla had prepared for him rose from the basket on the back seat and gave him an idea—perhaps it wasn't the most sensible one, but he was tired and a bit lonely.

He stopped at a wine merchant, where they produced an excellent Cannellino di Frascati. On his way back to the car, he dialed her number. "Ciao, Sofia."

"I've got to talk to you."

His lips curved into a slight smile. If it was tranquility he was looking for tonight, Sofia wouldn't be the one to offer it. He rubbed his fingers across his eyelids, massaging them. "Something urgent?"

"Yes. Extremely."

No sweetness in her tone, no hint of seduction. He sighed. The woman was single-minded. Why on earth go on desiring her? But there wasn't a rational answer to the question; that wasn't how it worked. He almost laughed. This wasn't a promising prelude for a date. On the other hand, she'd done nothing but surprise him, entertain him, or make him furious. All he could do was wait and see. Fohr, his stepfather, and the rest of the world could go to the devil!

"Listen, what would you say to dinner together? But I don't want to go out. Your place or mine, you choose."

When Sofia arrived at his apartment, she looked around, enchanted. "It's like you."

"I'll take that as a compliment."

The high white walls gave off a sense of freedom. Sofia noticed the light-filled windows, the simple furnishings with their clean lines, and recognized him. But what struck her most was the writing desk in the corner. It was large, solid, and majestic. She couldn't take her eyes off the desk, on which she spotted all the tools of calligraphy. She imagined Tomaso bending over a sheet of paper, his hair falling over his forehead, his hand grasping a pen. The sound of the pen on paper.

"You can look around if you'd like."

His voice took her by surprise. He came closer, stopping at her side. She could feel the warmth and smell the scent of him. She shivered and moved away.

"You know that letter you wrote me, the day you left for Munich? I couldn't believe you'd written it yourself." She didn't tell him just how struck she'd been by the handwriting. She kept that to herself.

Tomaso followed her. He was barefoot, his white shirt open at the neck, his expression relaxed.

"Writing makes your thoughts concrete, gives them a form, conserves them. It allows your creativity to influence reality."

It was true. Sofia considered how loaded the simple gesture of writing was.

"To write in a fine hand," he continued, "you need total concentration; the slightest error can ruin everything. The work grows letter by letter; you build it up and how far you decide to go depends exclusively on you."

Sofia stroked the surface of the desk. Even the scratches on the wood were revelations. It was as though someone had written a story there. A silence fell, in which breath followed breath, and thought followed thought, just like the looks she and Tomaso exchanged.

"Why don't you sit down? There's a sheet of paper there. And the right pen and ink too. Try it, Sofia. Write whatever you want." His voice was soft, almost a whisper.

She observed him there, a little distance away.

"It's just us; you don't have to prove anything to anyone."

She was about to protest, but then he winked as though promising to never pass judgment on her. Sofia felt confused, agitated. Was it possible that Tomaso was right? Had she been looking at herself through other people's eyes?

Images of her previous life appeared to her, marking every lost opportunity, every silence when she had wanted to scream. The most upsetting thing of all was that she had adopted that way of living. It hadn't been born in her. It'd been an adaptation to her situation, a compromise. It was detestable.

Rebellion boiled up; it didn't matter that it was Tomaso standing next to her and not Alberto. She raised her head. "I'm not afraid of anyone's judgment, even yours. I'm not afraid of you."

He held her gaze, squinting slightly. "That's a fine thing, don't you think?" He bent his head to one side. "Fear is a terrible way to start a relationship."

She stared at him, amazed. She had never known anyone to be so direct.

"Fear's a prison we hold the key to," he added softly.

If she had stretched out a hand, Sofia could have touched him, but she feared another sort of intimacy—the way the man could get around her defenses, as though he knew her most intimate thoughts.

"Of course, I don't know much about calligraphy," she said, sitting down at the desk. It was more comfortable than she'd imagined. She settled herself, gaining confidence. The pen was light in her fingers. She tried pressing it to the paper. Carefully, she dipped it into the ink and tried again.

Tomaso observed her silently.

"I know that the downward strokes are thick and the upward ones slender," she continued, "and that there are English italics, *italico*, and Gothic—"

"Yes. Every style has its own rules, but the first principle, the essential one, is that you should be able to feel yourself through your hand. The pen is you, Sofia; what you write are your thoughts. When they touch the paper, they leave you and go to others. It's a bond or at least a beginning."

"Like Clarice's letter."

"Like Clarice's letter."

She didn't reply. Slowly, a letter appeared on the paper, then another. The pen rustled, making a series of dry sounds, as if angry.

"May I?" Tomaso sat beside her.

Instinctively, Sofia drew back.

"This desk was designed for two people. There's room for us both."

That wasn't why she had pulled away, and they both knew it. It was what remained of the old Sofia, the one who withdrew from everything she desired.

His words, tossed out lightly, allowed her out of her dilemma without seeming hysterical. She was grateful for the kind gesture.

She focused on Tomaso's hand, which had started to move across the paper as though dancing. The lines appeared in harmony and with surprising strength.

Sofia Bauer. She had never seen her name written that way. It was a work of art.

"Do you want to try?" He handed her the pen.

She would never be able to match that style. "I don't think I can do it."

He studied her. "What you can or can't do depends on your determination to pursue your objective." He paused, then stretched out a hand in her direction. "May I?"

Sofia nodded, and he put an arm around her shoulders, wrapping her in his body. The embrace was not casual. There was seduction in Tomaso's slow movements, his gentle embrace, pulling her back toward his shoulders, closing the hand holding the pen in his own. It was in his

173

breath on her neck, his strength, and their synchronized movements. It was in his face, warm against her own.

"Let yourself go. Don't think of anything."

His embrace was both a challenge and a promise, and she let herself accept it. As he moved and she followed him, the name appeared. It wasn't like the one he had traced before. He had shown her the way, but she had been the one to write it.

He had moved behind her now, his heart beating fast. Sofia could feel it through the material of her dress. She shivered. She knew exactly where Tomaso was, knew that if she turned she would find him there to welcome her. Her breath caught in her throat.

She felt desire overcome her, need. Touch and smell. How long had it been since she had desired something this intensely?

Tomaso remained still, his head against her head, his hand resting lightly on hers. He was waiting. He would accept her decision, Sofia knew. No words, no declarations. Just an offer.

Slowly, she turned her head until she found Tomaso's mouth.

Her first sensation was the warmth of his breath and then the taste of him, the gentle caress of his lips. But the delicate gestures lasted only for a moment.

Tomaso's kiss deepened, and he plunged his fingers into her hair, clasping her to him. When she responded, he picked her up and took her to his bedroom, the place—he realized then—where he had always wanted her. Sofia did not object. They shared the same energy; the urgency in her gestures communicated beyond words or thoughts.

They sought one another, skin against skin, amazed because the sensations were like nothing they had imagined. They had no measure by which to understand what was happening. It was as though everything was new, everything different. They lost themselves in one another, as all their questions vanished, driven away by the desire that had united them since the start.

Afterward, as their breathing slowed and the world regained its contours, they stayed, embracing one another, determined to hold on for a moment longer to what had been created between them. They didn't know each other well, and at the same time, they knew everything.

Despite the moment of joy, despite the desire that still pulsed inside her, Sofia felt doubt rising. The certainty that had guided her movements was shaken. Life had taught her that, perfect though some things might appear, everything came to an end. And she felt it coming, along with her doubts. She grabbed the sheet and pulled it over her body, getting out of bed.

Quickly, Tomaso gripped her hand, pulling her back. "Whatever happened to you in the past has nothing to do with us."

She stared at him, ready to run away. "You know nothing about me."

His grip relaxed, and he smiled at her. "I'm hungry. What do you say we tell each other a bit more about ourselves over dinner?"

Before she could reply, he let go of her and turned around.

She watched him get dressed. Trousers, shirt, still no shoes. There was something special in that man, the way he related to the world, she thought.

There was a clear note of bitterness in his voice when he said, "I won't say I'm sorry for what has happened, because that would be a lie, but I have no intention of wasting time, tormenting myself when I could spend it more profitably or more pleasantly."

Sofia reflected that she likewise knew nothing of what had happened to him, of the life he carried on his shoulders. How could she have behaved so rudely? But this thought was immediately replaced by another. Why had Tomaso responded like that?

"I'm not sorry, either, but that doesn't mean anything in the end."

He stopped, looking back at her over his shoulder. "You think so? Seems to me it means everything." He took a few steps, then turned around. "Let's eat."

Sofia got dressed and found her way to the kitchen, stopping in the doorway. It was like the rest of the house, elegant but almost spartan, essential. Light colors, a lot of space. She looked around. There were flowers in a green vase on a shelf. Tomaso had put on an apron and was moving around confidently, glancing at her every now and again.

She entered slowly, wondering at every step what she was doing there and what had possessed her to let herself go with him like that. Cursed doubts that had wound themselves around her like a snake.

"Do you want some?" He handed her a stick of celery with sour cream and a prawn, then went back to the stove.

"Where do you keep the plates?"

Tomaso pointed to a shelf. Sofia set the table and then sat while he prepared the food. The tension between them had eased some, but it was still there. He uncorked the wine, making her jump. She lifted the glass to her lips, then raised her eyes. He was staring at her. The wine was dark with a rich bouquet. He waited until she had finished her sip before sitting down.

"Relax, Sofia. Let's eat now."

She hadn't realized how famished she was. Tomaso took over the conversation, slowly, like an expert, finding the place where she was hiding and drawing her out with keen observations and lighthearted comments. And so, slowly, Sofia's smile grew broader. In the end, she found herself laughing.

The thought that she could fall in love with a man like this was intoxicating, and yet fear rose in her, laying out a whole series of consequences, none without obstacles and danger.

"I was married for five years." She said this suddenly and then put her hand to her lips, reliving the alienation she'd felt, even from her own skin. She swallowed and forced herself to go on. "We weren't happy. I—I recently decided to leave. It's difficult."

Tomaso poured her a little more wine. "Five years is a long time. I think it's normal to be upset."

"I'm angry with myself."

"Sometimes we make one bad choice after another. But our survival instinct propels us forward."

Sofia thought she heard great sadness in Tomaso's voice. His gaze was distant, but it only lasted a second, then he searched her eyes again.

"Now he is the past."

He said it with such certainty that she stared at him, perplexed. Tomaso lifted his glass in a silent toast. "It's good to have you in my home. This is not a place where I normally bring people—but you mean something to me. Thank you for being honest with me."

"I don't want to talk about him."

"You don't have to. Frankly, I must say that of all that's happened this evening, it isn't your ex-husband that I'd like to spend time discussing."

She smiled, gazing at her wine. The glass was cold to her lips, the wine good and full-bodied. It brought her warmth, and she recovered a little courage. She breathed in deeply, concentrating, and then said, "I think the third volume is in Vienna."

Tomaso's smile broadened. He didn't answer, just gave her a steady look.

Her eyes flew wide open, and she jumped in her chair. "You knew already!"

"You just got lucky in Munich, girl."

She burst out laughing. "I'm convinced the books are bound to the places where Clarice lived."

Tomaso smiled. "And it just so happens that Vienna has the biggest center for the study of German Romantic writers. I've already called to make an appointment."

"When do we leave?"

He stiffened. "As to that, I have a couple of things to tell you."

"And what might they be?" Sofia had no intention of being left out. "Before you go on, Tomaso, consider that this is my story. I was the one who got you involved, and I was the one who found both letters. You need me."

He leaned back in his chair. "Need? I would've given it another name." He didn't give her time to reply. "Anyway, it's worth reflecting on."

Sofia stood up. "Why don't you reflect on whether you'd rather have me by your side or at your heels."

"I'm confused. It seems to me that I've amply expressed my appreciation already."

Intense heat rose to Sofia's cheeks. She wasn't used to that sort of dueling. She never considered that intimacy could be a subject of discussion, or a game. She was agitated and on edge. But when she met Tomaso's eyes, he was smiling at her.

"We leave tomorrow evening. I'll come by and pick you up."

"No, we'll meet at the airport. Thank you for—for dinner."

She started to pick up her plate, but he took it from her. "I'll do that." The message was clear and unequivocal.

Sofia went to the door. He was at her side. "Can I accompany you to your car, or would that be an attack on your independence?"

"I can find the car on my own," she muttered, trying not to laugh.

She was already outside when suddenly she turned back. She seized him by his shirt and stood on tiptoe. She kissed him gently. "Ciao, Tomaso. Thank you for everything."

He closed the door behind her and turned off the light. In the darkness, he pulled back the curtain and watched her get into the car. When she disappeared at the bottom of the road, he kept on staring at the point where she'd vanished.

He finally turned back to the room to gather a vinyl record, shiny as obsidian, in his hand. Delicately, he placed it on the turntable. He closed his eyes, blocking out everything, until the vibrations reached his soul and echoed inside him.

Only then did he return to the writing desk and, after picking up the paper Sofia had written on, let his eyes wander over the signs she had traced. He looked right inside her through her writing, trying to capture what she was hiding. He followed the lines, pausing now and then, his gaze suspended by the place in his mind where he had stored all the sensations, all the emotions he had felt since she'd entered his life. Now that they had moved beyond friendship, what would she do? What would he do? He shut his eyes. He was tired, and the next day was going to be very difficult.

He needed time, and he needed a whole heap of money.

CHAPTER NINETEEN

They who dream by day are cognizant of many things which escape those who dream only by night. In their gray visions they obtain glimpses of eternity, and thrill, in awaking, to find that they have been upon the verge of the great secret.

—Edgar Allan Poe, "Eleonora"

Vienna was like a woman of indefinable age with a parasol in her hand as she sped along in a sports car. It wasn't the Baroque palaces with their gargoyles and elaborate decorations that defined her, nor the crystal of the modern buildings towering over the squares. It was the union of many senses: the sound of music playing on the cobblestone streets, the sight of regattas racing on the Danube, the scent of chocolate demonstrating how a profession can become an art, the echo of conferences attracting academics from all over the world. Vienna's profound culture was an elegant robe draped around her.

Sofia knew the city. She had lived there for six months as a child while her parents were teaching at the Technische Universität. Yet what she saw now was very different from what she remembered. At her side, Tomaso walked silently. Since they'd stepped off the plane, he had uttered only a few words. The same had happened in the hotel, where they had booked separate rooms. He seemed to understand that she wasn't ready to share his space. She needed to become familiar with herself again, and she needed time. Tomaso hadn't put any pressure on her, but Sofia knew that, if she needed him, all she would have to do was stretch out a hand. Something she would take care not to do.

She desired the man like air, like water, with the same intensity and the same need. It was something she couldn't explain, completely different from anything she had experienced before. But she was afraid of it. Not of him, but of what he represented. She was afraid of herself, afraid that the sickness that had bound her to Alberto might repeat itself. She was afraid that desire might cause her to annul herself again.

Now and again he would look at her, as if to make sure she was really there, and then he'd seemingly take up the threads of his thoughts, advancing confidently, easily, toward the world. She didn't feel left out; they were companions and partners in the story.

"This is the place." Tomaso led her through a carved wooden door beneath a portico supported by neoclassical arches. "We have an appointment with Director Schulz," he told the man at the desk, handing over their paperwork.

After taking a look at his computer screen, the clerk gave them back their documents and said, "Third floor."

As they climbed the stairs, Tomaso seemed to regain his good humor for a moment. "This is the most probable place to find news of our book."

Sofia liked that "our." After coming across Clarice's latest revelations, she was dying to know what had happened to the woman. The desire was so intense as to relegate the discovery of a mysterious, unpublished work by Fohr to second place. "Do you think the director can give you some sort of clue?"

Tomaso nodded. "They have a huge library, the most highly specialized on German literature of the Romantic period, as well as a detailed catalog of works in the possession of others—both institutions and collectors."

"That's excellent. So why do you seem nervous?"

He gave her a dark look and a mere hint of a smile. "If the volume belonged to a public library or academic institution, it would be a disaster. We must just hope that, as they were odd copies, they remained on the antiques market."

Sofia knew it wasn't like him to be so pessimistic. Tomaso was a realist, but never lacking in faith. Now he seemed strangely vulnerable. Sofia wanted to lift him out of his distress, but she couldn't let herself get involved like that. Instead, she concentrated on Clarice.

"I haven't come this far just to give up."

Even if the book were in the custody of third parties, she would find a way of obtaining Clarice's letter somehow. After all, she owed her new life to Clarice. The woman had held out a hand, and Sofia had seized it with all her strength. The detail of their living two centuries apart was of no relevance at all.

Tomaso looked at her. "I'll remind you of those words."

Upstairs, they were welcomed by a young man who bombarded them with questions. Sofia was amused by the way Tomaso managed to give vague answers while extracting a whole lot of highly interesting information. The Institute for Studies on German Romanticism gathered information on private collections all over the world. "We have copies of every edition. We examine them, restore them, and put them back into a circuit of libraries on request."

"We're interested in Fohr's *In Praise of Perfection*. To be precise, the third volume of the work, the first edition by Cotta, Stuttgart, 1816."

"Ah! Christian Fohr. He's not a favorite of mine. Too sentimental. I'd go so far as to say anachronistic."

Sofia almost snorted. "He was ahead of his time. His respect for nature, the importance he placed on every living being, his interpretation of love being the inspiration of the purest sentiments. It isn't anachronistic; it's a profound expression of the soul."

The young man observed her skeptically. "From a purely literary point of view, Fohr is an emotional writer with flashes of innovation."

Sofia detested people who accepted the theories of others instead of using their own minds to tackle a text. "That old chestnut was already circulating when I went to school."

Tomaso suppressed a grin, and the young man blushed. He was about to reply when Schulz appeared in the reading room, if that title could be applied to the immense formal salon with frescoed ceilings, high walls, and lush furnishings.

"Mr. Leoni, welcome. I'm pleased to meet you."

Tomaso shook the man's hand. "The pleasure is mine. This is Dr. Bauer, the researcher I told you about over the phone."

The man observed Sofia with interest. "Christian Philipp Fohr—a curious choice." Schulz led the way, showing them into a side room. "I must confess I'm surprised by your interest in an author we really do know everything about, in view of the scarce amount of work he produced." He paused. "Unless you believe the legend about the unpublished work that disappeared."

Tomaso remained impassive. "Are there new developments on that front?"

Sofia shot him a surprised look. She had expected greater discretion on his part.

"None."

"Exactly."

Schulz smiled. "Of course not. Forgive me. We often come across dreamers with the most imaginative theories. It's embarrassing."

"I can imagine."

The director showed them to a desk. "If you'd like to explain in more detail what you're looking for, I'll see what I can do."

Tomaso described the volume. Sofia added a few details, taking care not to mention Clarice. The director's expression became more and more doubtful.

"We only keep complete works here, and that's an intentional choice. It doesn't make sense for us to purchase odd volumes. The same criterion applies to our catalogs too. I'm afraid I can't be of any help to you."

Tomaso stood up and shook the man's hand, and then it was Sofia's turn. She could hardly conceal her frustration. It had all been so quick and so disappointing.

They had only gone a few steps from the building when it started to rain. He took her hand, and they ran to seek shelter. They stopped under an arched doorway, their eyes on a foreboding sky swollen with clouds, their breath condensing in front of their faces. Tomaso put his arm around her shoulders, and Sofia clung to him. They stayed like that, listening to the rain batter at their feet and watching it dissolve into dark streams of water. Sofia felt closer to him than ever.

Tomaso stroked her face. "It's never easy."

Again, that feeling of serenity that allowed her to open up and confide in him. She shook her head. "That's not why I'm sad."

"No?"

"We might never find that damned book. I won't be able to keep the promise I made to Clarice."

He raised her chin. "It's a promise you made to yourself."

"That doesn't matter. I found her letter; I took up her story. No one made me do it. But I decided to take it on, and I shall go on looking. Tomaso, no matter how crazy it is, it's a promise, it's—"

He closed her mouth with a kiss. Surprised, Sofia went quite still, then put her arms around him, returning the kiss. Suddenly, that was what she wanted more than anything else. It was comfort, the present with a promise of the future.

They took refuge in a café, still shivering with cold.

"It takes a lot of patience, Sofia. The search for a book often takes years. What will you do in the meantime?"

"I know what I don't want to do. Is that all right too?"

He sat back in his chair. "It is."

They sat in silence, looking at one another, as she worked to give order to the words clamoring to be let out like crazed birds from a cage. "I won't leave Rome. I won't make decisions until I'm fully convinced. I won't follow other people's rules."

"Who was keeping you prisoner?"

She looked away, her fingers playing with the embroidery on the table napkin. Why did he always have to be so direct?

"I could say that it was him, my husband. But that wouldn't be true."

"Who, then?"

"Me. It was me." Her voice cracked. She struggled to hold his gaze, to keep back the tears.

"Why?"

"In the beginning, I thought that was how it worked. Isn't it out of love that we put the desires of the person we love before our own?"

"No. That isn't love, but go on."

Then why had she done it, if not out of love? Yet he must be right. There was nothing good about limiting oneself to please someone else. It had been fear, not love. She raised her head, meeting Tomaso's eyes again. They read inside her effortlessly.

Sofia was seized by panic. She didn't want him to know everything about her. There were things she herself hadn't faced yet, things she had to come to terms with. "Why do you even want to know?" She knew she shouldn't attack like that, but she couldn't do anything else.

"Out of love."

It was like being punched in the stomach, having the wind knocked out of her. She started to get up, but he grabbed her hand.

"Tell me to go to hell if it makes you feel better, but don't run away."

He let go, but it was too late. She reacted instinctively, backing away.

"Don't you dare tell me what I can or can't do!"

She left him sitting there, along with the shocked waitress, who had just come to the table with their order.

It took her time to get her thoughts together. She spent it walking in the rain, hands in her pockets, shoulders hunched. She felt like laughing; the trip had gone all wrong. She wandered aimlessly, and the city took her in its arms, its arches surmounted by richly decorated walls, its narrow cobbled streets, its lawns with fountains singing, immune to the passage of time. She could almost hear violins, the clatter of horses' hooves, laughter and song.

When she got back to the hotel, she was soaked through, but the anger and fear had eased. Still, her heart beat hard again at the memory of Tomaso's words.

Out of love. She didn't want his love.

Max would have told her that you should never ask a question unless you have the strength to face the answer. And Sofia didn't feel strong enough right now to welcome someone new into her life. She didn't even have a life.

She went slowly up the stairs, and at the landing, Sofia saw him sitting in front of the door to her room, his back against the wall, his head on his arms.

Tomaso stood up, a tense expression on his face.

"The things I want are the ones that terrify me more than anything," Sofia blurted out, then immediately regretted being so transparent.

His expression softened. "I'll take it as a compliment." He approached, kissing her wet hair and chasing the drops of water down her face with his lips. "Nothing tried and tested works with you. I tremble at the thought of giving you gifts like flowers or chocolates."

It was so good to feel him close to her. She sighed. "I'm sure you have better ideas." She paused. "I'm sorry. Really."

"So am I. But now you'd better go and get dry. I have an idea."

"Would you order dinner? I'm famished."

It took her a matter of minutes to shower and get dressed. It was the first time she'd felt lighter, more hopeful after a quarrel. Now she felt cheerful, full of vitality. She was in the hall when her phone rang. "Are you ready?"

"Yes."

"Where are you?"

"In my room."

"OK."

A savory smell of greens and stew greeted her, along with a smile. "Well, what shall we do now, then?"

"Go on vacation."

"What?"

Tomaso poured her a glass of wine. "We need to take a break. Tomorrow we'll take a walk around the city and make peace properly, OK?"

The time they spent together at dinner and afterward, driven by their mutual need, seemed to amply serve that purpose. Yet they both knew there was a lot more to resolve between them.

They woke up to a wet, unsettled morning, but if Sofia thought for a second it would get in their way, she was mistaken. When Tomaso smiled and stretched out a hand to her, she took it, and it was as if the sunlight inside her overpowered all the rain. At that instant, she decided that she would live her time with him moment by moment.

"Ready?"

"Yes."

As she and Tomaso toured Vienna together, their usual reticence fell away. Tomaso had always been very reserved and private in his past relationships. With Sofia, he'd begun to crack wide open.

This time it was she who would resist opening up—that he understood. So Tomaso had to decide how to proceed. In the end, he decided on one more day of rest. The hours they spent together would either be the end or a new beginning. He was honest enough with himself to know that, much as Sofia moved him, this was not sufficient for a relationship, and he had no intention of pursuing someone who didn't want to be caught.

"They don't even look like sweets." They had stopped in front of a shop window full of magnificent chocolate sculptures. "The idea that you can eat them is stupefying."

Tomaso agreed. "It seems impossible that anyone would go to those lengths to make something that can be destroyed in a second."

"Eaten."

"Yes. Beauty is ephemeral, yet it becomes part of us."

Tomaso took her hand and pressed it to his lips. "Let's go, there's so much more to see."

They still had time, and this kept them going. She showed him the places she loved most in the city. It was as though they both wanted to contribute moments to the day.

When Tomaso awoke the next morning, Sofia wasn't at his side. He looked for her in the shadows and saw her next to the window, her eyes staring out at nothing. He felt a sudden pain in his chest; she was so far away. Then, as if she could feel his gaze, she turned around and smiled at him.

"We'd better hurry, or we'll miss the plane," she whispered.

"I changed our flight. We have another day of vacation." Tomaso went to her, caressing her face. "I like the way you spend your time."

"I know."

A few hours later, just as they were about to leave the hotel, Tomaso received a phone call. Sofia watched him stiffen and then, after ending the call, walk slowly toward her.

"It was Schulz."

Hope lit her eyes. "Do they know where the book might be?"

"They have it."

Her jaw dropped.

"They searched through a lot left to them two years ago that they hadn't finished cataloging."

Sofia realized Tomaso didn't seem happy with the news. "So, why that face?"

He sighed and rubbed a hand over his brow. "It's irremediably damaged. Beyond any hope of restoration. But in any case, it's available. I've asked them if they could leave it to us to study. We'll see if they agree."

"They don't know what we're looking for."

He smiled at her. "No, they don't."

A few hours later, the young man from the Institute for Studies on German Romanticism brought them a cardboard box. "I warn you: it really is in a pitiful condition."

"It's more than we hoped for. Thank you."

Sofia lifted the lid of the box and winced. The edition looked right, but it really was in bad shape. "The spine's come unglued. The stitches are ruined, and the leather's come off the cover."

"It looks as though it's been in water."

Slowly, Sofia opened the volume. "Springtails and silverfish. Looks like they've been feeding off this book for generations." The paper was tattered, and whole pages had crumbled completely. "The only thing worse than this is an amateur attempt at restoration with glue and double-sided tape."

Tomaso nodded. "But the endleaves have survived." With a hand that trembled slightly, he pointed to Clarice's symbol—the circle with the two wings inside.

It was true. Encouraged by this discovery, Sofia proceeded. There was no need to force it; the cover came away like a door with no lock, revealing its secret. As she stared at the little pocket she'd come to recognize, her hopes grew. "The letter isn't damaged."

"No."

Delicately, Sofia took out the sheet of paper, trying to control her breathing, terrified the fragile paper would crumble.

"There it is."

Tomaso cleared the table and waited for her to place the sheet of paper on top of it.

In that wonderful country where people talk as though singing, I came to know the meaning of solidarity and friendship.

My companions, one of whom possessed the noblest of origins and spirits, welcomed me, and I once again became a sister and a daughter.

There are events that change our existence, like the one that occurred on our long journey from Vienna to Rome. I must pause—I am overcome with emotion. I must wait for the trembling of my fingers to pass, or I shall not be able to continue my story.

Of all the books my new friends read to alleviate the tedium of the long hours spent in the carriage, one showed me the light. Its author spoke to me through his prose, as only a dear friend can. In Christian Philipp Fohr's writing, I found myself reflected as in a mirror. The intuitions that had guided my actions took on contours, acquired significance, and soon became certainties. Freedom, equality, education, future. Words present in so few hearts. Fate then acted for us. That young and celebrated author asked me—an unknown bookbinder—to bind his personal volumes and create a cover worthy of them. But it was not me he was putting to the test, so much as himself. I came to know him as a man, a friend, and a lover. I finally discovered that love is light and gentleness, joy and happiness. He had a desk made that would seat both of us during the hours we spent writing together. He showed me that that, too, was love. And out of our love, a child of ink, paper, and words was born. And hope for a better world.

Our hope had to remain secret, but now I wish to leave a clue so that it may someday be found . . .

CHAPTER TWENTY

How many a man has dated a new era in his life from the
reading of a book! The book exists for us, perchance, which
will explain our miracles and reveal new ones.

—Henry David Thoreau, *Walden*

En route, 1815

As the carriage rolled on toward Munich, whence the baroness would
depart for Italy, Clarice forced herself to put one instant behind the
next, counting the minutes, the hours, and the days. She didn't speak,
except to answer the questions she was asked. She needed all the energy
she had to force the air into her lungs and keep her heart from breaking
with pain and fear. Even the company of the baroness and the women
with her was overwhelming. Yet it was their conversations that finally
penetrated the chrysalis she had closed herself in and slowly, slowly
drew her out.

"A pyramid, you say?"

"Not just one but three—much bigger than cathedrals."

At every one of Margareta von Neumann's pronouncements, the
ladies exchanged amazed glances. "Like castles?"

"In a sense. Soon, you'll see them."

It was Egypt the baroness had her sights on. Since the excavations by scholars dispatched by Bonaparte, many new discoveries awaited visitors. Clarice began to listen, and every day her curiosity grew. She admired everything about that tall, bony woman with her blond hair wound severely around her head and her thin lips—every word, every gesture. More and more frequently, the baroness ordered the coachman to stop and let her admire the sun glinting off mountains still covered in snow, or follow the progress of a herd of wild sheep—"in holy peace," as she put it. She devoted the same attention to a meadow full of flowers and an unexpected waterfall. Clarice had never known anyone so highly cultured and generous. The women accompanying her, apart from Janice Laimer, the widow of a cousin to Margareta who had fallen in the Battle of Reims, were all unmarried and determined to remain so. They would have had to support themselves on small incomes if the baroness hadn't provided for them.

Seeing that Clarice bore the signs of brutal mistreatment on her face and body, they had all been very kind and discreet, showing their solidarity and showering the young woman with attention. They were interested in art, and often, on the longer stretches of their journey, as the carriage bounced along with difficulty, they read the many books they'd brought with them. Clarice's favorite was Christian Philipp Fohr, a young Prussian author whose work had created a good deal of scandal. There was something special about the way he used words, as if they were colors in a painting.

Sometimes Clarice had the impression that she understood him in a way she'd never understood anyone before. It was as though she were made of the same stuff as those books. She, too, saw nature as a refuge, as well as nourishment, for humankind and believed that knowledge was essential, and everyone should be able to have access to it. But it was the concept of freedom that she most identified with, the equality of rights and dignity. For Fohr, femininity was a characteristic, not a defect.

At last they were in Italy when Margareta leaned out of the window. She ordered the coachman to stop and, once out of the carriage, took deep breaths of the fresh mountain air.

"The Count and Countess de Bertoldi are dear friends of mine, and their residence is called La Costa. You'll enjoy staying with them."

Their stay proved to be far more than pleasant, and instead of the agreed-upon two weeks, they stayed in Belluno for three months. Luisa de Bertoldi and her husband, Giovanni, overwhelmed them with kindness. Clarice borrowed Christian Fohr's books from Margareta and spent the warm hours of the afternoon reading in the peace of one of the villa's gardens.

When they finally left, Giacomo de Bertoldi, the count's adolescent son, who had become Clarice's shadow right from the start and taught her basic Italian, gave her a portrait and an octavo-sized notebook. Together with that precious Fabriano paper, he also gave her a wooden rod for mounting metal nibs and a bottle of ink, ready to use. "With this, you'll be able to free yourself of the thoughts that make you so sad." She had embraced him at length.

After Belluno, they stopped in Ferrara and then in Florence. "We'll visit Venice on our return journey. Now I want to stop in Rome." Margareta looked up, her eyes straying to Clarice. She'd grown fond of the girl, ever since she had seen her climb into the carriage, tortured by pain, driven by extraordinary courage. "My dear child, do you know that your beloved Fohr lives in this city?"

The idea that the man really did exist troubled and fascinated Clarice. That evening, bending over the writing desk at the inn where they had stopped, she committed her thoughts, her dreams, and her impressions of the long journey that had changed her so much to the first of her diary entries. And then she wrote about him—Christian Philipp Fohr—the man who believed in a world of equality and freedom.

Florence had seemed magnificent to her, but she was stunned by the beauty of Rome. It was like a collection of jewels laid out across a cloth. It was a city full of contradictions. The precious sculptures that rose above the variegated crowds seemed completely unaware of the chaos surrounding them. The city elicited exclamations of amazement from travelers, as well as indignation. Yet, unlike her companions, Clarice saw beauty everywhere. She was charmed not only by the landmarks but by the colored skirts of the peasant women, the thick black braids that flowed over their shoulders as they lugged full water bags, despite their access to the oldest aqueduct in existence. The ancient ruins covered with wild roses provided a backdrop for gold carriages drawn by horses with festively decorated harnesses and driven by uniformed valets. To Clarice, it was all to be admired. Margareta showed her the monuments, the Trevi Fountain, the Corsini Palace, the churches and gardens. The noblewoman had concentrated her full attention on the girl.

"Frederik asked me to take you to Rome and said you would know why, but I'd like you to continue the journey with us. I don't have the heart to leave you here amid all this danger."

But Clarice had already faced evil, and she had managed to free herself. Now she'd been swept away by the kindness of her companions and the words of an unknown man. Christian Philipp Fohr's words settled deep within her, forcing her to reflect and to leave pain behind. She knew that the only way to live was to move forward.

Clarice was tempted to tell the generous baroness about her past, but she resisted. She alone must bear that burden. So she simply replied, "I'll think about it. Thank you."

Clarice often escaped her companions, who preferred the parts of Rome frequented by other foreigners, and walked the little streets of the old city center. She loved strolling between the Colosseum and the ruins of the Roman forum. She only had to close her eyes to see the city as it had been in ancient times. Soon, she ventured farther: Palazzo

Sacchetti on the beautiful Via Giulia, the Casino del Bel Respiro and its secret gardens, the magnificent Villa Piccolomini.

"May I take the carriage this afternoon?"

"Of course. But promise me you'll be careful. But now that I think of it, I don't have any commitments, so I can take you wherever you want."

In fact, Margareta did have several appointments that afternoon; Clarice had heard her arranging them with her dressmaker and the other women.

"There's a bookbinder's I'd like to visit," she said, hoping that the baroness might let her go alone. It was a place Frederik had told her about; he had a bookbinder friend in Rome who might hire her in his bottega.

"Ah, wonderful, I've got a couple of books to be mended." The noblewoman tapped her fingers to her lips. "It's all decided then; I'll come with you."

"But I can mend them for you!"

"So it's true that Frederik taught you the profession."

"Yes, and I assure you I'm quite capable."

The woman studied her. "Why not? Fine. We'll buy everything necessary at the shop."

Clarice had imagined spending the day by herself, but if there was one thing she'd learned over the past few months, it was how to adjust.

No one seemed to know Raimondo Farina, Frederik's friend. After an hour searching through the lanes surrounding the Chiesa di San Luigi dei Francesi, Clarice started to lose hope. They were passing in front of a high door closed with iron bars when she saw the symbol: the outline of a book chiseled into the architrave. The wooden door was blackened and flaking.

"Stop!" she ordered the coachman. She got down and knocked on the door a few times, looking around.

"Master Farina has gone away. The bottega's closed." This came from an elderly woman sitting nearby on an old stool, her knotted fingers skillfully weaving a basket of reeds.

Clarice went up to her. "Can you direct me to the owner of this place?"

"Certainly," replied the woman. "It's me."

Clarice had already noticed the old woman's well-made clothes. She looked like a commoner, but the woman sitting beside her, handing her the reeds, was her servant. "What happened to Master Farina?"

"A fire."

"Did the bottega catch fire?"

"No, the apprentice's trousers. Master Farina tried to pull them off him, but the boy had gone crazy and pushed him, so the poor old thing fell into the fire. Then there was a right old rumpus. Farina's gone back to Bologna. He's shut up shop. Anyway, why are you asking? Do you want to rent it? I'll give you a good price, you know."

Clarice ignored the doubtful look on Margareta's face. "May I see inside?"

"You think I'd rent it to you without showing it to you first? Whom do you take me for?" The old woman disappeared behind a curtain on the ground floor of a nearby building and came out a moment later with two keys on a ring. The clinking accompanied Clarice's racing heart. "What would you make of it, anyway?" the woman asked suspiciously, stopping in front of the door.

"Another bookbinding workshop."

"Run by whom? You?"

"Precisely—us," replied the baroness haughtily, giving the woman a sharp look.

Clarice turned to the noblewoman in amazement.

"Is there any law in Rome to prevent women from opening a business?" It had taken Margareta a moment to grasp Clarice's intentions, but after her initial bewilderment, the idea appealed to her.

The old woman shrugged. "No, no. If you have the money, you can do what you like with it. Decent things, of course."

Once inside, Clarice felt her eyes fill with tears. The smell carried her back in time to when she herself had worked at tables like these, cultivating her dreams. She hurried from one side of the room to the other, touching the machines and tools, the surface of the tables. Apart from the general confusion and the objects that had ended up on the floor, the equipment seemed to be in good shape. Clarice opened the crates. Under covers of felt, the skins seemed to be in perfect condition. Red, green, and cobalt morocco leather. It was a real treasure house. Her eyes moved over the ample chamber with its arched ceiling of stone and brick. The glass windows leading to a courtyard at the back were dark with layers of dirt and soot. The weeds in the garden seemed to reach as high as the treetops.

"Never seen such a disaster," muttered the baroness, wrinkling her nose.

"I think it's marvelous," whispered Clarice.

"Really?" Margareta gave up trying to lift the hem of her dress, letting it fall with a sigh, then she turned to the owner. "How much do you want for this place?"

As the baroness negotiated energetically, Clarice chose what she needed to mend her benefactor's books. She paused a moment in front of the paper machine, smiling as though at an old friend. Then her thoughts took shape, driven by a force and an enthusiasm that she hadn't felt in years.

Her new life was right there in front of her, in her hands, the same ones that were capable of creating wonderful, unique bindings. She wouldn't be going to Egypt. Rome was her opportunity and her future.

It took her a week to redo the binding of Margareta's books. Into the leather she stamped the mountaintops, fountains, towers, flowers, and streams they had seen on their journey. She finished them in gold. The baroness regarded them, her mouth gaping. "I've never seen such elegant work, my dear. I'm speechless."

The bottega opened on the first of June. Thanks to the help from Margareta and the money Frederik had given her, Clarice hired three women from the baroness's entourage, choosing those who seemed to have the greatest need and competence. One of the three, Lauren, proved to be an important friend and ally, standing up for her when the baroness had a change of heart and tried to convince Clarice to continue on with them to Egypt.

Clarice faced Margareta's objections in silence, and then embraced the baroness, telling her just how important she had been to her, but how she must choose her own path. Clarice moved to the second floor of the bookbinding workshop that same evening. Lauren occupied the third, following her into their new life.

Resigned, the baroness lingered in Rome, introducing Clarice to the salons frequented by intellectuals, artists, and bored aristocrats. In her bag, she always carried a little book of Clarice's with a precious gold cover, which she would take out as if casually, arousing the envy of the other ladies.

And so the workshop's first books began to circulate among the ladies of Rome. Now and then, Margareta would visit Clarice, bringing with her fellow aristocrats curious about the girl's story. It was unusual for a woman, particularly a young one, to be the head of such a business, and it was the scent of scandal that, together with Margareta's support, brought in the first big orders. The rumors about Clarice were encouraged by her elegance and delicate beauty. The fact that she attended exclusive salons yet never favored the wealthy men increased people's fascination. In a short time, the bookbinding in Piazza di San Luigi was abuzz with orders, friends, and curious onlookers.

"Good morning, can you tell me where I can find Signorina Clarice Schmidt?"

She had changed her surname and still wasn't used to the new one. Clarice raised her head from the frame, where a little girl was intently watching the needle she moved over the sheets of paper.

"Good morning, sir." A lock of hair fell across her face. She cleaned her hands on the damp cloth Lauren handed her and approached the man. "That's me. What can I do for you?"

He was tall, dark, and simply but elegantly dressed, standing in the shadows. In his hands, he held bundles of papers. He seemed tired, his face drawn, but surprise filled his eyes. He studied her intently, then looked around. "Are you really the bookbinder?"

"Yes. Can I help you?"

He didn't answer immediately, as though reflecting on the question. Then he lifted his head. "It's a pleasure to meet you, Fräulein."

Clarice's smile died on her lips. She was silent for a moment, sustaining the questioning gaze of those clear blue eyes. She moistened her lips, her heart hammering in her breast. "For me too, *mein* Herr." How did he know she spoke German? Fear clawed at her. She must keep calm and breathe. August had nothing to do with this man, she told herself. She was free, her husband nothing but a bad memory.

"Baroness von Neumann directed me here. It seems you are the most amazing and talented bookbinder in all of Europe." There was no mockery in his words, just deep curiosity.

Clarice laughed softly, so relieved that she didn't notice the frightening admiration in the man's eyes.

"Margareta is my benefactor. Her opinion is profoundly influenced by the affection that binds us."

"That may be, Fräulein. Nevertheless, I can assure you that, as regards the amazement, the baroness has been absolutely right. As to the talent, I'm more than ready to believe her." He drew nearer, smiling, and took her hand, raising it to his lips.

Clarice couldn't stop staring at the stranger. There was something infinitely sad in his eyes and voice. She hastened to withdraw her hand, hiding it behind her skirt. "It's an honor, mein Herr."

"Allow me to introduce myself. Christian Philipp Fohr."

Clarice's eyes darted to the sheets of paper the man had placed on the table. The author's name was clearly printed on the top page: *Christian Philipp Fohr*. She was seized by awe; for a moment she couldn't speak. "Please excuse me. You couldn't know, but I owe you a lot. I owe you everything."

"This is most interesting and very peculiar. I'm certain I've never seen you before. I'm sorry to say so, but that's how it is."

He continued to regard her with that pained look, the polite smile that did not come from his heart. Clarice found it unbearable. He shouldn't suffer like this, not the man who had held her spellbound with the eloquence of his prose, the profound justice of his affirmations. Not him—capable of bringing to life thoughts Clarice didn't even know she possessed.

"Your books—they kept me company in a difficult period of my life. The things you wrote . . ." She paused. "To me, you were indispensable. You gave me faith."

He fell silent. His expression hardened, and his eyes became fierce. "You are a young woman, and hope lives in you by its very nature. Don't imagine for a moment that it was I, or what I wrote, that granted you faith, because you would be mistaken." He was quiet again, his breathing as rough as his look. A moment later, he sought her eyes. "Surprise me, Fräulein. I'm asking you to bind this new edition of my books as well as you can. But don't forget that they're just words. Life is something quite different, my lady." He bowed again and strode away from the bottega. Outside, a servant was waiting for him, holding the reins of a chestnut horse.

Clarice remained still, staring at the point where the man had disappeared from sight, until Lauren touched her shoulder. "What did he want?"

She showed Lauren the loose sheets. They had been printed by Cotta of Stuttgart. "A special binding."

"It was Fohr, the writer, wasn't it?"

"Yes." She smiled. "We shall bind his books. Is the paper vat ready? I want to put in some extra endpapers."

Her mind was already spinning through the designs she would create for each volume. Red morocco, gold decorations. The thought that Fohr would carry her symbol with him filled her with joy. A circle with two wings in it was her family's coat of arms. She'd worn her mother's pendant around her neck all these years, and now she found its true significance in Fohr's books. *Freedom is what humankind needs, like water, air, food, sleep.* Reading that in one of his books had helped her realize she wasn't a madwoman for escaping; she was a human who wanted to guide her own fate.

Over the next few days, Clarice worked incessantly. She wanted to find the perfect design for each book. The endpapers that included her symbol with the filigree were drying between pieces of felt. She prepared them herself, making the paper from soaked rags. On one side of the drying paper, she had placed a wire in the shape of her symbol. Like this, it would remain impressed in the fibers of the paper. Everything she used for the books she made herself. She even softened, stretched, and cut the leather personally. She worked feverishly without a break.

When her work was finished at last, Clarice wrapped the three volumes in a silk cloth that she had embroidered herself and organized their delivery to Fohr. Little Matilde, an orphan child she had taken on as an apprentice, was waiting for her at the entrance.

"Must I wait for an answer?" Matilde shifted from one foot to the other nervously.

"Are those shoes still hurting you?"

The little girl's eyes opened wide, then she blushed violently. "No, signora, and thank you for buying them for me."

Clarice bent down and stroked her cheek. "One day you'll be a bookbinder too, and then you'll be able to buy whatever you like, thanks to what you earn from your work."

The child nodded, her eyes shining with emotion. "You're the only person who wanted me."

"I would have been stupid to let such a good apprentice get away, don't you think? But tell me, what are you worried about?"

Matilde sighed. "If the gentleman wants me to tell you something, how will I bring the message?" Lauren was teaching the child to write, but the language gap slowed their lessons.

"You're quite right, you know." Clarice took the package out of her hands and smiled. "Go and help Caterina. This evening I want to see how many sheets you can sew together."

Matilde bowed and curtsied at the same time and went back inside, limping a little and running a little. Smiling, Clarice watched her go and then walked outside.

She was welcomed by the hot morning sun, and it was so pleasant that she decided to stand there, without her hat, for a moment. Her golden hair reflected the sunlight. She exchanged a few greetings along the way, making an effort to understand the words and repeating them softly. Her accent wasn't so strong now, but she still struggled with the fluidity and musicality of Italian. She stopped in front of one of the many fountains, her eyes on the jets of water that, flowing freely out of the statues of animals or mythological creatures, always charmed her. She had almost reached the building where Christian lived when she saw him riding his horse on the street. He dismounted and handed the reins to his servant, clapping him kindly on the shoulder. "Good morning, Fräulein, I didn't expect you so soon."

"Good morning to you, mein Herr." She bowed her head respectfully. Then she waited, a little embarrassed by the looks from passersby.

Christian pointed to the front door. "Come, we can sit in the garden."

Clarice took his arm and let him carry the books. "Thank you."

Beneath an elm tree, its silver leaves dancing in the sun, was a stone bench in front of a table and a little round fountain. "Here, Fräulein, make yourself comfortable."

The sadness that Clarice had noticed at their first meeting was still there. Christian placed the package containing the books on the stone table, opened it, and froze. Slowly, he took the first volume and held it in his hands.

Clarice was a bundle of nerves now. She couldn't see his expression, to see if he was satisfied or disappointed, but she knew she'd put her whole heart into that binding. She'd let her emotions lead her, creating a series of designs representing the key concepts of the work.

After a few minutes of silence, in which he intensely examined all three volumes, Christian raised his head, his eyes moist. "You continue to be mistaken about me, Fräulein."

Clarice leapt up. "You don't like them."

Of course, it was obvious. The work was too personal; Frederik would have been ashamed of her. How could she have broken the rules? These weren't her books; they were supposed to represent a universal work. Instead, she had personalized them, turning them into an expression of her own heart and soul.

When Christian made no reply, simply stared at her, Clarice muttered her apologies and rushed out.

When she got to the bottega, she raced up to her apartment, ignoring the workers' surprised looks. She didn't cry, although her throat was tight with disappointment. After a few minutes, she got up, fixed her hair, which had come loose around her shoulders, and splashed water over her red face. A while later, her friend knocked discreetly at the door.

"Remember, we're attending Margareta's party this evening."

She'd forgotten. In her devotion to binding Fohr's books, she had neglected everything else. "Thank you, Lauren." She had no desire to go to a party; instead, she felt like hiding, just like she'd done in the past.

The thought caught her unprepared, and she pictured herself huddled on the floor in a little ball of pain. No, that's not how it was anymore. She would not allow life's adversities to make a fool of her. She had made a mistake with Christian, but next time she would do better. Only death was definitive. And she was alive.

She took a long bath, braided her hair, and put on one of the dresses the baroness had had made for her. Around her neck, she still wore her mother's necklace with the diamond wings that had belonged to all the women in her family. She found Lauren waiting for her beside a hired carriage. "I'm happy to see you looking better."

Clarice didn't reply. She concentrated on what her friend was saying. That was the secret—to distract yourself, putting as much as possible between you and the pain. "The writer has sent the money to pay for the binding. Doubled the fee you agreed on."

Clarice shook her head. "There must be some mistake. He didn't like the work."

"Well, he paid for them, and very generously."

They spoke no more of it. But the news that the great Christian Fohr had commissioned Clarice to do the covers of his own personal copies of his books had already spread, causing some clamor at the party. And so, between the dancing and the refreshments, Clarice gained some new orders.

Time passed, business flourished, and Clarice often thought of Christian. She told herself he'd probably gone back to Munich and his wife, though, according to the gossip, she had left him for another man.

Clarice preferred not to think about what had happened between them, yet it returned to her mind regularly. Why had she behaved so inappropriately? The intimacy she had allowed herself in the bindings went beyond the confines of simple acquaintance, and she knew that very well.

Although she regularly took part in the receptions given by Rome's old aristocracy and bourgeoisie, Clarice preferred the folk dances and neighborhood festivities, where you could see the real face of the city. One evening, she was taking Matilde to one. The child was chattering away with excitement, drawing smiles from the taciturn Lauren, who was holding her hand.

"I've forgotten my shawl," Clarice said, rushing back inside. When she came out again, Lauren and Matilde turned to go.

"May I speak to you?"

The voice took her by surprise. Christian Philipp Fohr emerged from the shadows into the lamplight. "It's important."

Clarice was amazed. "Of course." She returned his bow and turned to her companions. "You go on ahead; I'll catch up with you later."

Lauren nodded. "We'll wait for you in the square."

Clarice was about to say that wouldn't be necessary, when Christian broke in. "I'll accompany the signorina personally. It won't take more than a minute or so."

Christian waited until they were alone to speak. "I have come to apologize, Clarice. May I call you that?" Without her permission, he went on, as though he'd been waiting out there in the dark, preparing his speech. "Your interpretation of my work showed amazing insight. It was like looking in a mirror, no, not a mirror. It was like looking at a part of myself. And that"—he paused, looking around as if searching for words—"had never happened to me before." His attention turned back to her. "My silence was due to my astonishment. You have been illuminating. You have been precious." He fell silent, in the grip of emotion. "So you see, my dear lady, you are the one who has given me back my faith in the world."

"I don't understand."

Christian drew closer and took her hand. Surprised, Clarice turned her wrist, and his lips touched her palm. Although she hastened to withdraw it, she could not ignore the turmoil she felt at that strange kiss, the sweetest she had ever received.

"I have come to thank you and to bring you a gift. I hope you can accept it." He handed her the three books she had bound. "They are for you. I've written something in the margins. I hope that, in this way, you may understand more about me."

Clarice opened the first of the volumes and, in the faint golden light of the lantern, observed the elegant handwriting accompanying whole chapters. Her eyes fell upon a striking sentence: *It is by sharing thought that the soul is enriched, grows, and prospers.*

"I have left empty spaces—they're for you."

She looked up, questioningly.

"Write what you think, I beg you. I would like your thoughts to be joined with mine." His fingers ran through his hair, which kept falling across his face, and a feverish need seemed to radiate from him like a magnetic force. He came nearer again, this time with greater determination. Clarice backed away, turned, and opened the door. "Come inside. We can talk more calmly in the garden."

She'd had a little fountain built there, and she tended personally to the roses that covered the old stone wall. In just a few months, the weed-choked courtyard had filled with floral perfumes. The space was divided up into little colored flower beds, and there was a central path covered in fine gravel that led to a giant elm tree. Under the branches, Clarice had placed chairs. She hastened to light the lanterns and then turned to him.

"It's beautiful. Is this where you spend your free time?"

She nodded. "This is where I read." Clarice sat down. The silence was a blanket, similar to the one she used to place her precious sheets of paper on.

"I wrote these books because I wanted people to know that inner strength, humanity, and compassion are indispensable to change our society for the better. The social gap is cruel and alarming. There are masters and servants. Nothing in between. This is intolerable."

"I understand you."

Christian was sitting beside her. He was so close that Clarice could feel his warmth, the scent of leather and soap on his skin.

"But I have learned that there is no humanity, no redemption. Even those who guide society lie. There is no common good; each individual pursues his own. Mine are simply illusions."

Yet Clarice could see that his immense suffering didn't come from his analysis of society alone. It went far deeper. It belonged to the private sphere. To a blow dealt by someone who had been much loved.

Those were the wounds it was hardest to recover from. That was the pain that left the deepest scars. Evil disguised as good. Because it takes you by surprise, and no one has sufficient defenses against it.

"I thought everything was lost," he continued. "And then you, you who are so young, created something extraordinary. You gave shape to my ideas, transformed them into images, decorations. I've never seen anything like it." He paused, looking into her eyes. "Thank you from the depths of my heart."

Clarice stretched out her arm and touched his face. Not a caress, because there was no tenderness in the gesture, or seduction, either. Hers was a primitive need to make contact.

Christian pressed her hand to his face, then to his lips. "I'm a married man. I don't have much to offer you."

"I don't need anything." It was true: all she needed was his presence. Because love had already filled the gaps, becoming hope and then certainty. It had been the words she'd read on her journey that spun the first binding threads and later, when she'd met Christian, his eyes and his gestures had done the rest. There was no more doubt in her, just profound well-being and a joy so great it swept away all the rest.

And in her words, Christian Philipp Fohr found the love he had been looking for all his life. Love free from the economic and dynastic calculations that had dominated his marriage. It was simple to take her in his arms, feel her breathing, find himself again in that girl who had understood him before they'd even met.

Was that love? He would soon find out, he decided. He would find out in the arms of this bookbinder, who had made her way into the depths of his heart.

Autumn followed summer. Clarice spent her days waiting impatiently for the few moments she could spend with Christian. They were very discreet, not wanting what they shared to be soiled by gossip. They knew that society would not condemn them if they kept within decent limits, but theirs was a bond that no one else was invited to know about.

Clarice's life hadn't changed outwardly and neither had Christian's. Apart from Lauren and Margareta, no one in Clarice's circle knew about them. The baroness continued to speak of her journey to Egypt, but never quite made up her mind to leave. In the meantime, Janice had remarried and was expecting her first child at the end of the spring. The baroness watched over her acquired cousin, the only remaining family she had, as fiercely as a tiger, so much so that poor Paolino Visconti, Janice's new husband, feared the days she came to visit. Then, with the delivery imminent, the timid count insisted his wife should move up to his country estate in Tuscany, where the climate was healthier. To the man's dismay, the baroness followed them a few days later, bringing her ladies, a doctor, and a midwife with her. Little Edward's birth was a joy to everyone and brought a note of cheerfulness into their lives.

A year had gone by now since Clarice and Christian had become lovers. There were moments when the intensity of their emotions frightened them. They would stay in one another's arms, watching the sky and asking questions about the present, while carefully avoiding the future they knew didn't belong to them. They couldn't get enough of one another. Sometimes they went beyond all limits, riding through the countryside, challenging each other in daring races over rough hills or along placid streams. And there were special moments when their souls were calm. They would write together, imagining what their existence would have been like if fate had not connected them.

Christian had a desk specially made so that it would seat both of them. He'd spend hours leaning over it, leaving a trail of loose leaves that Clarice would gradually bind into blocks. He named the new book *The Age of Joy*. He had dedicated it to his love for Clarice, and friends who knew about it were enthusiastic about the first few pages he'd shown them. Christian couldn't wait to reveal the whole truth about the work, and was determined to do so as soon as the situation allowed.

But the past could not simply be overwritten by love. One night, amid sobs and tears, Clarice awoke, defending herself from a nightmare—and Christian found out about August. He cradled her for a long time and then made love to her, as though desiring to cancel out the brutality with gentleness, the violence with tenderness. But his own anger couldn't be erased, either. "Men who make use of their greater physical strength to inflict suffering," he told her, "are the scum of society."

From then onward, he had become more distant and took to riding out alone.

Clarice knew that the idea of August still having legal power over her drove him mad. But August was a long way away. No one knew she had taken refuge in Rome, and even if he had found out, the city was immense. He would never find her.

In July, Christian had gone to Munich to attend to some urgent matters. Clarice watched him go, repeating to herself that she had had far more than she'd ever dreamed of. Still, she was choked with suppressed tears at the thought of him seeing his wife again, even though the woman was little more than stranger to him now.

The last few days they had spent together had been unforgettable. Clarice didn't bear the man's name, but she knew his heart. As for the rest, for a long time now, she had been used to living day by day, investing complete passion in everything she did.

One morning while she was in the garden, drawing some sketches for the cover of a family Bible, Matilde called her. "They're asking for you, my lady."

Usually it was Lauren who looked after the customers, but her friend was away, visiting Janice. For a moment, Clarice thought of telling the child to say she couldn't receive anyone; then she sighed, laid down her pen, and patted her hair into shape.

"Did he say his name?"

"No, just that he wanted to speak to you. He's a foreigner."

"Show him into the little room. I'll be there in a second."

Who could it be? She wasn't expecting anyone. Plus, she was tired. She should have shut up shop, as Margareta had asked her to, and taken the opportunity to join them all at the Visconti estate. It was incredible how fond you could grow of a baby in such a short time. A few days of rest were what she needed. She would leave the next day, she decided, just in time to make the last deliveries and give the workers some time off. Matilde would be delighted about the trip.

As she approached the room where she talked to customers, she glanced around and gave a pleased smile. Everything in the shop was going splendidly. Soon, she would write to Frederik to return the money he had given her and tell him all about it. She took off her apron and hung it on a hook with the others, smoothed the folds of her skirt, and entered.

"Good morning, you were asking for me?"

The man, who had his back to her, was tall and imposing. He had a large hand on the windowsill, his gaze directed out of the window.

Clarice's smile fell. She couldn't breathe. When he turned around and looked at her, she thought she was going to die.

"Did you really think I wouldn't find you?"

She forced herself to keep still, although instinct told her to run. When August approached, she sustained his gaze.

"What do you want?" She forced the words out, one by one. She was dazed. Had August managed to force Frederik to give up her hiding place? She pushed the thought away. She didn't want to consider the possibility. She couldn't. Or she would start to scream.

He smiled at her. "It's self-evident, isn't it? I've come to take you back home."

She mustered every ounce of strength in her body. "You've come a long way in vain. I shall not go with you."

He looked around. "Seems you've got yourself well set up. I'm impressed. I thought I'd find you in poor conditions, but instead you're running a business. Surprising."

"Because I'm a woman?"

He shrugged. "Of course."

She'd had enough. "We have no more to say to one another. Go back to Vienna. You have everything you want now, don't you?"

"If you're referring to money, now that Kurt and his wife are dead, I have a lot more." He paused and went on smiling, pleased with the effect of his words on the woman. She was his; she'd just forgotten it. But now he had all the time in the world to remind her, and the sooner he reestablished his dominance, the sooner everything would be settled. "But you see, Clarice, it's not enough. Why should I content myself, when I can have everything I desire?"

Clarice knew that expression. She backed away quickly and opened the door. She had to escape, had to get help. What a fool she'd been to think she could face him. She'd only taken a few steps down the corridor, when she felt herself being grabbed from behind. August's hand pressed over her mouth, stopping her from screaming. When he pulled her back into the little room, she knew what he was going to do before he whispered it in her ear. She struggled, bit his hand, and went on defending herself until she tasted blood. Finally, he let go. He laughed out loud, but his eyes were cold.

"Aren't you curious to know how I found you?"

She panted, her back against the wall, her breath like fire in her throat. She didn't want to listen to him; she didn't want to know any more. He had just flung the deaths of her aunt and uncle in her face, and pain burned a black hole in her breast.

"Go away, August. Get away from here and never come back."

"I'm going to tell you anyway, Clarice. It'll be a lesson to you because, believe me, my love, it's all your fault that I had to do those things to a poor old man." He sighed, straightening his tailcoat, his eyes not leaving hers for an instant. He smiled again, satisfied. "It was chance that led me to the bookbinding workshop. Or fate. I think there is a sense of justice in everything. Toward the end, Vogel was accusing me of not being able to control you. I liked listening to him: his suffering put me in a good mood." Another pause, another smile. "It was while he was raving like that, that he referred to an episode in the past. 'I have never understood your wife,' he said. 'When I stopped her from becoming a bookbinder as she wished, I offered her teachers, an education.'" August laughed softly. "It took me some time to put all the pieces together. It was odd how the servant at the front door didn't see you go out when you escaped. And, in the end, I found the passage behind the barrels. The rest was easy."

She didn't reply, her eyes glazed over with pain.

August studied her for a long time. "But it wasn't Schmidt who betrayed you. He held out; he told me nothing." He shrugged. "It was a worker of his—I forget his name. He was afraid I had the same fate in store for him. He wouldn't have lasted so long." He chuckled, and when Clarice fell to her knees, weeping and hugging her belly, he went to her side. He pulled her up into his arms and brushed her lips. "Think, next time you decide to run away. I have no intention of losing you, and I will never lift a finger against you again. You see? I've changed." He kissed her again. "You will come back to Vienna with me, and you will be my wife again. Perhaps we'll take the girl who let me in with us. That will help you keep calm and make you behave."

When the three of them left, it was together. Clarice took no more than a few clothes, piled into a bag, together with Christian's books. She'd sent all her helpers home, and they hadn't asked too many questions. The bottega was empty. August made the child climb up next to the coachman, and though Clarice tried to make her stay, little Matilde ignored her.

"I'll never leave you," Matilde swore.

Clarice was confident that she would have an opportunity to escape on the journey to Vienna. But instead, August took her into the Roman countryside to a villa he'd rented. "We shall stay here for a while."

August had hurried from Vienna to Rome, stopping only to change horses at the posthouses, and in the company of a single servant. However, he could not make the return journey the same way. He needed time to arrange a carriage and a driver.

Clarice thought she knew all about hell, but the place she was shut in with August was a bottomless pit with no escape. If she didn't throw herself into the murky waters of the Tiber, which flowed alongside the villa where they were staying, it was only because she feared for Matilde.

She must be patient and find a way for them to escape.

As for August, she didn't exchange a single word with him. All he would have of her was her silence.

Her voice belonged to Christian, and her heart, her light, her love.

Over the following days, her husband became more and more irascible. Hard as Clarice tried to avoid him, he would find a way to catch her off guard. When she realized that he liked terrorizing her, she stopped trembling. At night, she forced herself to go limp in his arms.

Every time he touched her, she fled to a place inside where he couldn't reach her.

Convinced that he had her in an iron grip, August relaxed his surveillance.

Clarice took advantage of this to study her surroundings. And when he wouldn't let her out, Matilde took on the task. With the child's help, she studied the roads and paths, realizing it was impossible to escape overland. The river was their only chance. They had to find a boat, to reach the port. From there, it wouldn't be too hard to disappear onto one of the departing ships. The idea of starting over again didn't frighten her; so long as she had the use of her hands, she could earn enough for herself and the child to live on.

Finally, Matilde succeeded in her task. "The appointment with the boatman is for tomorrow evening," she told Clarice. "He'll wait for us until sunset, then he'll continue toward Rome."

Everything was ready. They would take advantage of August's afternoon ride. Sitting in the shade of a ruined wall that, centuries before, had been a temple to a god of the woods, Clarice stared at a distant point. She had accounted for all the details, but worry stopped her from thinking clearly. There were thousands of things that might go wrong. She was so frightened that she had to clench her fists to stop her hands from shaking. She didn't fear for herself but for the child. She had persuaded Matilde to hide her things in the garden, including Christian's books.

Now Clarice told Matilde to go to the river. The child protested, but Clarice was firm.

"You have to go ahead, because if something happens to me, you are my only chance of being rescued. You must return to Rome and wait in hiding in Margareta's palace. When the baroness returns in a few weeks, you must tell her everything. Swear that you will go to her."

She took the girl's face in her hands, letting her feel her concern so that Matilde would understand the importance of her task. The little girl nodded, and Clarice began to hope that she, at least, would manage to save herself. She kissed her, and the child set off.

She herself still felt trapped, a prisoner of that evil man. He had tormented her all morning with stories of what he would do once they were back in Vienna. He had joked about all the children they would have, and how he intended to restore the von Harmel castle so that they could move there during the summer.

"What are you doing out here?"

She jumped. She'd thought her husband was already out on his ride. As August strode up to her with a smile stamped on his face, desperation rose up inside her.

"The driver I hired to take us back is free at last. We depart tomorrow."

She nodded and lowered her head, afraid of giving herself away.

August took hold of her chin and lifted it. Then he narrowed his eyes to study her. "What's going on inside that lovely little head, my darling?"

"Nothing." She said it softly, trying to appear calm. When he kissed her, she didn't draw back, praying to God to give her just a little more strength.

He walked off whistling. Not until he was far away did Clarice start breathing again. If the boatman didn't take them that day, there wouldn't be another chance. Fortunately, August was wearing his riding clothes. He hadn't changed his mind, so perhaps he was just leaving later than usual. She prayed intensely that he wouldn't give up his ride.

She waited a little while, her eyes on the villa, her heart pounding in her chest. She walked slowly along the bank of the river and then, once beyond the boundary of the estate, she started to run, lifting her skirt, with hope lending her wings. Finally, she saw the cove appear. At that moment, she heard the thunder of galloping hooves.

August had found her out. No, she couldn't stop, not now. She launched herself toward the trees. The grass whipped her legs, tripping her. A branch hit her face, drawing a scream; she lost her balance and rolled over onto the ground, grazing her hands. But she pulled herself to her feet and started to run again.

The horse was nearer now, sending clods of mud flying.

"Stop, for heaven's sake. Stop, Clarice!"

An arm grasped her waist, pulling her up into the saddle.

That voice!

She turned her head and met Christian's eyes. She flung her arms around his neck and clung tightly.

"Good God, Clarice. I was going mad. What's happened to you?" Christian reined in the horse, bringing it to a halt. He took her face in his hands and kissed it, panting and desperate.

"Christian, you must go; he'll kill you. You don't know what he's capable of."

"You mustn't worry about that. These are matters between me and your husband."

"No, no. You don't know, you don't know him."

Christian ignored her protests. He dismounted and pulled her down. He held her face, pushing her hair back from her neck. Bruises stood out like the beads of a necklace on her pale skin, descending toward her breasts beneath the lace of her dress. He caressed her face.

"It's over now. Get on my horse," he ordered. "Go to my house. And stay there. I'll deal with him."

He had never spoken to her like that.

Then everything happened at once. Clarice felt his presence even before she saw him. She turned around. August was bearing down on them at a mad gallop.

"Who the devil are you? Let go of my wife immediately."

Christian grabbed Clarice and pushed her behind him, sheltering her with his body. "Go, Clarice, go, take the horse and go. Now!"

August charged at him, but Christian dodged. They went on like that for a while, sizing one another up, feinting and striking at the air.

"So my wife has found a knight in shining armor! I'll kill you, you bastard, right in front of her. And then I'll teach her how an honest woman should behave."

Christian knew about men like August. He'd almost gone crazy when he returned from Munich and found Clarice gone. It was the elderly owner of the workshop who put him on the right track. "That man was a devil, and the lady was so frightened she didn't even dare turn around. Believe me, sir, the devil himself came to take her away."

Christian knew there was only one man who had the power to terrorize Clarice. After that, it was simple enough to find out which houses had recently been let to foreigners.

"I'll kill you, you bastard."

He didn't reply, continuing to dodge the blows, fully focused. When August drew out a knife, wounding his shoulder, Christian shifted his position. They struck at one another, charging, running, and dragging each other through the tall grass, then falling into some rushes. Clarice watched them, powerless.

In the confusion of the fight, the two men had edged toward the river. When August threw himself forward, Christian grabbed his shirt and dragged him down with him. They struck violently at one another, rolling around on the ground. All of a sudden, the bank gave way, and they both slid into the water. Horrified, Clarice watched them struggle in the mud. It was over in a matter of seconds: the current sucked them under into a whirlpool.

CHAPTER
TWENTY-ONE

Yet with how many things are we upon the brink of becoming acquainted, if cowardice or carelessness did not restrain our inquiries.

—Mary Shelley, *Frankenstein*

It was a calculated risk. Some you won, some you lost. Tomaso had taken this into account right from the start. Yet the awareness did nothing to lessen the sense of desolation he felt. The defeat felt like impotence, the end of hope.

Every now and again, he glanced at Sofia. She seemed serene, a relaxed expression on her face, and she was breathing easily. If it hadn't been for the way she stared obstinately at the clouds outside the window of the plane taking them to Rome, he would have thought she hadn't taken it too much to heart.

He sighed and ran his hands through his hair.

Fohr's book had delivered Clarice's third and last letter to them. But the last page was damaged, right at the end, where she seemed about to reveal the location of the secret work. The paper and ink had been ruined by dampness, which also made a good deal of the book itself indecipherable. Sofia had put the letter back in its place, and they'd returned it to the institute, leaving in silence.

Clarice's story had been rudely interrupted. Now their adventure was over.

"I'm sorry." The words were banal, but he had no others.

"I know. So am I. But I'm glad to know that they were happy together, even though Christian died so young." She smiled at him, and Tomaso thought that, despite everything, it had been worthwhile.

What would happen with Sofia from then on was impossible to predict, but Tomaso felt there was something unique and undefinable in her, something that bound him to her. The sum of many little things, which, taken all together, destabilized him, forcing him to put himself to the test, to let go of his certainties and dare to go further. And what was he to her? That question, he realized, terrified him.

"I feel as though I've lost a friend. Someone I was fond of. That must seem ridiculous to you."

He took her hand and kissed her fingers. "Why on earth? Your sensitivity is a gift, not a defect."

They dozed for the rest of the flight, now and again touching hands. The silence was once again a place where they could be together. Not a confine, but somewhere their thoughts joined. Sadness cast a shadow on both of their faces.

They took a taxi from the airport. Sofia still didn't feel like talking. As they drove off, Tomaso glanced at the messages on his phone. Frank was back in the hospital, desperately ill. His mother had already lost one husband—why must she suffer through it again? Powerlessness gripped his chest, crushing him. *I'm on my way.* He typed the message rapidly. He would just take the time to drop off Sofia at her home and then go on to the hospital. He considered telling her about it, but then had second thoughts.

Suddenly, anger gripped him. He covered his eyes; it was absurd to blame Frank for being sick. Tomaso's mouth was dry. He felt as though he were balanced on top of a mountain with landslides in every direction. First, Fohr's unpublished book—gone forever. Now, his stepfather in intensive care. The agency on the brink of bankruptcy.

What next?

The city was ablaze with lights and familiar noises, in which they both found comfort. As they crossed the avenues, he looked at the bare trees silently spreading their branches across the black sky. In spring, they'd be covered with leaves, and life would start its course again, but at that moment, it was hard to believe.

They were almost at Coppedè when Sofia turned to him. "I'm not giving up, Tomaso. We know a lot, and we can continue the search."

He sighed. "We'll talk about it tomorrow." At that moment, his thoughts were on a man who was leaving this world and toward whom he continued to feel resentment. He didn't like what that said about himself. He would have preferred to feel other emotions; he would have liked to love Frank—the man who had taken his father's place. But all he could think about was his own grievance and his mother's devastation. Of course he would go on looking for the lost book. He didn't have any intention of giving up, either. But this wasn't the moment.

"There's someone who can help us. In fact, he already has," Sofia went on.

Tomaso gave her a confused look. "Whom are you referring to?"

If she had caught his tone of voice, Sofia would have realized that he'd reached his limit. But her desperate need to pursue the promise she'd made to Clarice and to herself made her insist.

"Tomorrow morning I'll go and see the bookseller. Andrea Vinci knows a lot, perhaps he can help us."

"What the devil are you talking about?"

Sofia fell silent, startled by his harsh tone. "The man who gave me the book, remember? I told him everything. He's been very important to our search."

"You—what?" Tomaso was bowled over. "You shared information on our research with a perfect stranger, despite our agreement on privacy?"

"He isn't a stranger," she protested. "He *gave* me the book, and without that we'd have nothing. It was my duty to inform him. And anyway, it has nothing to do with you," she added. "If there were money to be made and Vinci wanted something, I'd share my part with him."

He stared at her in disbelief. Discretion was the only thing he'd asked of her, and she ignored it. Yet as he looked at her, his anger diminished, leaving him defenseless. He felt an urge to hug her and apologize for having raised his voice. It was because of that hurt look she had, he thought, her delicate and vulnerable appearance.

But now something in Sofia's expression changed. Her eyes were stern with indignation. She hadn't kept her word, and now she was offended because he was upset with her for it? Tomaso lost control.

"Is this just a game to you? Don't you have any idea what you've done?"

That wasn't how he'd intended on responding. That wasn't the way to try and understand one another.

Sofia's eyes narrowed. "I told you, I'll deal with the bookseller."

"Stop talking nonsense!" He rubbed a hand over his eyes, then looked at her again. "There's nothing to be shared, understand? Nothing, Sofia: no money, no book, no story," he hissed. "But that doesn't change anything. You can't be trusted."

And once he said that, it was too late for anything else.

Sofia recoiled as though he'd hit her.

It took so little to break things, thought Tomaso, and then he raised his eyes to look at her. Who was this woman? Had he been mistaken? Had he just seen what he wanted to in her? Had he been stupid—a romantic fool? Nausea filled him. "Stop," he ordered the taxi driver. "Pull over right here."

He got out of the car, pulled out his bag, and went around to the driver's window. "Take her to Coppedè." He handed the driver a bunch of bills. "Go."

He didn't so much as look in Sofia's direction. He called for another taxi and waited in the dark, his hands plunged into his pockets, his morale shattered.

The intensive care ward was a highly functional place but cold and aseptic. After taking the stairs two at a time, Tomaso desperately scanned the crowd in the waiting room. He spotted Luisanna in a corner with Carla. They were embracing, supporting one another. He realized it was too late.

Frank Hobart was dead.

He reached them in a few strides, a lump in his throat. "I'm sorry, Mother." He wrapped her in his embrace. "I'm here now. Everything will be all right."

She wiped her eyes with the back of her hand, and suddenly Tomaso saw her as she really was, an aging woman who had once again lost her life companion. She was alone because she would no longer have the only presence she really desired.

"It doesn't matter anymore." Luisanna's whisper was lost in the buzz of the waiting room, amid faces exhausted by waiting, shoulders heaving in sorrow at their own losses. Tomaso supported his mother, gripped Carla's hand, and they left that place of suffering and last hopes together.

It was true. As he drove his mother back to the villa, Tomaso thought about what his mother had said. Nothing mattered. Everything ended in death. Everything.

Over the next few weeks, he had to deal with a series of complex formalities. He managed everything, splitting his time between his mother and the lawyers. The funeral was challenging for Luisanna, yet she withstood everything courageously, her eyes dry behind her dark glasses, with a strength that amazed him. As for him, he didn't allow himself, even once, to indulge in thoughts that weren't strictly necessary; he ate because he had to, he worked until he was dead on his feet, he listened and made the decisions that his mother couldn't. The only thing that kept him on his feet, the only thing that mattered, was duty.

When he attended the reading of the will, even the little hope he had been harboring subconsciously vanished.

Good old Frank, he thought. *Consistent right up to the last minute.* There was nothing left.

He would have to sell his own home to save the agency. He didn't even want to curse his stepfather anymore. All he felt toward him was pity.

"I need to get back home for a while. You can reach me on my cell." He kissed his mother and made for the front door.

"I'm sorry, my dear."

He turned around with a confused expression. Luisanna smiled at him. "Go home and rest, darling. Thank you. You've been the only thing that's kept me going. I love you."

"Love you too, Mother." He left quickly. He hated the idea of bursting into tears like a little boy. But he felt very close to it.

A few hours later, as he was wandering around his grandmother's place, he thought about what he would keep. The old photographs, of course. He would have to rummage through the attic to find them. He would sell the furniture, hoping to get a good price, everything except the writing desk. It was part of the Leoni family; the rest could be replaced, but he wouldn't let that piece go.

He looked around, heavyhearted. He would miss this place—it was his home—but there was nothing else he could do. With the money from the sale, he would pay for the agreement with the Baldini heirs, cover the agency's outstanding debts, and help his mother. Hopefully, there'd be enough left over to allow him to get by for a while.

In the kitchen, he poured himself something to drink, his eyes on the stove. He should eat, he thought. He couldn't remember the last time he'd had a proper meal. Instead, he went to lie down on the bed, his arm covering his face.

As the tension ebbed away, the events of the last few days came flooding back into his mind. One image stood out—the shock and anger on Sofia's face.

He rubbed his chin. He'd been hard on her. But when she'd said she would share her part with the bookseller, it had infuriated him—the implication that Tomaso's sole concern was the money.

Tidy up. That was the first thing Sofia did after she got back from Vienna. She started in Max's conservatory, after she called to make sure he and her grandmother were well on their trip to France. Then around the apartment, although everything was already in perfect order. It was as though she wanted to regain control over everything she knew belonged to her—her family, her living space—because all the rest was out of her hands. It had escaped her, including her relationship with Tomaso.

She'd polished the mirrors, dusted, washed the veranda, and finally called her mother and father. She hadn't heard from them in far too long, and though that wasn't unusual, she realized she desperately needed them.

"Ciao, darling, is everything all right?"

"Yes, fine, Mother, and you?" They chatted for a while, and when Adèle asked once again how she was, she lied again. "I'm working on something very important. I'll tell you all about it another time." She felt the need to be close to her as never before, yet she knew that both her parents would disapprove of the entire business with the book, the letters, the search. They were paladins of logic and pragmatism.

She, on the other hand, was not and never had been. This created a gap between them that nothing, not even time, had been able to bridge. They loved one another, but when their differences arose, it could spark flames. That was why Sofia avoided conflict at all costs.

She realized then that her existence had always been a constant series of compromises. With her parents, with her grandparents, with Alberto. Only with one person had she felt truly free; only with Tomaso had she managed to be completely herself.

Family was something you carried inside you. It was the first test you had to pass, the first judge, the ballast for everything you were. And paradoxically, family was also what encouraged you to run away in search of autonomy.

The only person who had really stood alongside her, not as a friend but as a true companion, sharing her objectives, understanding her without ever judging her, had been Tomaso. She felt her stomach tighten. She missed him dreadfully. How had he managed to make his way to her, to such profound depths? They had only spent a few days together. There hadn't been enough time to fall in love, but was time really the right way to measure?

Love was something that came from inside. And the lack of it had set off a turmoil inside her. Tomaso, she realized, had created an absence she would never get used to. And then, once again, she thought back over the last angry words they exchanged.

Why had he behaved like that? What had made him so furious? It couldn't really have been because of the bookseller.

If only he had given her time to explain. Nothing about Andrea could endanger their mutual enterprise. In fact, he was one of their keenest supporters. Hadn't he sent her to Tomaso?

But she hadn't had time to explain.

Frowning, she went over their fight yet again. How long had it been, a month? No, three weeks. They hadn't been in touch for three weeks. But she didn't want to think about it, not then. There was something else to consider: the divorce documents were ready. She had her own problems to deal with; she didn't need any more. Her husband had been a good objective lesson in a way. You could do everything in your power and more, but nothing could persuade someone who didn't really love you to do so.

She dried her eyes, breathing slowly.

She had given Tomaso all the time he might need, but he hadn't been in touch. And she was hardly going to reach out to him. She remembered the look he had given her the moment before ordering the taxi driver to go. She had no desire to see that again.

"Go to hell, Tomaso!"

She glanced at the clock. Time to hurry up and get to work. She'd accepted Andrea's offer to look after the bookshop. He would have liked to sell the business to her, but Sofia knew that no bank would give her a loan at the moment.

Still, looking after the bookshop made her happy. It allowed her to dream, imagining that one day she would do something that was all hers, just like Clarice, who had fought for her freedom in a time when such a thing was scarcely possible. How close she felt to her, that modern woman who had lived centuries earlier. In the end, it'd been Clarice who forced her out of a marriage that was destroying her. "Clarice Marianne von Harmel, wherever you are, thank you from the bottom of my heart," she whispered to herself.

Andrea hadn't been in the shop for several days, and Sofia was growing concerned. Recently, he had aged dramatically. He no longer possessed that spark of vivaciousness that had marked their first few meetings.

When she'd told him about Clarice, and how their search had been interrupted, he had been very disappointed.

"But there must be another way forward." He'd said it with moist eyes and a desperate expression on his face.

Sofia, who had gone to him in search of consolation, had found herself having to provide it. "If there is a way, I shall find it."

And indeed, she spent hours looking through margin notes and reading everything about Fohr she could lay her hands on. She'd gone back to the Bibliotheca Hertziana several times. But so far, her research had led to nothing.

She went downstairs and greeted Felipe. Turning the corner outside, she came out onto the road leading to the bookshop. She was halfway there when she glimpsed a figure sitting on the bench next to the door. She recognized the bookseller, and her steps hastened. "Good morning." She waved to him. "Why are you sitting out here?"

Andrea replied with a tired smile. "Ciao, Sofia. I forgot my keys. It's age. I was just resting before going home to get them." The bookseller looked up at her. "Are you all right?"

She didn't reply immediately. She took advantage of the time it took to open up the shop, hoping to blink back the tears that were unexpectedly welling up again. When she turned to him, she was smiling.

Once they were inside, Andrea sighed and took off his hat, leaning heavily on the counter. "I have a feeling your sadness isn't just about Clarice."

She didn't reply.

"I see," replied the old man after a while. His eyes wandered over the floor, following the design of the tiles. Then he stood up straight again, closed his eyes, and recited a long poem.

"That's beautiful. What is it?" asked Sofia.

"A poem called 'After a While.' I find those lines illuminating in their simplicity. They're a guide for how to live courageously."

"Do you think I don't? Do you think that I'm a coward?" Sofia felt the pressure of the tears coming again—someone else's judgment and then the one that weighed most heavily: her own.

The bookseller's eyes widened in amazement. "Was that the impression I gave you? If it was, I apologize immensely; my intentions were quite different. I just wished to share with you something that did me a lot of good at one time."

She hadn't thought of that. She was so intent on her problems that she had mistaken a caress for a blow. She was ashamed. She fell silent, twisting her hands.

"My dear, the people who get hurt are those who surround themselves with the highest walls and stop themselves from enjoying life."

"But what if I chose the wrong person again?" There, she'd said it. After Alberto, how could she trust her own judgment?

Andrea shrugged, grimacing. "Love belongs to those who dare." He paused. "They deserve it, don't you agree?"

Sofia remained silent, emotion welling in her throat.

"Look at me, my dear. I'm alone. But it wasn't always like that. I know well what it means to love, and even better what it's like to give up." He smiled at her, but there was deep sorrow in his eyes. "I know every aspect of regret, even the color. Regret is gray. It doesn't have the strength of black or the grace of white. It has no shades. Regret is one single, infinite stretch of sadness. It's barren. It doesn't even have the ability to prepare the soul for something greater."

His words made a breach in Sofia's most deeply hidden fears. "Not everything is the same for everyone."

"No, that's true. But some things are identical all over the world. They're part of something called humanity—joy and pain, hope, regret. Love."

She looked at her hands: they were empty, nothing there. "Perhaps it'd do me good to reflect a bit. Do you feel well enough to watch the shop today?"

"Go, my dear, I'm sure that there are far more important things out there than keeping an old man like me company."

She embraced Andrea, then let him return her hug with a pat on the back. There were times when the simplest of gestures managed to give the most strength.

Sofia easily found the eighteenth-century building again. She rang the buzzer and waited. Her hands were shaking, so she put them in her pockets, silencing her protesting mind and refusing to listen to the hammering of her heart. She wanted an explanation. She wanted to know what had driven him to behave so horribly. She wouldn't pretend that Tomaso had meant nothing to her, but she wouldn't give him anything more.

The door opening surprised her. He hadn't asked who was there, simply opened up. Tomaso stood, one arm against the frame, his hair falling over his face. He was wearing a T-shirt and a pair of jeans. He didn't look surprised, not one bit. But that wasn't what struck her. It was the pallor of his thin face. What had happened to him, for heaven's sake?

"I'm not here to apologize." That wasn't what she had intended to say. Or rather, it was exactly what she'd intended to say, and she'd repeated it a thousand times in the car on the way here. But that had been before she saw him like this. If he'd shut the door in her face, she would have deserved it.

Instead, his face lit up with a beautiful smile. "I've missed you." He stood aside so that she could enter. When she passed, he grabbed her jacket and pulled her toward him, gripping her in an embrace that was a cry of pain.

Sofia returned it with the same urgency, recognizing his suffering as her own.

None of the words she'd thought she must say were said; the reasoning she'd carefully constructed was not displayed. What spoke for them, apologizing, loving one another, were their bodies, which knew all there was to know about one another and desired no help from words.

Hours later, as they lay together, Sofia kissed him again. "I'm sorry about your stepfather." In the light of the new facts Tomaso had told her, she understood his reaction. If only she had known earlier . . .

"Me too. You know, I didn't think I'd ever say such a thing, but honestly I'm very sorry he's gone. He could never be my father, but maybe he could have been a friend. Anyway, my mother loved him very much. It's the second time she's lost her companion. I don't know where she finds the courage."

"You know, I don't think anyone really knows what they're capable of. We find out over time, when we're tested."

"Was it like that for you too?"

"For me, for Clarice. And for you. You found the strength to love a man who didn't really deserve it." She realized she had overstepped and waited for him to stiffen and tell her off, but instead Tomaso remained relaxed beside her. He seemed to be reflecting on what she'd said. And she realized then with crystal-clear certainty that they might argue forever, but they'd always want each other. She felt as though she had freed herself of a weight that had stopped her from flying, just like in the bookseller's poem.

"I've lost everything, you know? I have nothing anymore." Tomaso's voice was light but pained.

She laughed at him. "That's the most ridiculous thing I've ever heard." She sat up cross-legged. "Everything you are is here." She touched his chest. "And here!" she concluded, touching his forehead. "You don't need anything else."

"Have you ever thought of becoming a motivational speaker? You're extremely good at it." Yet, despite his lighthearted tone, they were both moved, amazed at how much better they felt. It hadn't taken much to pick up where they'd left off.

Love had been sufficient.

"I'm starving!"

Tomaso smiled and stretched. "Would a quick *pastasciutta* do?"

"Sounds perfect."

As he headed to the kitchen, Sofia went to the writing desk. "I hope you're planning to keep this."

Tomaso looked around the door to see. "Yes. That, yes, and a couple of other things. I'm selling the rest."

Although he was trying to downplay everything, Sofia could sense the suffering behind his words. It wasn't easy for him to sacrifice so much.

She put out her hand to touch the old wood, the surface, the little drawers. She adored that piece of furniture. It exuded an almost-magical air of serenity. Clarice and Christian had had their own desk too, sharing it just like she and Tomaso had. Warmth filled her as she recalled that evening when he taught her to write her name in italics.

She decided she wanted to try again. This time, however, she would do it alone. She needed a piece of paper, the pen, and ink. She was carefully moving some old photographs out of the way, when she froze and cocked her head to one side. Then she picked up a photograph, staring at it for a long time. She opened her mouth, then closed it again.

"Whom do these photos belong to?"

Tomaso came to the doorway again. "They belonged to my grandmother. I'm starting to sort through and decide what I want to take with me after I sell everything. Let's see."

He came up to her and pointed to a slim, elegantly dressed girl with a determined look on her face. Next to her stood two young men. "There, that's her."

That couldn't be. Sofia moistened her lips. "Tomaso, the man with his arm around her shoulder is named Maximilian Bauer."

He frowned. "You know him?"

She nodded. "He's my grandfather."

The silence grew as they both tried to make sense of the discovery. "Our grandparents knew one another?" He turned the photograph over and read the inscription: *Max Bauer, Ludovica Devoto, Andrea Vinci. Rome, 1953.*

"My grandfather, your grandmother, and Andrea Vinci." Sofia took a deep breath. "The bookseller. The man who gave me Clarice's book."

CHAPTER
TWENTY-TWO

"Tell me everything right from the beginning, please." Tomaso poured her a drink, then filled his own glass.

Sofia picked distractedly at her food. "I've told you before. The bookshop had been closed for a long time, but on that particular day, it was open again. I just thought I'd browse a little. Then I started chatting with the bookseller. He showed me Fohr's book and said it needed to be restored before he could sell it. I loved the writer, so I made him an offer."

"Didn't he give it to you as a gift?"

She nodded. "Yes. First, he tried to persuade me that it wasn't a good buy, and he couldn't possibly sell it to me in the state it was in."

Tomaso observed her over the top of his glass. He swallowed the wine and poured himself more. He needed something stronger, he thought, but then he also needed to be as lucid as possible.

"Sofia, if Andrea Vinci gave you that book, it cannot have been a coincidence."

They went over everything they knew. Sofia couldn't believe it, but what Tomaso said was right. He analyzed everything calmly. He never got carried away by anger or returned to the argument they'd had coming back from Vienna. He examined everything with a healthy detachment and great care. And in the end, a precise picture emerged, incredible though it might seem: Andrea was behind almost everything that had happened in their search for Fohr's books.

The man had played the part of an invisible puppeteer.

"I insisted on paying for the book, but he wouldn't agree. That I remember very well." Sofia mused. "Then, all of a sudden, he gave it to me. It seemed strange, but I didn't pay it that much attention."

"Was it before or after you told him your name?"

She thought about it, then her eyes widened. "It was after! You're right." She had talked about her grandfather and the fact that he lived in Coppedè. If the two men knew one another, as the photo showed, then he would have known who she was. "All of a sudden, he didn't want me to pay for it, and then he asked me to come back and see him. To show him the book, once I'd restored it." She remained silent for a moment. "And he was the one who sent me to you."

"What do you mean?"

She raised her head. "When I told him all about Clarice's letter, and that I needed a specialist, he advised me to contact you. He said you were the best."

The hair on the back of Tomaso's neck stood up. "But how on earth does he know me? I don't know him—"

They stared together at the photograph of their grandparents and the bookseller. The link between them all was undeniable. Andrea had met Sofia by chance, it was true, but only upon realizing she was the granddaughter of Maximilian Bauer had he given her the book. And then he'd insisted she should come back and see him, fortifying his connection to her. The strange thing was that neither then, nor later, had he mentioned the fact that he knew her grandfather.

"Why? I mean why did he need to manipulate me? Maybe he already knew something about Clarice?"

"Perhaps not. The book is interesting in itself. Don't forget the handwritten notes. He might already have suspected they were in the author's handwriting." Tomaso paused. "And my grandmother was a graphoanalyst too!"

"A bookseller, a graphoanalyst, and an academic—my grandfather was a professor of German literature. They would have been the same age, maybe studied at the same university. But why didn't Andrea tell me he knew Max?" She rubbed a hand over her face. "The only thing to do is to call Max and ask him to shed some light on the situation. Then I'll talk to Andrea." She shook her head. "There was no need to deceive me. If he'd asked me to help him in his research, I would have."

Tomaso sighed. "I know what you mean, but he couldn't have known about Clarice's letter. And he couldn't have expected that you would be so passionately interested in anything regarding Fohr. Let's say he made a bet when he entrusted the book to you, and he won."

Sofia nodded. "When we got back from Vienna and I told him the third letter was damaged, I was afraid he was on the brink of heart failure. He was deeply disappointed that we'd given up our research. He became less responsive, and then he suggested I help him with the bookshop. Today I saw him again; he hadn't been to the shop for some time." She cleared her throat. "While we're on the subject, I have something to tell you." Suddenly, she was troubled and nervous.

"Look, you can tell me whatever you want; at this point, nothing would surprise me."

"It's probably thanks to him that I'm here now."

Tomaso smiled. He didn't tell her that, with or without any help from the bookseller, they would have seen one another again in any case. "So I'm indebted to him." He kept his voice lighthearted, even though his heart was beating hard.

But Sofia didn't laugh. "I'm angry with the man, but I'm also very fond of him. I just want to know what made him manipulate us like that. I have to know the reason for it."

"It's three o'clock in the morning, Sofia. We'll think about it tomorrow." He held out his hand. For a long moment, they looked at one another, but Tomaso didn't give in. In the end, she did. He pulled her to him in an embrace. "You continue to surprise me." He kissed her slowly. "I wouldn't mind if it became a habit."

They went back to bed, hand in hand.

Maximilian Bauer was dumbfounded. "Wait, wait, Liebling. I can't keep up with you."

Dawn had hardly broken, but Sofia knew that her grandparents were early risers. She'd delayed calling as long as she could so as not to alarm them. "Grandpa, just give me a simple answer to my question. Do you know a man named Andrea Vinci?"

Silence, then a choking sound. "Yes, of course. He was an old university friend. But how do you know that name? He doesn't even live in Italy. He left decades ago and never came back." A sigh. "His father had a bookshop in Coppedè. I used to take you there when you were a child."

"Exactly."

"You mean he's back? Did you meet him at the shop? Of course, of course. It's plausible. But, Liebling, why do you need to talk to me about him so urgently?"

"He gave me a very special book."

Silence again, but this time, it was tense and heavy. Max knew something. "Grandpa, are you there?"

He coughed slightly. "What book?"

"An old edition of the first volume of Christian Philipp Fohr's work, the *Discourse on Nature*."

"Listen carefully, Liebling." Max's voice was urgent now. "Is the book in question bound in red morocco leather with notes in the margin?"

Her heart leapt and her head spun. "Yes, that's right."

"The bastard! If I get my hands on him, this time I'll kill him. Take the book back to him immediately Sofia. He stole it. Give it back to him. No, no, give it back yourself. Go to the Bibliotheca Hertziana and tell them that—no—that won't do, either." A long pause, but she could hear Max talking to someone else. Finally, he said, "I'll get on the first plane. Don't do a thing until I get there. I'll take care of that damned—I won't let him compromise you too!"

"Grandpa, wait, listen. Hidden inside the book, I found a letter."

"What?"

"It was written by a woman named Clarice. She was the one who bound that copy of Fohr's trilogy. In each volume, she hid a message."

"Why?"

"She wanted to hand down a secret so that it wouldn't get lost." Sofia chose her words carefully. "I'm convinced that Fohr left an unpublished work. Clarice loved him, and I think she desperately wanted the work to be found later, even though, at the time, it had to remain hidden. She wanted everyone to be able to read it, so the world would know too."

"But why, in heaven's name? Fohr was one of the most famous writers of the 1800s. Any editor at that time would have leapt for joy at the idea of publishing a new book by him."

"I don't know why. I just know that they loved one another deeply until his death, and that later, Clarice decided to write their story down in black and white. In the last volume—we managed to find all three, and each one contained a letter—there should have been instructions for finding the unpublished text, but the letter's damaged, and the crucial part is illegible."

Max took a deep breath. "Of course, we have to consider the period to understand the woman. If she had been left to safeguard the book after an illicit relationship with Fohr, that could explain the secrecy. Reputation in society was everything at that time." A sigh. "But we'll see about that later. Just give me time to get there, Liebling. Don't talk to anyone and wait for me to arrive. An unpublished work by Fohr—amazing!"

Sofia stood there with the phone in her hand for a moment, her eyes on Tomaso still in bed. "Did you hear all that?"

"Sounds like the time's come to show our cards and have a chat with the bookseller."

Yes, Max might have asked her to wait, but she had to act immediately. She'd had enough of secrecy.

"I wonder what part my grandmother played in all this," wondered Tomaso out loud.

"I think we're about to discover that."

After they had breakfast, Tomaso put off his appointments with two prospective house buyers until the afternoon. He wasn't going to leave Sofia alone with the old man. And Tomaso, too, wanted some explanations.

They found him at the counter, bent over a book, as usual. Andrea Vinci lifted his head and looked first at Sofia and then at Tomaso. His eyes lingered on him a moment longer, then he smiled, muttered something to himself, and gently shook his head.

"Good morning."

"My dear Sofia, I see you've brought me a friend."

"I think introductions are superfluous," Tomaso shot back, "seeing that you know me, and you knew my grandmother too."

"You've got her eyes, you know. So penetrating and expressive—one always knew what Ludovica was thinking." He laughed softly, leaning on his stick. "I was expecting you. Let's take a seat. The business of Clarice and Fohr is enchanting, but it's a very long story, and I can't stay on my feet for too long." He coughed and pointed to the corner with the armchairs. "Your grandmother detested me and didn't bother to hide it. I was everything she despised." He looked toward Sofia. "Max was her favorite." His smile vanished.

Sofia realized he was immersed in his memories, in a past that belonged neither to her, nor to Tomaso.

"But please, be seated." He sat down, his bony knees almost visible through the material of his trousers. "Where shall I start?" he muttered. Then his face lit up. "Before we start, I want to tell you something. I'm happy it's over. I don't think my heart would have held out much longer. Too much excitement—that's what our Clarice von Harmel has given us, far too much excitement." He leaned back in the armchair, which seemed to swallow him up.

"Why?" Sofia's question was quite clear.

The old man thought for a moment before replying. "You know, once I read about a fellow who always carried with him a book that he would never read. He didn't really care about it. All he really wanted was to possess it." He spread his arms, amused. "Books are like that. Everyone sees something of themselves in them. They can be answers to questions that torment us, even those that haven't yet entered our minds. They have great power." His voice faded for a moment. "For me, Fohr's book meant the end of my youth. For a while, it had been the symbol of freedom and rebellion against injustice. Then, when I freed myself of the power it had over me, it proved to be a friend. It became a warning. A border I must not venture beyond." He chuckled, and his attention returned to them. "You must excuse my ramblings. I have too many things in my head; it isn't easy to know which to choose and which to neglect."

"Try. I can assure you we're very patient."

Vinci became serious. "My dear Tomaso, it was your grandmother who spoke to us about Fohr. I don't know how she managed to locate it in the Bibliotheca Hertziana, but, you see, Ludovica argued that this copy contained notes handwritten by Fohr himself and that the other writing belonged to a woman. An unknown woman who had shared the margins with him, filling them with a series of reflections and thoughts." He made a face. "Nobody believed her, of course. First of all, because she was just a girl, even though she was at the top of her class. And then her skills were a little too far ahead of handwriting analysis at the time. Her conclusions seemed like mere suppositions." He stopped to catch his breath. "Our professors dismissed her, but I saw a possibility. The discovery of a book about which there had been rumors for centuries."

"You knew the legend."

The bookseller shrugged. "My dear Sofia, it was far more than a legend, and that book, with notes by the author, might have provided clues to its whereabouts. We all knew German. Ludovica and I because we'd studied it, and Max because it was his mother tongue."

Tomaso's eyes narrowed. "Go on, please."

"All three of us became very keen on Fohr and that strange book. But while it was personal for Ludovica, and Max was interested because it made him look good to the girl he was in love with, I saw it as a way to prove myself in the academic world." He leaned toward them, his scrawny hands clasping the sides of the armchair. "I wanted to be acknowledged as the one who made a great discovery, who found Fohr's lost book. I wanted glory, honor. I wanted a place on what I considered the Olympus of knowledge."

Now that she could see more clearly, Sofia could detect the signs of obsession in the old man. It was there in his wide eyes, still animated with that feverish light, even after so many years.

"And then what happened?"

The bookseller's face darkened. "What always happens when the arrogant realize that those beneath them might be right after all." He shrugged his shoulders. "After laughing at us, they tried to steal the results of our work and our dreams. A sad fate, don't you think?"

"Explain."

His lips tightened, as though even now, decades later, Andrea could still taste the bitter anger. "One of the teaching assistants who was keeping an eye on our research on Fohr informed the professor. He asked to see the book. He didn't believe Ludovica's hypotheses—no one did—but he wanted to be sure. From that moment on, we were prevented from accessing it."

"So you stole it."

The bookseller stiffened. "Yes. At the time, I was even proud of it—a blow to the arrogance of the system. Later, well, later is a different story." He sighed. "That rash act, my dear, cost me my country and my family. And the friendship of two people I really cared for." He turned to Tomaso. "Afterward, I regretted it, you know. I could have come back to Italy, but I didn't have the courage. The disappearance of the book was never reported—there was too much else going on at the time—but my shame for the problems I'd caused my family kept me away. Then, my father discovered it. Life finds ways to entangle you in incomprehensible designs."

"But what do I have to do with all this? Why did you give me the book?"

Sofia pushed it toward him.

The bookseller didn't touch it, looking at it as if it were a living thing that he wanted nothing to do with. "When I realized who you were, it seemed like a sign. The book could go back to its rightful place. A few days before we met, I'd been looking for Max. I wanted him to help me take it back to the library. I couldn't go myself. Even though the theft was over sixty years ago, how would I have explained?" He glanced at her. "I thought if I gave it to you, he—Max, I mean—would recognize it sooner or later. I was certain that, with all his contacts, he would manage to sort things out discreetly." He was silent for a moment, wiping his lips with a handkerchief. "I wanted the circle to close at last. But then you came back and told me about the letter you'd found. It was as if fate were offering me a second chance. Before I died, I would finally find out whether or not my work was in pursuit of a dream or a mere illusion."

"So I was your puppet."

The bookseller shook his head. "It isn't that simple. There was something else that made me give you the book."

"And what was that?"

He ran a hand through his silver-gray hair. "You, Sofia Bauer, are extraordinarily sensitive. You're kind, you listen when people talk, and you're respectful. You, my dear, came into my life like a ray of sunshine."

He wasn't flattering her. His sincerity shone clearly in his eyes. But Sofia still had so many questions, and most of all, she had to decide whether she could still trust the man. "You weren't honest with me."

"Is there any choice between a lie that allows you to live and a truth that causes you to die?"

"Enough of clever talk. I trusted you. You should have told me everything; there was no need for you to manipulate me. You manipulated us all."

"My dear Sofia, that was not my intention. I beg you to believe me."

She didn't reply, her eyes wet with tears and disappointment. Tomaso stood up and held out a hand to Sofia.

"Please don't judge me too harshly. You know what it means to pursue a dream. As to what I stole, you can always take the books and letters to the library and tell them everything you've discovered. I think you'd be doing a good deed, far better than I would have by giving back a single book, in its pitiful state, no less. As far as I'm concerned, my story's over."

He was testing them; Tomaso knew it. Yet, as they left the bookshop, Sofia's hand held tightly in his own, he couldn't stop himself from smiling.

"That diabolical old man had the last word."

"I think he's right, you know. It's the best thing to do. As soon as my grandfather gets back, we'll try and find a way to return the book. We'll tell them everything, even about the damaged book we found in Vienna." Her face lit up. "Maybe they'll acquire it, and the trilogy will be together again, Tomaso. And who knows, maybe in light of all this, someone might find a way to restore the last letter. Maybe someday they'll even find Fohr's unpublished text—if that's the secret Clarice was talking about."

Although there were still questions to answer, Sofia felt satisfied. She was grateful to have come across Clarice and her story, and for how it had restored her to herself.

Clarice taught her to not give up, to embrace change, to be courageous. Clarice, who had taken her fate into her own hands and fought for what she desired.

And now Sofia would follow Clarice's example.

CHAPTER TWENTY-THREE

I do not wish [women] to have power over men, but over themselves.

—Mary Wollstonecraft, *A Vindication of the Rights of Woman*

The plane was on time. When Maxim and Therese appeared, Sofia couldn't wait and ran toward them. She hugged her grandparents, happier than she'd felt in a long time.

"Liebling, let me look at you; you look marvelous."

It was so wonderful to see them and so sweet to feel part of a family once again.

"I'm very sorry you had to interrupt your trip."

Max waved her off. "We should have come home some time ago. Age is a great bother. It's difficult to put things off, you know? There were so many things we'd intended on doing and seeing that it would have taken us years." He paused, his hands squeezing his granddaughter's. "I'm so sorry you came to know about Andrea Vinci and this regrettable matter. Frankly, I thought the story had been forgotten."

"Actually, Grandpa, I have to—we have to tell you so many things." She turned to Tomaso.

Therese's eyes lit up. "This must be the person who's been helping you in your research, am I right?"

Sofia smiled and took Tomaso's arm, leaning against him. The gesture was more than an answer; it was a fact.

"It's a pleasure to meet you, Mr. and Mrs. Bauer." The two men shook hands and sized each other up. "My name is Tomaso Leoni. Perhaps you remember my grandmother, Ludovica Devoto Leoni."

Her grandmother took a step forward, a smile on her face. "Oh! Really? What an incredible coincidence."

Not a bit, thought Sofia. And suddenly, only a slight trace of the recent bitterness she'd felt toward Andrea Vinci remained. Joice's words came back to her: things happened because they were supposed to give rise to others. Like her meeting Tomaso. Sometimes you had to stop thinking about the before and after and concentrate on the present.

The bustle around them had increased. Groups of passengers were arriving, welcomed by parents and friends. The loudspeakers echoed, reminding passengers not to leave their luggage unattended. The crowds were like successive waves thundering past.

Sofia cleared her throat. "Should we continue this at home?"

When they finally got back to Coppedè, they gathered in the library. They had to wait for Max to check on the greenhouse, but fortunately, it took him only a few minutes. The two books were right on the table where Sofia had left them, along with her transcription of the third message found in Vienna.

"That's the book Andrea stole." Max pointed to it. "Ludovica and I were terrified; we thought we'd be expelled from the university at any moment." A smile.

"Go on, Grandpa."

Therese sat down in an armchair next to her husband. Sofia stood next to her grandfather, Tomaso behind her.

As the memories rose to the surface, Max's voice deepened. "Ludovica persevered in her research, despite everything, but I'd had enough. I didn't want any more to do with it. And she wouldn't forgive me for that." Silence and then a sad smile. "I hadn't seen her for a while when she told me she'd changed her course of study, and after that, I never heard from her or Andrea. It was a bad period; I won't deny that, Liebling." As he spoke, Max continued looking from Fohr's books to Clarice's letters. "I can't believe that Ludovica was right about the book." He paused. "It was quite by chance that she got so passionately involved in that story. Her professor suggested a thesis on a Romantic writer, and she chose Christian Fohr because his tomb had made such an impression on her. She'd seen the tombstone in the English cemetery, under the pyramid." He sighed. "I took you there once, remember?"

Yes, she did remember—the atmosphere, the light filtering through the trees, and all those flowers growing in the dark soil. Sofia, too, had been impressed by Christian Philipp Fohr's tomb. She nodded and Max continued.

"That young man who drowned made a deep impression on her. She often wondered about him and about the rumors of a lost book. When she came across those notes in the library, she became convinced it was true: the writer had continued working. She maintained that a woman and a man had both written in the book, and that they'd done so together, not one after the other. She'd say, 'If we find them, we'll be able to find the missing book.' And Andrea, well, he was very ambitious; he wanted to make his mark. Finding Fohr's book became an obsession." He fell silent for a moment. "And life, as far as I can see, has not tempered his ambition. He's learned nothing."

Tomaso stroked Sofia's shoulder. "Actually, he would have liked to give the book back. It seems he tried to contact you several times when he got back to Rome. As soon as he realized Sofia was your granddaughter, he entrusted the book to her, but he really hoped to reach you, Professor Bauer. He was certain that a man with your influence, who'd held important posts at the university, would somehow find a way of returning it discreetly, making up for what he'd done."

Max sighed deeply. "The library will be happy to get back a precious book like Fohr's. But are you sure you want to give up the other volume as well? And the letters?"

They'd discussed the matter at length, she and Tomaso. "We think the library should have them."

Everyone would come to know the story of Clarice and Christian, and Sofia was glad about that. They hadn't found the lost book, it was true, but the historical discovery was of great importance nonetheless. And Clarice's wish to emerge from the shadows had been fulfilled.

"I imagine you've asked me these questions because Ludovica can't give you answers anymore, Mr. Leoni?"

"You can drop the formalities with Tomaso, Grandpa. You're going to be seeing a lot of him."

Max gave his granddaughter an indulgent look. "Tomaso, I'd like to know about your grandmother."

"She's been dead for several years now. She was happy. My father used to speak of her as a courageous woman, always ready to fight for what she believed in. Nonconformist and modern."

Max remained silent, his fingers on the table. "She was always writing. She had whole notebooks filled with her marvelous handwriting." His gaze was far away. "Dozens and dozens of them." He squeezed his wife's hand. "They must have been indispensable to your research."

Sofia shook her head. "Actually, Grandpa, we only just found out about your friendship—from a photograph in Tomaso's house of the three of you."

"Really?"

"Yes!"

Soon the conversation turned to more personal matters. After a quick supper, they said goodbye and agreed to meet the next day. Max would call a few friends at the university and decide how to contact the library.

Soon, there were meetings, appointments, documents to sign. Sofia and Tomaso decided to keep their names out of it as much as possible. They had no desire for fame. The important thing was for Fohr's works to be finally reunited and Clarice's letters made public. It would then be up to the Bibliotheca Hertziana to come to an agreement with the institute in Vienna on the third volume.

Max's anger and resentment faded day by day as he remembered the friendship that had bound him to Ludovica and Andrea. It was too late to say anything to Ludovica; he couldn't apologize, couldn't laugh about what had happened. It was final, a clear break. But he could still talk to Andrea, close a troubling chapter that had never left him.

One afternoon, Max finally found the courage. He entered the bookshop rather uncertainly. Two customers were at the counter, buying books from an old man. Max realized it was Andrea, the dreamer. Andrea, the ambitious one, always ready to see the amusing side of things, to debunk accepted truths, to rage against the system; he was also the fragile one, capable of tears and great emotion. Max realized he'd forgotten all that. He'd only remembered the unpleasant aspects of him.

When the couple walked outside, leaving them alone, Andrea raised his eyes toward Max.

Silence, shock. "Is it really you?" Suddenly, he was shaking, clinging to the counter.

"Ciao, Andrea, what a long time it's been."

They met halfway in an embrace, and all that Max had imagined saying to him vanished into thin air. Then they looked into each other's eyes, and beneath the tears and the inevitable signs left by time, they saw one another for what they'd been.

"I wanted to tell you it's all over. Fohr's book is back where it belongs."

Andrea nodded. "I'm glad . . ."

With her grandparents back in Coppedè, Sofia decided to find an apartment of her own. Although Max and Therese told her to stay as long as she liked, she wanted her freedom. So she moved into a small studio. The space was divided into a bedroom and a kitchen, and she covered the ugly walls with books. It was her very own space, where she could think and dream.

And with a new place came new opportunities. Sofia was offered a job. The discoveries regarding Fohr convinced the directors of the institute in Vienna that it was time to open a branch in Rome. She would oversee the library.

"You just don't want to miss any opportunity for finding something else hidden in those old books," Tomaso had joked, and he wasn't entirely wrong.

The past few weeks had been exciting. After returning the stolen book to the library, donating what she'd found in Munich, and revealing the location of Fohr's third volume with its precious contents, Sofia had won the admiration and esteem of several institutions.

Many would have liked to have her on their staff, but those positions would not have allowed her to work in such close contact with books.

"Clarice imagined Christian's book as a ship capable of sailing the waters of time," she explained to Tomaso, "a bottle with a message inside, and many others did too, in their own ways. And I want to gather those messages. I want the books entrusted to me to go on conveying those stories. To speak of the people who wrote them and also of those who read them."

Tomaso, of course, had the agency to run. He was about to conclude the sale of his place and was relieved to know he'd soon be able to pay the Baldinis, cover all the agency's debts, and help his mother with the villa. He would also tell her the truth. After Frank's death, he realized he'd let himself be affected by his stepfather's distorted perspective. His mother was an intelligent woman, and she would understand.

But that conversation didn't go as planned.

"What on earth are you thinking, my dear?" she said during a dinner he'd organized so she could meet Sofia. "I don't know who put it into your head that I'm your responsibility, but I can assure you it's absurd. And I already put the villa up for sale. It's too big for me now. Half the money will go to you, naturally. Perhaps you'll reconsider selling your place? As for me, I've decided to go to America. I'll stay with your uncle." Then she had squeezed Sofia's hand. There had been instant warmth between them, as Tomaso had expected. "I think you two should go on with your research. It really is exciting." She paused to think.

"Your grandmother, Tomaso, once told me that Fohr was the most modern writer that Romantic literature ever had, that he was a hero. She said she could have fallen in love with a man like that, and believe me, she wasn't a sentimental woman. But perhaps you can see for yourselves. Somewhere up in the attic are Ludovica's diaries. She liked writing; she said it put her in touch with herself. Go look for them and show them to Sofia."

The search took several days, but the discovery was extraordinary.

It was just as Max and Luisanna had said: in Ludovica's numerous notebooks, she'd also written about Clarice and Christian. After breaking away from her two friends and fellow students, Ludovica had continued her research alone. By means of painstaking archival research, she'd discovered the mysterious bookbinder Clarice—going by the name of Clarice Schmidt—in Rome, and following the stamp with the pair of wings, Ludovica had traced her back to Vienna and even Munich. The last stage in Clarice's wanderings, according to Ludovica, had been England—more precisely, London. The last notebook contained an address that corresponded to a villa, a historical building now converted into a hotel. After that, the notes stopped. Ludovica went no further.

"We could go to London, my love," Sofia said in a low voice.

It was the first time she'd called him that. He observed her from beneath his eyelashes. Sofia caressed his face with her fingertips and then kissed him slowly. "Love belongs to those who dare, did you know that?"

It took him some time to answer, because when your wishes come true, the sensation is like flying. It would take them some time to recover their balance, if ever.

"I was waiting for those words."

A week later, they were standing hand in hand in front of a villa in the London suburbs, looking at the impressive Georgian building.

"Come on, let's go in," said Sofia. They went up the path leading to the entrance, with their souls in turmoil and hope in their hearts. "Do you think we'll find something?"

"If we don't go in, we'll never know. Relax."

Sofia was on edge. There was something about the place that disturbed her. It was as though she recognized it—the garden, the big windows, even the pillars at the entrance seemed familiar.

They were welcomed by a middle-aged woman wearing rather out-of-date clothes. "Welcome, please come in. I'm Matilda."

"We have a reservation."

She raised her eyes a moment, then glanced down at the documents they had handed her. "Yes, we were expecting you. This is a small hotel. We don't have many rooms. Actually, my family and I live here."

"So you're the owners." Tomaso looked around, gazing at the high walls and the decorations.

The woman broke into a proud smile. She pointed to the frescoed barrel ceiling with the tip of her pen. "That's right. The house has always belonged to our family. It became a necessity to convert part of it into a bed and breakfast." She sighed. "These old buildings need expensive maintenance, and we love our old lady far too much not to provide her with it, so we've had to adapt. But it's all for the best. We like having guests." She photocopied the documents and handed them back. "You can leave your bags; my son, Frederik, will take them up to your room." A tall, very blond boy with blue eyes smiled timidly. "Come with me, please."

They crossed the whole house, passing little lounges, storerooms, kitchens, and a large, formal drawing room. "Here they used to dance in my great-grandfather's time." It was an enormous room with a high ceiling and spectacular crystal chandeliers that reflected the soft afternoon light.

"It really is magnificent!"

"And this," Matilda said, flinging open a pair of double doors, "is the library." She showed them in, pleased by their interest. "I admit this is the part of the house I like best, and not only because of the books. There's something heartwarming about it." She turned to her guests and followed the direction of their eyes. "Ah! The people in the portrait are my great-grandparents, both Prussians. They had the house built, you know. She was Clarice Schmidt, and those are her seven children standing around her."

Tomaso and Sofia stood stock-still in front of the portrait.

"His name was Christian Schmidt."

Matilda went on with her story, but Sofia and Tomaso didn't hear a word. Clarice, that beautiful, sweet, and courageous woman, and beside her was Christian Philipp Fohr. They'd seen his face countless times in literature textbooks. It was them, without a doubt.

But what did it all mean? Why had they changed their names? Hadn't Christian died?

Their hands entwined. Their hearts beat together.

"Clarice," whispered Sofia.

"Yes. A truly beautiful woman. But he's charming too. He was a cousin or something. That's why they had the same surname. At that time, it was quite frequent for relatives to get married. They loved each other madly."

Tomaso squeezed Sofia's hand.

"Behind the glass on that shelf are some of the family books. Maybe you'd like to look? Actually, the library contained many volumes, but over the years, some have been lost."

Still incredulous and almost trembling, Sofia went up to the glass case. The spines were arranged according to shape and color. Was it possible that Clarice might have bound them herself? She imagined her bending over the frame, sewing the sheets, and conceiving the wonderful covers. They were the same gestures she herself loved, she thought. It was their bond, the link between them. It made her even dearer to Sofia.

Suddenly, her breath caught in her throat.

Her eyes had fallen on a spine, with a title that made her shiver: *The Age of Joy*. And the symbol was stamped on it.

A circle surrounding two wings, resplendent in gold.

Tomaso immediately realized something had happened. "What's going on?"

She pointed to the book.

He stared for a second, then turned to Matilda. "Do you think we could have a look at that book?"

After a moment of confusion, she opened the bookcase. "Why not?" She took it out and handed it to Sofia. "If you like, you can examine it on that table over there."

Sofia couldn't believe her eyes. There were their names on the frontispiece. This was it, Fohr's unpublished book. She opened it gently, trembling with emotion. Clarice's symbol was on every page.

"They wrote it together." Tomaso's voice echoed her thoughts.

Bending over the pages, yellow with age, they discovered the rest of the story. They'd written the book together, Clarice and her beloved Christian. A man and a woman who shared their lives, creating the perfect union of two human beings, completing one another. The book's introduction explained everything.

"It's the only one in the collection that's handwritten, you know?"

Sofia and Tomaso were overcome with emotion. They were standing in front of a work that celebrated life and did so through the love of two people who had faced many trials and still managed to be citizens of their time without ever betraying their ideals.

Tomaso took the book from Sofia's hands and gave it back to Matilda. Then he embraced Sofia and—in front of an amazed Matilda, half smiling—kissed her passionately.

"Oh, Tomaso! We found it!"

They told Matilda everything, and she begged them to stay longer—there was so much to find out. Together they would decide how to make the whole story public.

As they wandered through the city a few hours later, their hearts and minds were still full of questions, conjectures, and wonder. First of all, the details of how Ludovica got that far without Clarice's letters was something they would unfortunately never know. And wasn't Christian supposed to be dead? Somehow, he and Clarice had left Italy and taken refuge in London. They had lived out of the public eye, changed their identity, and brought up their family. They'd even written a book together.

"But why did they hide it? Just because they didn't want to be found?" Tomaso suddenly broke the silence.

Sofia reflected. The famous unpublished work wasn't a second study by Fohr, as they had imagined, but a completely new work written by Clarice and Christian together. "They must have feared for the safety of their family, which would have been illegitimate in the eyes of society. But there's also the fact that they'd written a work that was virtually unacceptable at that time. Even the notes in the margin of the first volume were on that very subject, and perhaps those were the ideas that brought them together: the celebration of female identity and women's right to independence."

"The work wouldn't have been accepted then; it had to remain hidden until society was ready to understand." Tomaso took her hand and kissed it. "Until one day, someone found the letters and followed the trail."

They continued talking, opening their hearts to one another. Sofia marveled at how easy it was now to express herself and the joy she found in sharing what was inside her. Fear had vanished, and for the first time, everything was vivid, vibrant, full of emotion. One day, she'd found a letter in a book, and her life had changed. Still, she was the one responsible for that change. Like Clarice, she took her fate in her own hands.

Sofia was overcome by emotion again. "I've always thought that the book somehow carried a message. That it had chosen me."

"That's what books do when you're very lucky. They choose you."

As they strolled together, he kissed her hand. Warmth spread through every inch of him, even those hidden places where he had never allowed anyone to venture.

It was a good way to start again, thought Tomaso. The best. The only one worth fighting for. To match your steps with the person you loved, lengthen them, slow them down, and then run again.

It was the secret to happiness.

EPILOGUE

A hope that had to remain secret, but now I wish to leave a trail so that it may be found . . .

One day, everyone will understand that the only path leading to joy is love and that equality and respect are indispensable traveling companions. I have so much faith in the future and in change, and so I am entrusting these pages to time. One day, someone will pick them up and know. I shall send the three books harboring them out into the world to seek a person capable of understanding and revealing the secret. Nature, humankind, and thought will guide their steps through knowledge, and thus, what we have done and dreamt together will be passed on. The Age of Joy, our book, will see the light of day. I shall keep it safe in London, the city that gave us shelter, in the library of the house where I lived such happy years and brought up my children. When it is no longer a threat to them, I shall hand it down to my unwitting heirs, whilst waiting for you, reader, to find it. Our thoughts will become those of others, who will adopt them as their own, and the ideas will travel on the wings of freedom. Women will have the same rights as men and that new world will experience prosperity.

Because this is true love, to be free together. For always.

Clarice ran along the bank of the river, her skirt hoisted. Not for a second did her eyes leave Christian's, as he continued to disappear and reemerge.

Then he vanished from sight.

Desperately, Clarice flung herself into the river, but her skirt, heavy with water, kept her from swimming. She dragged herself back to the bank, her heart bursting in her chest, her fingers clawing at the grass in an attempt to escape the current. She pulled herself up with difficulty, her eyes darting along the bank, and then she froze. A little farther on in an inlet, covered with mud, a body was floating, caught on a branch.

A deep moan shook her to the core.

Seized by desperation, she ran toward the man, dropping to his side. With shaking hands, she turned him over and shut her eyes. It was August; it was what remained of her husband. She covered her face with her hands. And now what? Now what would she do?

A sudden burst of energy drove her to get up and search again, frantically, desperately. And when she glimpsed Christian trying to reach the riverbank, she pulled him out, crying and shouting, and fell onto the grass beside him. She hugged him, rocking him until, exhausted, he opened his eyes. He was filthy and scratched up, with blood running down his face, but he was alive! He was alive, and he was smiling at her.

"It's all over." He embraced her, holding her tightly to him.

Later, when they were both able to stand, Christian stopped beside August's body and made his decision. He would never leave her side again, his brave Clarice. In the eyes of the world, he would die, and the drowned man washed up by the river would bear his name. He put his own signet ring on August's finger and left him to the current.

His new life began right there. Christian Philipp Fohr abandoned fame for a new and different world. A new age—the age of joy.

ABOUT THE AUTHOR

Cristina Caboni is the international bestselling author of *The Secret Ways of Perfume*. One of Italy's best-loved authors, she has sold more than one million copies of her books worldwide. *The Binder of Lost Stories* is her second novel to be translated into English. When Cristina is not writing, she devotes herself to her family's beekeeping business. She currently lives in the province of Cagliari with her husband and three children.

ABOUT THE TRANSLATOR

Patricia Hampton, a graduate in modern languages at the University of Birmingham (UK), taught at the University of London, King's College, and worked in London as a translator. In 1973 she moved to Italy and perfected her knowledge of the language "in the field." An expert in linguistic mediation and transcultural issues, she taught English at Milan State University and collaborated on the production of English-language textbooks, and she now focuses on translation within academia and cinema.